Accepting Agatha

A BOMBSHELLS OF BRENTWOOD NOVEL BY

VICTORIA BLUE

Accepting Agatha

A BOMBSHELLS OF BRENTWOOD NOVEL BY

VICTORIA BLUE

WATERHOUSE PRESS

For David, my best friend, my other half.

I love you dearly.

CHAPTER ONE

AGATHA

Bright. *Too* bright. So bright, even with my lids still closed, the obnoxious light beams were making my head throb worse.

Oh my God, my head.

This had to be the literal worst part of excessive drinking. The morning after was brutal, and this one was no different from the times I'd done this to myself before.

Cautiously, I patted the mattress beside me.

Shit.

There was definitely another person in bed with me. Luckily, when I listened a bit longer, whoever it was continued sleeping. The soft sounds of air moving in and out through parted lips made panic rise. Was that a chick?

Not again.

I had no idea what *that* was about lately, but on more than one occasion, I'd taken a woman home with me. It had never been my thing before, but to be honest, I'd been pretty fed up with the male population.

We couldn't all be as lucky as my oldest sister, Hannah. The incredibly fine specimen she had sunk her teeth into could right the wrongs for so many douchebags before him. If I could just sit and stare at that guy, it would be suitable penance for all of mankind.

Infinitesimally, I turned my head, not wanting to wake my bedmate and deal with the awkward morning-after conversation. At the same time, curiosity killed this cat every single time. I needed to know who I so carelessly shared my body with the night before.

Although... after a quick assessment of things beneath the blankets, I was fully clothed. And ewww, I needed a shower in the worst way. There was my out—I just had to be stealthy when exiting the bed.

But first, I had to figure out where the hell I was.

Parts of the room seemed familiar, or at least what I could see from my current vantage point. I slid my hand across the mattress to estimate how close I was to the edge. If I could slither off the bed without creating much motion, I could get to the shower to freshen up. Nothing worse than having the morning-after conversation with a stranger when your mouth tasted like you might have barfed a time or two.

So, fine, this was not my proudest moment. And also fine, this kind of bullshit was happening a little too often lately. I needed to stage an intervention with myself and stop this shit before I did something really stupid.

I made it to the bathroom without waking my party pal. At least there was some relief when I saw it was a guy and he was someone I knew. Probably explained why my clothes were still on. Carmen Sandoval was a straitlaced mama's boy who would never take advantage of a drunk woman.

Even if she were—

Wait. What the fuck am I wearing?

My stomach roiled as I gaped at my reflection. Whether the letters were backward or not, even an idiot could read what my T-shirt said.

BRIDE

No. Please no.

I instantly dropped my eyes to the cheap green jelly band on my left finger. Well, at least drunk me got the color right. Green was my favorite...

I was desperate to find bright spots in what was looking like a monumental disaster. Trying to calm down, I stripped off the offensive shirt and angrily threw it into the neighboring sink. It had to be a joke.

This is a joke, right?

I tugged off my leggings and left them in a heap on the floor. The massive showers in these villas were glorious, and this one was calling to me like a siren.

Under the spray, I tried in vain to recall the events of the night before. My sister and one of her bosses, Rio Gibson, married the men of their dreams, shotgun style, at a cheesy little chapel on the strip. Afterward, we had a fantastic meal in one of our hotel's restaurants and played many hands of poker until everyone was shitfaced or exhausted.

Guess which one I was?

I remembered doing a lot of shots in that card room, and things went really fuzzy from that point of the night onward. I leaned my head back farther to rinse the suds from my long hair and racked my brain a bit more.

Did I leave the property? I must have at some point, because this chichi hotel didn't sell tacky souvenirs like the one I woke up wearing. Maybe it was Hannah's and I borrowed it after a spill or vomit episode. That sounded pretty reasonable, so I held on to the concept with all the functioning parts of my brain and stepped out of the marble enclosure to dry off.

I startled when the door pushed open and a sleepy Carmen

staggered in. One eye still closed, he rubbed at the other one. His hair was rioting in every possible direction from a hard sleep, and the erection tenting his boxers couldn't be missed.

"Morning," he mumbled as he shuffled past me to go to the separate toilet section of the villa's expansive bathroom. He closed the door behind him, and in a few beats, I could hear him relieving himself. The occupants in the neighboring villa might have heard him as well, because the sound was incredibly loud.

Is that a man in there or a horse?

I chuckled at my nonsense and leaned in closer to the mirror to survey the damage.

Normally I would expect bloodshot eyes and super dry skin, but this morning I actually had several bruises on my face, neck, and what I could see of my body peeking out from the towel.

Was there a brawl?

Wouldn't be the first time for that, either.

While I quickly searched around the bathroom for the luxurious white robe the hotel provided, Carmen shuffled to the sink to wash his hands. Even after peeing, his dick stood at attention.

When he cleared his throat, I realized I had stopped mid-tie of the robe's belt to stare at his physique. Not going to lie, the man looked good . . . until I noticed his shirt.

GROOM

I shot my eyes to his left hand, and sure enough, a green jelly band was on his ring finger too.

I popped my eyes up to find him staring at me via the mirror, and my shoulders dropped low.

"What did we do?" I croaked in the most pathetic voice, rubbing my throbbing forehead in distress.

"Got irresponsibly drunk, for starters," he answered cautiously.

"And?" My voice pitched higher by the slightest bit, but my volume shot considerably louder than it had been.

He recoiled from the decibels and answered sheepishly. "Looks like we caught the wedding fever that's been going around."

"How can you be so calm?" I barked.

"Should I be overreacting like you?"

"Overreacting? You think this is overreacting? Dude, you haven't seen overreacting," I warned with a bit of smugness.

"Oh joy," he muttered while drying his hands.

I stood and glared, but getting upset was amping up the pain in my brain. I needed to calm down before I burst a blood vessel. Instead of continuing the pointless conversation, I pushed past him and stormed out into the room.

There had to be a minibar in here somewhere.

Hair-of-the-dog approach was not one I normally practiced. But if ever an evening of alcohol-soaked mistakes needed to be forgotten, it was this one. I'd just throw back a shot or two and be in a much better headspace to deal with this fuck-up.

Of course the high-end hotel didn't just have a minibar in the room. Nope—this bad boy was fully stocked with normal-sized bottles. I struggled with the top of the vodka I randomly grabbed until my husband easily snagged the bottle from my grasp to help.

Well, I thought he was going to help.

He set the glass bottle on the end table with a definitive

thunk and met my confusion head- on. And whoa ... not sure what was going on ... Could the residual liquor in my system have been messing with me? The guy seemed to have gained about three inches in height as he stood defiantly guarding that Ketel One bottle.

I assessed him, starting low at his bare feet and moving inch by inch up his muscular body. How had I not noticed this body before? Carmen wasn't hulking and beefy, but he was fantastically toned and, dare I say ... very appealing.

I had already brushed my teeth, so I couldn't blame the sudden dry mouth on last night.

I tried to speak, but all that came out was a squawk of a sound. "Wha—" After a solid throat clearing, I gave it another go. "What are you doing?"

"I don't think that's the way to handle this," he said while giving me a disapproving scowl. Honestly, the expression looked a lot like something my parents would bestow upon me when they disagreed with my behavior.

Instantly I was irritated.

"Well, I don't recall asking for your input. Do you?" I bit back.

"Okay, you do you, then. But I'm going to see about getting back to LA while you're getting shitfaced. Again. And we can worry about living arrangements when we get home."

"Living arrangements?" I laughed before tilting the bottle to my lips. After a hearty swig, I grimaced and shivered as the burn hit my throat and irritated my sinuses. Yeah ... there had definitely been a vomiting episode recently.

He watched me poison myself with a second swig and shook his head.

"And I can do without the judgment. If you don't like what

I'm doing, don't stand there and stare at me while I do it."

Carmen let out a heavy breath before speaking. "Look. I'm not judging you or whatever. It's just that we seem to be in quite a situation here"—he held up his left hand, and I thought for a moment that the green band actually looked nice against his skin tone—"and it would be nice to feel like we're both working on trying to figure things out instead of having to take care of you while you're drunk. Again."

"Stop saying that!"

"What? *Drunk?*" He laughed. "With the amount you drink, and the frequency you do it with, how can the word describing the problem be what's hanging you up?"

"No, the word *again* is the one I'm objecting to. And what do you know about how often I drink?"

"Here's what I know. We've spent, what, a total of five days together since we met, give or take a few hours? You've been intoxicated at least four times in those five days! Looks like a problem from where I'm standing, girl."

"And where is that? Up on your high and mighty platform of judgment? First of all," I said, holding up one finger, "we met at my sister's birthday party. It was a paaarrttteee. People over twenty-one often drink at parties. So what? Secondly"—I added my middle finger to the first—"we've been at a weekend-long destination wedding in Las Vegas for fuck's sake! Vegas by its city charter says you have to drink while in the city limits!"

I scanned my brain for a third point but came up empty. Those swigs of vodka were fast tracking through my body, and the warm fuzzy sensation I loved most about consuming alcohol was setting in.

So I hit him with the time-tested oldie but goodie. "And three, who the fuck asked you?"

"Apparently the state of Nevada, for one. No wife of mine is going to be a lush. Especially at our age." He paused suddenly and got that sheepish look on his face I was now recognizing as one of his go-tos. "How old are you, by the way?"

I burst out laughing. Or cackling, more accurately. My darling husband immediately cupped his hands over his ears.

"That's a very unpleasant sound, wife."

"Stop calling me that."

"I don't know..." He shrugged and casually strolled over to the small table arranged with two chairs. On top of the round surface sat a piece of white paper, folded in half, and then again. "Says right here"—he unfolded the sheet and tapped on the bottom portion—"that's exactly who you are. As of"—he squinted as if reading very small print—"four o'clock this morning." He looked at me and shrugged again.

"That's bullshit, and you know it. There's no way they can legally marry drunk people," I insisted. And then was hit with a wave of sadness. I really thought I could like this guy before all this happened.

We certainly had a good time together. He was very handsome, and shit, now that I got a good look at his body, other parts of me wanted to really like him too.

"Let me see that," I demanded, forgetting any form of manners. I could picture my mom's scowl for that one.

Before saying anything, Carmen slowly shook his head. "No. I think I better hold on to this for safe keeping. With your current problem—oh sorry, not problem—who knows what will happen to it?"

"If you make one more reference to my drinking habits, I'm going to knee you in the dick. How does that sound?"

"Painful," he replied dryly.

After glaring at him for a bit, I huffed and said, "I need to call my sister. We're supposed to fly home today."

"Wow, you were really out of it, weren't you?"

"What did I just tell you?"

"Your family left this morning or at least were getting ready to leave when we stumbled into the hotel from our"—he looked heavenward as if the word he was searching for would be handed down by God himself—"excursion last night."

I had zero recollection of seeing my family this morning. None at all. That should probably worry me, and on some level it did. But probably for the wrong reason. If we saw them earlier, that meant they knew two of their daughters were married this weekend, not just one. Cradling my face in my hands, I thought of all the shit that would rain down on me when I spoke to them next.

"You okay?" My doting husband was right in front of me when I looked up.

"Oooohhh . . ." I groaned. "This is bad. So very, very bad."

"Which *this* are you talking about? There seem to be several really bad things going on here."

Rather than providing clarification, I dropped into the closest chair and rested my head on my crossed arms. I likely looked like a toddler throwing a tantrum, but I didn't want to get into the dynamics of my family at the moment. Honestly, if he weren't being such a wet towel, I could really go for another shot or two.

Where's that damn bottle?

But that thought was erased when warm arms wrapped around my shoulders. I picked up my head to find Carmen standing beside me, trying to provide some comfort.

"Stand up, baby," he said, and his voice was deep and throaty.

"Huh?" I croaked while looking up the length of his toned body.

"I want to hold you, and it would be easier if you stood up," he explained with way more patience than I deserved.

"I don't need to be held. I'm fine."

Easily, he tugged me from the seat, and I stumbled into him. He put his arms around my waist and pulled me against his body.

My brain was shouting at me to protest. *Be the independent, fierce woman everyone knows you are.* But my psyche and libido ganged up on my foggy gray matter and listened to his unspoken command. I sagged into his chest and gave in to the warmth of his embrace. Instinctively, I wrapped my arms around his waist then too, and we stood like that for long minutes.

He swayed from side to side like we were sharing a slow-motion dance, and it all felt so good.

"You smell so good," I muttered into his shirt and then looked up to find him staring down at me.

"You know something? You're beautiful. I mean, really, really beautiful. You have this all-natural look locked down. I like it better than if you wore a lot of makeup."

"Is that right?" I grinned so he would know I was teasing and because it was genuinely nice to be complimented so innocently.

My four sisters and I all looked very similar. We all knew we were pretty girls. Hell, we'd been told that our whole lives. So in addition to that natural confidence, I'd always had a healthy self-esteem. It didn't hurt that I could usually walk into a bar or club alone and not buy my own drinks all night. Typically, I didn't have to go home alone either.

I tried to finally pull away, but he held me tighter. "Okay, thank you." I tried to pull back again and still got nowhere. "That was lovely," I said quietly.

"I could stand here with you in my arms for hours," he declared and buried his nose in my hair.

I didn't want to touch that comment with a ten-foot pole. We didn't need to get confused with feelings. "That's all well and good, but if we want to get a ride home in style, I need to check in with my sister. If my family already left, we'll have to see if we can fly back with the newlyweds tomorrow."

"I doubt my boss will leave us here to fend for ourselves. No matter how pissed he is at me."

Finally, he released me with hesitation, and I walked back into the space with the bed. The thing was calling to me like a temptress. I turned back to find him right on my heels, so I reconsidered the minibar and chose the bed instead.

"I think I'm going to close my eyes for a bit longer. My head is really pounding."

"I'll get you some water. I think I have some sort of pain reliever in my travel bag. Do you want me to check?"

I answered *yes* a bit too eagerly, and that piqued his suspicion. I had designs on a quick chug from that bottle to really put me to sleep fast.

"Well, let's get you tucked in, and then I'll look," he offered with one brow arched.

"I don't need a babysitter," I snapped.

He added a tilt of his head to his doubtful gaze. "That's debatable," he muttered, but he went toward the other room for his toiletries.

There was no way I'd prove him right and drink now. But I was definitely growing tired of his bit. Already. And whether he had some stupid paper that said we were husband and wife or not, that did not make him my warden.

If that's what married life was like—you could keep that shit.

Carmen brought me two pain-reliever tablets and a glass of water. All three went down the hatch in record time. I was definitely grateful for both, though, so I made sure to thank him. I wasn't usually so bitchy to people and considered trying a little harder to be kinder to the guy.

When he went around to the other side of the bed and pulled the covers back, I widened my blue eyes at him.

"What are you doing?"

"What? I can't share a bed with you now? We've slept in the same bed all weekend."

"Fine," I huffed and turned to face away from him as he settled in.

"Should we cuddle or something?" he asked, seeming to have every intention of snuggling.

"Probably not a good idea," I said without turning over.

"Why not? You enjoyed it last night. I'm an excellent snuggler," he said proudly.

A grin split my face. "Is that right?"

"Yes. You even told me so."

That made me flip over to face him. "You're so full of shit."

"Scout's honor." He smiled and gave me the sexiest wink I might have ever seen.

"Sleep, Mr. Sandoval," I ordered.

"You too, Mrs.—"

"Don't even say it!" I laughed, and his eyes closed slowly when I did so.

"What?" I asked, regarding the way his face just

completely morphed.

"That laugh, Christ," he nearly choked. His voice had shifted back to the dark, silky tone again.

There was definitely chemistry between us, but this whole drunken matrimony would never stand a chance. No one started a life together that way. No one.

Then again, I always take pride in being a trailblazer.

CHAPTER TWO

CARMEN

This woman. God—this woman. Equal parts alluring, infuriating, and sexy as hell. I'd never had a woman's laugh give me a hard-on before. But, well, now here I was. Lying in bed alongside the little siren wasn't helping my cause either.

She fell asleep within minutes, and even her freight-train snoring was stirring my arousal.

I stared at her for close to thirty minutes by the time I drifted off myself. And what did I dream of? Agatha Christine, of course. How the hell had she burrowed under my skin so deeply and so quickly? I'd known her for a couple of weeks— three at most—and she was on my brain constantly. Out of the blue, I'd get a face-splitting grin from remembering something she'd said or done, and it already pulled me up short a few times.

People got nervous when you chuckle in an otherwise quiet room. Like last weekend, for example. While all eyes were on me in church, I had to make up some bullshit excuse as to why I was cracking up during the priest's homily. Lying... *in church* of all places.

I could still picture my mother's disapproving scowl when I apologized. Three times. And that was before I was trapped in the family car for the drive home.

Remarkably, Agatha was still asleep when I woke up. The vodka she chugged before our nap probably had something to do with it. The excessive drinking had to stop. My mind sailed right into that harbor as soon as I considered her sleep aid. She was too young, too bright, and too beautiful to become a wasteland. As long as she was mine, she'd be drying out.

And I had every intention of her remaining mine. I hadn't investigated the matter yet, but I assumed the marriage could be annulled. But with my family's religious background, there was no way that would be happening. Not if I wanted to stay in my parents' good graces.

First, I had to figure out a way to explain to them how I ended up with a wife and save her reputation at the same time. There would be no laughing over the story about how we got so drunk we didn't realize the place was a legitimate chapel.

I'd been digging through my jumbled memory of the previous night, and that was the best notion that made sense. There was a lot of laughing and shouting—mainly on my darling wife's part—and then some goofy borrowed wedding attire, and now we had matching green rubber rings on our fingers.

It didn't escape my notice that she hadn't taken hers off when she'd pieced together what those and our souvenir T-shirts meant. A faint memory of an argument over the shirts was teasing my consciousness, but I couldn't connect those dots just yet. I figured with more quality sleep and some nutrition that wasn't chugged, details would start to line up.

I groaned aloud and quickly clapped a hand over my mouth. Definitely wanted my little storm to sleep a bit longer. Just thinking of the hell I was going to catch about the marriage made that noise erupt from my body on its own, though.

Yes, I was old enough to live my own life. If my parents didn't approve of the choices I made, they should at least respect me enough to be kind to Agatha when they met her.

Not holding my breath on that one, though. My mother had been trying to set me up with several women my age that she had met at church, and she wasn't just going to accept a stranger.

My father was a traditional man. He ruled the house and everyone in it. He put in an honest day of work, six days a week, and the United States Postal Service was lucky to have him.

My mother was more opinionated than anyone I knew. She was a beautiful woman when she was young, but now she was bitter about everything, and her bad attitude made her unattractive. If you were excited or happy about something, she could strip you of your joy in one sentence or less. It made being around her very unpleasant. Now that I had my own place, I didn't visit them very often. Or at least as often as I should, according to her.

But Sundays in the Sandoval house meant church and family, and I still showed up for both. Week in and week out, I dreaded the entire day but did it anyway. The hell I'd pay for not going was way worse.

Graziella, my sister, was younger than me by just under two years. She still lived in their house, so she was still under their rule. Gray, as I'd called her since childhood, was a stunning young woman who had more boyfriends, friends who were boys, and boys who wanted to be her friend, than any one girl should have.

Remarkably, she'd remained a virgin—or at least my parents believed so. Honestly, I didn't know if she was or not. We didn't typically discuss our sexual escapades.

Not that I had them by the dozen or anything. I had dated the same girl from high school until last year around this same time. She finally got tired of me dragging my feet about marrying her and had left me for some dude in the Marines.

Funny, though, since we'd broken up, we'd hooked up around eight times for middle-of-the-night booty calls. Either she'd text me after getting home late from a club or I'd message her when I just needed a release that wasn't self-performed.

It worked out fine for both of us until the Marine found out. Then all hell broke loose. She vowed she would never do it again, and blah blah blah, and the dumbass took her back. She texted me two weeks later for a midnight run, and I turned her down.

It was shitty of me to be a part of her infidelity, and there were plenty of other willing, able, and single young ladies out there. I didn't need to be adding more meat to my guilt sandwich.

Then I met Miss Farsey and, well . . . here we were.

Thankfully, her snoring stopped, and I grinned widely as I looked at her buried up to her perfect pink lips in the downy comforter. Each feature on the woman's face was textbook perfect. Put all the components together, and my wife was completely beautiful.

As if she could sense my attention, she slowly opened her tired eyes. For a long, silent moment, she stared at the ceiling overhead and didn't speak.

I thought maybe she might drift off again, but she turned her face in my direction instead.

"Did you sleep? Or have you been staring at me the whole time?" She smiled as she asked, and missing from her tone was the acid that could lace any of her comments. The woman would definitely keep me on my toes.

"I slept a bit. Too much in here at the moment." I tapped on my temple.

Agatha rolled toward me completely. "We've got a big mess, huh?"

I then rolled toward her and propped up on a bent arm. Without thinking, I reached out and tucked a wild section of hair behind her ear. She didn't bite my head off or make a sassy remark. In fact, she might have liked my small gesture, because she slowly closed her eyes while I touched her skin.

I stroked the backs of my fingers over the soft skin of her cheek, and she hummed low in her throat like a content little kitty. I liked this version of her. Very much.

There was a good chance I would blow the sweet moment if I voiced the decision I'd made while she slept. But it needed to be said, and sooner rather than later. We needed to be on the same page as we mounted the war against our families.

"Maybe it doesn't have to be," I said by way of continuing the topic she introduced.

Her big blue eyes popped open wider, and she seemed much clearer and more focused than I'd seen her in days.

How much had this girl been drinking when no one was around?

"You're so beautiful."

We hadn't been physical beyond holding hands and innocent touches here and there. Something about lying in bed with her during broad daylight seemed to be sending signals to parts of my body that did not have permission to be involved in our conversation just yet.

"You're a really sweet man, Carmen. Thank you."

"Well, I'm not just saying that to be sweet. You have a

natural beauty I haven't seen in a long time. Most girls our age are more worried about makeup hacks on TikTok and plumping parts of their faces that aren't meant to be plump."

"Hmm."

I had no idea how to interpret that, given the context of our conversation. But from our past interactions, I knew she was a powder keg. If I questioned the meaning of her reaction, it could easily ruin the moment with a defensive outburst.

"So, what did you mean when you said 'it doesn't have to be'? What doesn't have to be what?" she asked to fill the growing silence.

Well, we might end up arguing anyway when I explained my comment. I should've kept my damn thoughts to myself and enjoyed this docile version of her a little longer.

"I was thinking maybe this whole thing doesn't have to be a mess. We could make the best out of ..." I rolled my eyes toward the ceiling, trying to get the wording right here. "An unexpected situation."

My gorgeous storm sat up and propped a couple of pillows behind herself. "Do you want to explain that?" Her eyes narrowed with suspicion.

I didn't want to be lying down if she wasn't, so I repositioned to sit cross-legged by her thighs. If this bombshell was about to detonate, I wanted to be able to brace for impact.

"We could give it a solid try," I offered cautiously. "Us, I mean."

"Were you hitting the vodka while I was sleeping?"

"No, but I did pour the rest of that bottle out."

Five. Four. Three. Two ...

"Why would you do that?" she snapped, but I'd expected as much.

"So you're not tempted to drink it."

"I'm a big girl, Carmen. I can do whatever I damn well please. And I don't have a problem. Alcohol doesn't *tempt* me."

Nodding, I said, "It's very true that you're an adult, in charge of your own life. But I think you drink too much, and I want you to chill out with it." I wouldn't cave on this.

"That's not up to you, for one thing. And you're not my babysitter."

"No, I'm your husband." My voice naturally dropped in register, and I held her gaze so she understood I wasn't backing down. I knew how to be stern when I needed to be. It just wasn't a version of my personality that many people saw.

I reminded myself of my father, but I didn't ever want to come off like the tyrant he had.

Agatha's breath hitched when I spoke, and I couldn't be sure what about, because instead of the comeback denying my position in her world that I expected, she snapped her mouth shut and stared at me.

I didn't really know what to do with her attention now that I had it. So we just stared at each other. For a long, long moment.

Strangely, of all the things that should've been running through my mind, I wanted to kiss her. Now more than any other moment we'd shared, I wanted to attack her and pin her to the mattress until she acquiesced. I wanted her to let me take care of her like a husband should.

I moved closer by leaning onto my arms, as if I were about to pounce on her the way I imagined.

"What are you doing?" she whispered after a rough swallow.

Watching her throat undulate that way was the final straw

for my common sense, apparently. Closing the last space left between us, I kissed her.

Finally.

Just as I'd imagined and had fantasized about over the past couple of weeks, her lips were velvety soft. Our kiss started with a simple peck to her bottom lip and grew from there. A longer, somewhat firmer kiss to her top lip coaxed her to join in the experience.

We both parted our mouths, and while hers was tentative, mine was more demanding. My body was working on autopilot and definitely had an agenda. I crawled forward, and she sank back into the pillows while reaching her hands out to grasp my shoulders. The new position provided a better angle to deepen the kiss. Our tongues found each other and stroked and prodded for more.

I had to pull back and assess how she was dealing with what we were doing and ensure I wasn't coming on too strong. But God, how I wanted to. I wanted to mount her and feel her body beneath mine.

Want it so badly.

"You good?" I panted and wanted to cheer when I saw her chest was pumping for oxygen too.

"Yes. Very good." She smiled up at me, and it was a version I hadn't seen yet. Shy? No way, not this girl. But her eyes were saying exactly that.

Do you like it? Do you like me? Do you want more?

Yes, yes, and hell yes.

"Am I crushing you?" I asked.

"No, but I wouldn't mind if you tried to."

She laughed, and that damn sound made me drive my hips forward to press my hard-on into her.

"Mmmm, yes, please." And just like that, the shy girl was gone, and the saucy, cocky, confident woman was back. Both had their pluses and minuses, and my mental jury was still deliberating which I liked better.

We made out for long minutes, and by the time we were groping at each other's clothing, I knew a decision had to be made. We either needed to commit to this attraction and go for it, or I needed to get off this bed immediately.

And probably go work one out under a cold shower.

"Tell me, Agatha Sandoval," I growled in her ear. Since my face was buried in her neck, I couldn't see her reaction to me using her new name.

"What?" she panted. "Tell you what?"

"Are we doing this?"

"Yes, God, please. I don't know how much clearer I can be here."

"Not what I meant, Storm." I liked that nickname for her. She was a tempest wrapped in a sexy body, with blue sky eyes and a tornado personality. It fit her perfectly.

She bit my neck where she'd been kissing, and I hissed. It felt so fucking good, and I was about to give in. Forget the talking and the promises I wanted her to make me while she was vulnerable and bury myself inside her alluring body.

Luckily, a cooler head prevailed than the one leading the charge thus far.

"I meant"—I kissed her once but pulled back when she tried to move in for more—"stay married. Give it a try being husband and wife."

Her eyes shot open wide, and I could see the thunderclouds move in. Lightning would strike next with a verbal assault; I just knew it.

"Is that the only way you'll fuck me? If we're really married? Are you some kind of religious nut and haven't told me?"

She tried to put space between us, but I wouldn't budge. I outweighed her by at least seventy-five pounds, and while she was fit and strong, I easily pinned her to the mattress. This time, when I attempted to kiss her, she turned her head to dodge my effort.

"Don't be a brat now," I said, and again, out of nowhere, my voice took on a dominant edge. Something about this woman was making even my unconscious traits morph.

"I'm not being a brat. I don't get you. Why would you do all this?"

"All what?"

"Get us both all ramped up and then basically throw a bucket of ice water on my pussy."

"Is that why it's so wet?" I grinned down at her.

"Ha. Very funny."

I slid my hand back into her little panties that were driving me insane. They were the sexiest white-cotton underwear I'd ever seen. Inside was the warm, wet paradise I needed to taste. Right now. I'd ask her again to commit to me when she was on the brink of orgasm.

Dirty tactics? Maybe.

Did I care? Not one single bit.

"I think I better take a closer look," I teased and backed off her body. With a hand on each of her hips, I dragged her down the mattress, and she erupted with a giggle.

"What are you doing? Just tossing me around like a caveman?" she asked through her laughter.

"I'm burying my face between these gorgeous thighs for a

while. I won't take no for an answer."

"No girl in her right mind says no to a man that adamant about going down on her." She looked down at me while I tugged her panties down to her ankles. I got distracted throwing the covers to the floor, and when I refocused my attention on her, she had kicked the little white knickers off the rest of the way.

"I like those panties. They're sexy. Though I imagine I would appreciate anything that's been touching this pussy all day."

"Less talk, more tongue. Husband." She gave me a sassy wink and pointed to the juncture of her thighs.

"You know, I'm not normally into punishing women, but I could make an exception for you." The threat was leveled playfully, but my dick didn't get the memo about the levity. Remarkably, the thing seemed to get harder with the thought.

Boom. Boom. Boom.

My worst nightmare became reality with that sound at our door.

"Rise and shine, newlyweds," my boss said from the other side.

"For fuck's sake," I muttered into my hands while Agatha scrambled faster than I knew someone could move. She had her panties yanked back into place and was looking frantically from left to right, obviously searching for more clothes.

Boom. Boom. Boom.

"Coming," I hollered toward the door. "Give me a minute. I just got out of the shower."

"If my sister is with him, I will die," Agatha whispered.

"Why? We've been sleeping in the same room all weekend. You don't think people think we're going at it in here?"

"Didn't I have a robe on before we took our nap?" she

asked while still searching through the bedding.

I picked the thing up off the floor where she had carelessly dropped it and thrust it toward her. Once she had it on, I went to open the door. I'd be tempted to punch his pretty face if he knocked like a madman one more time.

After one last check on my wife's degree of decency, I slid the deadbolt open, unlocked the door, and flung the thing open.

"Hello," I said as casually as possible.

"Are you guys ready?" He gave me a slow inspection from my face down to my bare feet and then continued. "Plane leaves when we get to the tarmac. Pilot texted me they're all fueled up and ready to go."

"Shit. No." I rubbed my forehead. "I guess we lost track of time," I offered weakly. "We can go back commercial if we're going to hold you up."

But my dearest had a differing opinion. *Of course she did!*

From over my shoulder, she shouted, "No, let's go. We'll hurry, Elijah. Don't leave without us. We'll be out front in ten."

"Sounds like a plan." He directed his comment past me to my bride. Then directly to me, he said, "I see who already wears the pants around here." He finished it with a playful wink, turned abruptly, and strolled off down the pathway.

We just spent an amazing weekend at what was likely the finest hotel I'd ever been to. So many places, hotels, restaurants—hell, even the convenience stores—were over the top with opulence in this town. Vegas had never been my scene, but now that this chapter of my life started here, it became a new favorite.

Agatha's sister, Hannah, had just married my boss, Elijah Banks. One afternoon, while packing up at the end of a workday, he'd shared the secret getaway plans with me. I'd let the beans spill to my girl the very next time we spoke. From there, Agatha insisted we accompany the party across the Mojave and even leveled a threat to expose their plans to their parents if we couldn't tag along.

Never in a million years would I have guessed I'd be coming back married like the rest of the men in Elijah's posse. We'd have to pay the piper eventually, but right now, I needed to pack my stuff and get out of our villa.

The gang had rented a beautiful and private mini compound for their vacation spot that was owned by the infamous Stone family from Chicago. It looked like every venture that family took on was a success.

We all shared one main house for the past three days that included an incredible gourmet kitchen, living room, and dining room. Each couple had a small, isolated villa where we slept. The concept was a great layout, especially for groups like ours.

The moment I closed the door, she set off like a hurricane. She barked out orders, drill-sergeant style, until I finally stepped in her path and stilled her movement with both hands on her shoulders.

"Darling," I said calmly and ducked my head down to meet her eye to eye. "Settle down. They're not going to leave without us, and you're whipping around here like a maniac. We're bound to leave something behind."

She exhaled, and her shoulders softened beneath my hold. "You're right. Sorry. I just know how my sister gets all worked up the minute something doesn't go to plan, so I tend to do my best to not kick that off. Especially now that she's knocked up. That anxiety of hers can't be good for the baby."

"I'm sure you're right, but I'm confident my boss will keep

her in line."

Just like that, a switch flipped.

Her hands flew to her hips, and she fired back, "In line?"

Damn, this woman was a spitfire.

"You know what I mean. He'll do what he can to keep her calm. Like I'm trying to do here," I said but then muttered, "for whatever good it's doing." In a normal volume again, I finished my thought. "I don't like seeing you so stressed out. Plus, it makes me tense watching it."

"Sorry." And the switch flipped back because she grabbed my hands and squeezed them. "I really am. Are you almost packed, though?"

"Yep. I'm ready. Can I help you with anything?"

"Actually, yes. That would be great if you could put the stuff in the bathroom into my makeup bag."

"Sure. Where is that?"

"It's in there on the vanity." She continued describing where while I headed to the bathroom. "Can't miss it. It's that quilted, floral thing that looks like a big purse."

I laughed at the image that painted in my mind as I hustled into the next room. I found the bag right where she said it was and gathered the things that looked like they didn't belong to the hotel. I reached for a small velvet square that looked like a thin wallet but knocked it to the floor in my haste. Her birth control pills slid out of the sheath and lay on the marble floor. Well, that answered a personal question I wouldn't have to pose now. But when I picked them up, I noticed she was behind in taking them by about three days.

"Wife!" I shouted and stalked back into the bedroom.

"Really, man. Stop calling me that. It's ridiculous."

Choosing to not address the topic, I held up the packet instead.

"Oh, shit. I need to take one of those," she said nonchalantly.

"Actually, looking at the packaging, you've skipped several days."

"Okay, I know you have your paper that is giving you this weird notion that things like this are your business," she said and snatched the packet from my fingers. "But this is definitely not your business."

"Are you sleeping with other people currently?" And this part definitely *was* my business. If my employer hadn't interrupted us just twenty minutes ago, I'd be coming inside this woman right about now.

"I really don't think this is the best time for a conversation like this, Carmen. I mean, they're waiting for us!" Her agitation was ramping up, and I couldn't help but wonder if it was truly about holding up the other couple or if she didn't want to tell me the answer.

"You know what, you're right. We can chat about it once we get on the plane."

She visibly relaxed and went to dart off in another direction, but I caught her by the arm and stopped her.

"What?" she asked with very little patience.

"We *will* have this conversation, Storm."

Her glare would've been lethal to someone else. She had no idea the experience I had with my father and the extent of the man's temper and foul disposition. I wasn't moved in the slightest by her amateur version.

The grin that spread across my lips seemed to really piss her off.

Agatha yanked her arm from my grasp and buzzed across the room to finish packing. I was momentarily transfixed by her energy and temperament. No idea what it was, or why it was this girl, but my dick swelled in my boxers. I wanted nothing more than to bring this little storm all the pleasure and ecstasy I knew how to deliver. She needed a reason to yield to me, and that just might be the way to do it. Keep her in a sex fog so she didn't have time to spark up all this manufactured drama.

For the most part, though, she didn't strike me as a drama queen. One of those women who turns every hill into a mountain simply because they thrive in chaos. No...I had a feeling there was an actual reason behind her hot and cold personalities, and I really had to ask myself before I got in any deeper with this fierce little lady... *Is she worth it?*

Only time could tell me the answer to that one. The problem with the wait-and-see mindset was I didn't have the luxury of time to wait.

When we got back to Los Angeles, some decisions would need to be made.

CHAPTER THREE

AGATHA

Finally settled in our seats for takeoff, I exhaled fully for the first time since I woke up this morning. The first time. Carmen was getting on my nerves with his doting attentiveness, and I tried to take the seat next to my sister on the plane, just to get a break from the guy. But her new husband was having none of that, and she was so googly-eyed in love with the man, she just did whatever he told her to do.

I had to hand it to him, though. He was super clever as he went about his controlling ways. He always made it seem like everything he did was for her, first and foremost, and she swooned a bit more each time.

A girl could puke from all the sugary sweetness between the newlyweds.

So why did it get on my last nerve when Carmen attempted the same shit with me? I recognized the pang in my gut every time I watched Hannah and her beau. It was jealousy, and I wasn't proud of the fact. I wanted her to be happy more than anyone else. She was beautiful, smart, and loyal to the bone. She deserved to have someone love her and gush about it to the world. My sister deserved that more than anyone I knew. The feeling wasn't a begrudging sort of jealousy as much as also wanting what she was lucky enough to have.

Maybe I didn't deserve that sort of pure joy, and that's why the universe kept it hidden away. Again, the man who was trying to bestow goodness upon me sat right beside me, and every one of his gestures of kindness or affection just irritated me.

During our other encounters, I had a good, if not great, time. When I tried to really examine what he was doing that was so annoying, it was the babysitting nagging combo regarding drinking that really stood out. In many senses—all right, in most senses—I barely knew the guy. What made him think he could appoint himself my sponsor?

Not that I needed one, anyway.

Yes, my partying had leveled up recently. But what about it? I was young, single—okay, scratch that one—and I was in that phase in my life where you're supposed to have fun. Make memories. Do irresponsible shit. If I had known he was going to come along and squash all that, I would've never agreed to go out with him in the first place.

Now that I had, though, I liked him. In fairness, he had many qualities on my list. My four sisters and I sat down about a year ago when we were all single and wrote lists of ten qualities we wanted in a guy. And I was talking about long-term partner, not just a roll in the sheets. That might be a different list all together.

My twin sisters, Sheppard and Maye, had lists at complete odds with each other's. Was that strange since they were twins? Weren't they supposed to share some wavelength or something?

The older of the two, by a whopping six minutes, was Maye. She was kind, responsible, and so smart it was intimidating.

Sheppard had to be pulled out of the birth canal with

some sort of labor room gear that left her head looking like a Hershey's Kiss. Of course, we teased her about it relentlessly for most of her life. But if nothing else, the girl was consistent. Stubborn from minute one.

Until recently. A switch flipped in that young lady, and now she was not a very nice human to be around. Truth be told, she was a total bitch. And no one knew why. We all talked about it, and no one could come up with a good reason for the change, but there had been one, because it was about a one-hundred-eighty-degree flip, not just changing preference from plastic to paper.

Our mother, bless the woman's soul for putting up with five daughters, insisted that she would snap out of it one day and either talk about what crawled up her ass and died or just simply go back to the way she used to be: nice. Or at least nicer than she was these days.

The sad part of it all was that by the time either of those two things happened, she wouldn't have any friends left. She was mean to everyone, not just the family. Even the people at Starbucks were afraid of her, and they dealt with assholes all day.

Hannah, our oldest sister, described Prince Charming of fairy-tale fame to a T on her list. Considering her new husband, Elijah Banks, she pretty much got what she was looking for. Although Mr. Banks had way better hair than the two-dimensional prince.

The baby bomb of our brood was Clemson. The bombshell nickname started with Elijah and his security team and spread to his friends after that. They said we were five blond bombshells and called us the Bomb Squad and other predictable nicknames related to explosives. Well, I'd been called waaaay worse, so at least there was that.

Breaking me away from my random thoughts, Carmen touched my arm with his left hand, and I saw that green band again. To be fair, I hadn't removed mine yet, either. I got some odd comfort when I looked at my hand and saw it there. Not diving in too deep about the meaning behind that, though. Was there a possibility, however slim, that we knew what we were doing last night?

Wouldn't be the first time I used alcohol as a scapegoat.

I looked up to his handsome face and gave him a small smile. I really needed to be nicer to the guy. He was in as much shit for this as I was.

"Do you want some water or something?" he asked but quickly added, "Not booze."

With an irritated scowl, I answered, "You need to stop. Day drinking isn't really my thing, anyway. Some water would be great. Thank you." My smile went from genuine to practiced and plastic in the span of one comment.

I watched him relay the request to the flight attendant and really studied his bone structure. First in profile while he spoke to the pleasant woman, then straight on when he handed me the water. I landed a hottie for sure.

Leaning past his body, I signaled to her again. "May I have some ice, please?" If I crunched on something during landing, my ears wouldn't clog. Otherwise, I'd drive myself mad trying to clear them for the next twenty-four hours.

"Sorry," he said with that sheepish, innocent-boy look he had perfected. "I didn't know, but we're still in the discovery phase."

"No need to apologize," I said and touched his arm.

He looked down to my left hand on his sleeve, and I

quickly pulled back. Or tried to. The handsome man took my hand in his and brought my fingers to his lips while I stared. Baffled. He softly kissed my ring and looked up to find me gaping at him.

"We can make this work," he vowed for just my ears.

I continued to stare. Speechless, really. It was a rare occasion, but it happened.

"Do you want to add anything to that?" he asked with a cautious smile after silence ballooned between us.

"I-I-I really don't know what to say," I spluttered.

"Say you'll give it a try with me. If we can't make it work in what? A year?"

My eyes bugged out at the time frame. He wanted me to commit a year of my life to fix a drunken mistake? Seemed a little extreme to me.

"Okay, nine months?" My husband paused for me to reply, but I still had nothing. Well, I had a lot to say, actually, but none of it would be productive in the given situation.

So he went on with his proposition, clutching my hand the whole time. "I don't think it would be fair to either one of us to commit less time than that. I still think it should be a year."

"Carmen—" I finally started. And came up short again.

"Yes, my beautiful storm?" He grinned, awfully proud of himself for coming up with that nickname.

"Be serious," I finally squawked and quickly looked around to see if anyone heard me. "We don't even live together. With both our hectic schedules, how much time would we even see each other?" It was the best reason I could come up with under the pressure of his undivided attention.

"Simple solution to that." He shrugged.

"Really? And what is that?" I muttered. "I'm almost afraid

to hear what you're about to say."

"You live in your parents' home, right?"

"Yes. I've been looking for my own place, though, because my commute is horrid."

"I have my own place. You'll move in. We can move your stuff this coming weekend," he declared, nodding while he spoke like the plan was as good as done.

"Uhh, I don't know, dude. I think I'd be a nightmare to live with. Just being completely honest here."

"It'll be fine. Married people live together, darling. People find a way to work through the little things every single day."

How could he be so nonchalant about all this?

"I don't know. I still think we should find a way to undo this." I held up my left hand. "There must be a cooling-off period or something in Nevada. People make bad decisions as a way of life in that city."

He turned fully toward me in his seat and held my stare for a few beats before speaking. Could he see I was about to have a meltdown? I usually hid it pretty well, but the guy was very observant, and I was operating on very little sleep.

"I don't want to undo it. I want to give this a shot," he said, meaning every single word judging by the gravity of his stare. He squeezed my hand, which I guessed was my cue to vow the same thing.

But I couldn't bring myself to make the commitment.

"Let me think about it. That's reasonable, right? It's a huge commitment, and we don't even know each other. That well, at least. What if you snore?"

The man's eyebrows climbed close to his hairline. "Storm, you sound like a freight train when you're sleeping, and I'm still on board." He chuckled. "You'll have to come up with something better than that."

Aggressively, I turned more toward him in the confinement of our seats. Even planted my hands on my hips to display my defiance. "I do not snore."

"Oh, woman. You most certainly do. Ask your neighbors. Even they can confirm it."

"You're full of shit, and you know it," I continued to argue.

My husband could barely answer through his laughter. "Fraid not, dear."

"No one has ever complained about sleeping with me before."

Carmen leaned in closer and dropped the volume of his next comment. "Oh, I most definitely would not complain about that either. Have you really made it to this age without knowing how men's brains work?"

I just shook my head at his very guy-like comment and couldn't really identify if we were playing or arguing. My pulse was racing and my breaths were coming quicker than at rest, but I couldn't grab on to anger where I normally felt it—in the pit of my stomach.

It looked like my man was having a similar war. When his nostrils flared on his inhalation, I felt heat in my core. Jesus, really? This was what turned me on these days? This whole weekend had every one of my senses scrambled. That had to be the explanation.

The small plane bounced through some turbulence, and the dip in the cabin beneath me startled me. Instinctively I grabbed on to Carmen's arm with the grip of a baseball slugger. I leaned closer to mutter an apology, and my husband smashed his lips to mine.

Shock from the action and arousal that had built from our

little tiff had me easily yielding to him. His tongue was urgent and demanding, finding mine with delicious skill.

I should've pulled back. We were on a small plane with a handful of other people. They didn't need to see us swapping spit the way we were. But I couldn't bring myself to stop. So many men I dated lately were terrible kissers. Maybe they were just inexperienced boys now that I had this benchmark experience for comparison.

This guy knew how to deliver a kiss. At least for my preferences he did. This was the first time we'd kissed while I was completely sober, and I could smack myself for missing all the nuances the times before.

When we finally broke apart, I couldn't help but notice how the side conversations that had been taking place around us had stopped all together.

"Mmmm," he hummed. "I think I could do this for hours. Your mouth is paradise, woman."

A smile spread across my lips, and I lifted my hand to touch them with my fingertips. Hell, it felt like my whole face was numb. I dug deep for a clever response but came up with nada. I was warm and fuzzy in all the best places and wondered if I could talk him into joining me in the lavatory for a quickie.

Although, bathroom sex was never really my jam. Too many germs to obsess over. Being yucked out about the location obscured any enjoyment of the activities taking place.

As if the moment weren't awkward enough, my sister popped up behind our row of seats.

"Well, isn't this cozy?" she said with a mischievous giggle.

Carmen tapped the *fasten seat belt* icon on the overhead display and told my sister, "You better stay seated, Mrs. Banks. For your own safety, of course." He sneaked me a quick wink, and I chuckled.

Hannah sank back down behind us into her own cushy seat but said loud enough for us to hear, "We'll talk when we get home, Dah. Don't think we won't." She gave the back of my seat a solid push with her foot, and I growled while jolting forward.

"Knock it off, Han, or I'll tell your honey an embarrassing story about your childhood." I teased with the threat, but the idea had merit.

"I've been meaning to ask you about that name," Carmen said. "What's that about?"

"You mean *Dah*?"

He nodded, so I went on to explain that the nickname came from my dear sister in the next row. When I was born, she was just two years old and couldn't say Agatha. But she apparently thought the syllable count or something—no one really knows—sounded like "Tah dah!" And it stuck from that point on. Most of my family routinely used the nickname.

"It's cute. It suits you," he said after my long-winded explanation, and he leaned over and kissed the tip of my nose.

This kissing thing could get out of hand. But I liked it too much to tell him to stop. There was a part of me—a pretty big part of me—that liked his attention. If he would just get better at picking up on the cues I threw off when I wasn't in the mood for physical affection, we'd be golden.

We were on the ground in less than two hours. Normally the flight from Las Vegas to Los Angeles was shorter than that, but apparently we circled the airport a few times waiting for other air traffic to land. I hadn't really paid attention to the duration of the trip, though. Carmen and I easily passed the time chatting and laughing and, yes, stealing kisses whenever the opportunity arose.

Legitimate dread rested right behind the carefree joy I decided to allow myself on the second half of our flight. Knowing the shit was really going to hit the fan when we got home prompted my decision to just enjoy the man's company while it was still unburdened.

Now that we were on the ground, I felt like an elephant pulled up an easy chair on the middle of my chest. The desire for a drink was so strong, I found myself coming up with ways to get separated from the group as we walked through the terminal. I could always lag behind in the airport and hit one of the pubs sprinkled through storefronts and departure gates.

In the long run, it wouldn't do me any good, though. Plus, the moment we stepped onto California soil, my new husband swept my hand up into his and tugged me toward the exit. There were so many cool and convenient things about flying aboard someone's private plane. Not having to fight the masses of people in the baggage claim area or wrestle with suitcases bigger than me were the two best.

I really wanted to talk some things over with my sister and get her take on the mess I was in. Unfortunately, she slept for most of the one-state hop while her husband read quietly beside her. I guess the pregnancy was already affecting her physically.

So I was on my own to try to figure out the best way to handle breaking the news to my parents. Currently, the plan was to not deal with it and just go on about my life. Most nights, I got home from work and went straight to my room to shower the day away and crawl into bed.

Lather, rinse, repeat.

CHAPTER FOUR

AGATHA

My new brother-in-law's personal driver shuttled us to Brentwood in a tricked-out SUV that made me feel like I was a special agent in the CIA. He pulled up to my parents' home and hustled around to my door before my husband could get to it. The two men exchanged some friendly banter before the driver shuffled back to his spot behind the wheel and Carmen whooshed my door open.

"My lady," he said brightly and offered a hand to help me out to the driveway. I smiled at his boyish charm and let him assist me even though I was completely capable of exiting a car on my own. The one rolling bag I brought was already parked there, handle extended. I turned to Carmen to say goodbye, but he snatched the handle and started toward the front door.

"Hey! Whoa ... where are you going?"

"Well, no sense putting this off, right? You can introduce me and maybe just let me do the talking from there. Your folks seem very reasonable. I'm sure they'll be fine."

Again, his cavalier attitude left me speechless.

Until I jolted back to the moment. "What planet are you from?" I squawked, and the sound came out much louder than I intended.

"Mars, from what I've read, but I don't know if I can

buy into all that." His seemingly permanent smile grew after delivering that pitiful joke, and I groaned in response.

"I don't think we need to get into this with them already. Not the moment I walk in the door. Why don't you let this nice man drive you home, and I'll check in with you tomorrow?"

"No. You're moving in with me. We discussed this on the plane. I'll help you get a few essential things together now, and we can come back over the weekend to grab the rest." He said all that so carelessly, like this wasn't a life-changing moment here. Not to mention, he'd be lucky to not exit on a stretcher if he just waltzed into my father's home and uttered any of those plans.

"Storm, listen. We're home now. It's time to get serious about what's going on here. You said you'd been looking for a place to live. Bingo! You found one. You wanted to be closer to work. Check that box too. You won't drive a single mile on the 405 ever again if you don't want to." He couldn't have looked more pleased with himself while rattling off the reasons this was the best plan.

A big knot of—shit, I had no idea what it was—was forming in the pit of my stomach because I felt like a mean mother who was about to tell her kid there was no Santa Claus.

"Carmen," I said on a heavy sigh, and already his features wilted.

How could he truly believe this would work out?

With more emotion than I expected, he said, "Don't give up on us before we even try. I'm asking you sincerely to just try with me."

He wrapped his long arms around me, and I just let him. Why couldn't I stop sending the poor guy mixed signals? My handbag was squashed between our bodies, and I smiled into his chest about the awkwardness of the embrace. It suited us perfectly.

There was certainly a lot to like about the guy. His height, for one thing. He was at least six one, maybe six two. I was just shy of a foot shorter than that, so while in his arms, I felt very secure. Purse and all.

"I need time to explain things to my parents. You don't understand," I said, putting my flat hand up to stop his protest. Kindly, he held his tongue while I went on. "My dad has a medical condition... I swear I'm not making this up," I began to explain and heard what a lame excuse it sounded like.

"He's had a few cardiac events?" he asked, as if pulling the information from a database in his head.

I gave him a sideways look. "How did you know about that?"

"I don't know details, just something Elijah once told me while talking about Hannah."

"What did he say?"

"It was a while ago, before I met you, so, to be honest, I listened with minimal interest." He ducked his head apologetically. Or at least that's how I interpreted the gesture. "But I think he said your dad has had three heart attacks?"

Nodding along while he spoke, I answered, "Yes, that's right. But he's very sensitive to stress. His blood pressure shoots sky high at the slightest provocation. I don't want to put the man in his grave over a stupid choice I made while intoxicated. You know?" I tilted my head back to look up at him.

"That makes sense. I'm happy to hear how much you care about him, and the rest of your family as well. Family is super important to me, too. I can't wait for mine to meet you. They're going to love you instantly," he chattered on with a palpable affection for his relatives. It was really sweet to witness.

With renewed hope, I brought the topic back to the issue at hand. "So you understand why I can't just bust through the front door shouting 'Guess who's married?'"

While I grinned at the visual that created in my mind, Carmen acquiesced.

"How long do you need? I can come by tomorrow after work. That way we can pack both our cars with stuff." He winced before asking, "Do you have a lot?"

"Let's not get ahead of ourselves. I'm not convinced my folks are going to green-light this whole arrangement. I mean..." I thought about it for a moment or two and then chuckled. "I've pulled some pretty stupid stunts in my life."

He gave me a chaste kiss on the forehead before saying, "I can't wait to learn all there is to know about you, Mrs. Sandoval."

I groaned for good measure, but inside my stomach, and parts just lower, butterflies charged with static zipped and zapped every time he touched me sweetly or called me by that name.

Okay, so why am I sending myself mixed signals too?

If nothing else, I needed time to get my head screwed on straight about how I really felt about this man, this situation, and the future. The comment about pulling some harebrained shit in my short life was not an exaggeration. This arrangement, or whatever we decided to label it, needed real examination.

"Hey, wait a minute," I called to Elijah's driver. "Can you wait one more minute?" And then added quickly, "Please?"

"Yes, of course, Miss Farsey," the man responded with a quick dip of his head.

"Carmen, go with him. Let him drive you home, and I'll call you tomorrow."

I tried to take the handle of my suitcase from him, but he

blocked it with his body.

"Storm, let's go inside and talk to your parents. At least they can start getting used to seeing us together. You can drive me home later, and then you can see the apartment." His mien changed every time he issued instructions, and for some reason, I agreed.

"All right." I told myself it was the path of least resistance, and he could take an Uber home in fifteen minutes when I ushered him out.

"Never mind, Lorenzo, I'm going to stay here. We really appreciate the ride." Carmen strode over to the man with an outstretched hand.

The two shook heartily, like old friends, and then we stood on the front step for a moment while I tried to control my rioting nerves.

"They're going to kill me. They're going to be so mad. This is never going to work out," I continued to mutter to myself while my husband reached forward and opened the door.

"You're back!" my mom called from just inside the door. "I thought I heard some commotion out here."

"Hey..." I greeted and then trailed off.

Carmen, on the other hand, pushed us into the entranceway farther with a firm and calming hand to my lower back.

"Oh, Carmen!" my mother chirped in her brightest voice. "So nice to see you again."

I stood slack-jawed while my spouse charged forward and bussed my mother's cheek in greeting. Of course, never far from each other, my dad came from the living room to say hello too.

Somebody just shoot me. Please, make it quick and painless and put me out of my misery.

"Mr. Farsey, hello." Carmen offered his hand to shake. "How was your return flight yesterday?"

"What's to complain about?" My father laughed. "A guy could get used to traveling that way, right?"

"Definitely." Carmen smiled widely, and my heart skipped a beat or two. He really was a good-looking guy.

Thankfully, I snapped out of the lust fog and said, "Okay, thanks for seeing me home. I'll call you, okay?" I locked eyes with him and silently begged him to just go along with the exit strategy.

But my mother, with all her hostess grace, interrupted. "Nonsense. You two are probably exhausted. Carmen, won't you stay for dinner?"

My pleading stare turned to a threatening glare. I knew before he even spoke that he would take her up on the invitation. She'd played right into his plan, and we both knew it. I gave my head an imperceptible shake, but he answered for himself.

My youngest sister, Clemson, strolled past the huddle just inside the door at that exact moment, stealing everyone's attention with her comment.

"Nice rings."

I. Am. Going. To. Kill. Her.

And if I found out Hannah had anything to do with her keen observation, I'd be down two sisters.

While the others carried on with their conversation, I was frozen in place. Completely afraid to move in any direction and encounter an expectant stare. I studied my feet with keen interest until Carmen's strong hand was at my lower back again, confidently moving me deeper into the house.

"Why don't I help you unpack?" he asked with a stare of his own then that I hadn't seen before. He was both giving me the courage to escape this awkward situation and some sort of direct instruction on how to do it.

"Sounds good!" I chirped in an overly bright tone. I was barely finished with the comment before I took off down the hall toward my bedroom—hubby hot on my heels.

Behind the safety of my closed bedroom door, I looked up at the man as he pulled me into an unexpected embrace. It was going to take some time to get used to his touchy-feely ways. My body automatically stiffened on contact, but the moment I caught a whiff of his comforting scent, I relaxed.

Did this guy have magical powers? Magical pheromones, maybe?

"Well, that probably could've gone a little smoother." He chuckled while holding me against his firm body.

All I could produce was some sort of groan combined with a whimper. The sound was so pitiful, he leaned back a bit without breaking our embrace to assess my face.

"Don't cry, baby," he whispered sweetly and stroked some stray hair back from my face.

"I don't cry," I declared with an edge.

"Ever?"

"Pretty much. It's just another thing about me that's broken," I admitted with a shrug. Even when I was a child, my mother said I rarely shed tears. There were times I really wished I could or did. It seemed to make a lot of people feel better to express feelings so deep. But it just was a gene that skipped me, apparently.

"Not even over a lost pet?" Carmen continued in disbelief.

"I've never had a pet."

"Whaaaat?" He dramatically dragged the single syllable over a few beats.

"My mom said she had her hands full with humans; she

didn't need to deal with animals too. Hannah was heartsick about it for most of her childhood. To this day, she hasn't forgiven my mother for the childhood scar." I forced a laugh.

The fact that Hannah had to deal with so much trauma from her childhood wasn't funny. At all. The part that earned the chuckle was Carmen's reaction and how it was the exact reaction I got from everyone I told the story to.

Maybe sensing the topic was deeper than my glib attitude toward it would pretend, Carmen changed the subject.

"Let's unpack. That way you'll know where to start for the move."

"Listen…" I flopped down on my bed, then quickly scrambled back to sit against the headboard.

"May I join you?" my tall guy asked while standing on the other side of the mattress.

"Sure." I sighed. "Why not?" Christ, I was tired. The stress from this ridiculous fuck-up was starting to wear me down.

Carmen made an enormous production about getting situated on the bed beside me. Propping pillows and folding the covers back at a perfectly straight crease, he uncovered my journal where it was normally stowed beneath a throw pillow.

"Well…" He waggled his eyebrows at me, and I burst out laughing at the silly expression. "What do we have here, Storm?"

"Give it," I ordered in the most serious tone and held out my hand.

"Nope. I don't think so," he teased as I scurried up to kneel on the bed in front of him.

He held the small, blue, linen-covered book over his head so I couldn't reach it.

That little bound pile of pages held every single secret I kept inside, in the most private places I guarded with my existence. There were comments and stories and factoids that absolutely no one else knew about me—and never would if it were up to me. If that journal landed in the wrong hands, I probably would never leave the house again. I'd die of humiliation.

With a glare filled with every ounce of seriousness I was capable of, I issued a warning. "That would be an unforgivable breach of my privacy. Let that be known now." It was a fact that would never change, no matter what degree of closeness our relationship possessed.

"I'll trade you," he offered confidently. I probably exposed way too many cards with my threat and death stare, but he had me backed into a corner and knew it. At my crossed arms, he added, "You're really at the disadvantage here."

"I will never forgive you for this . . ." I trailed off, sensing his steadfastness.

"Take the deal I'm about to offer, Storm." He gave a cocky grin that reminded me so much of his boss, it was uncanny. After a cool shrug, he said, "Then you can have it back."

Nothing more than a wicked stare from my position directly in front of him. If I said one more thing, an emotional meltdown that was hovering just beneath the surface would crest. Not tears and blubbering like other girls, though. My freak-outs included yelling and throwing things—and breaking items if necessary.

Slowly, he closed the space between us and pressed his lips to mine. While still in contact with my lips, he quietly bargained, "Give me a year."

I didn't react. I couldn't. I was in a washing machine of feelings, and the spin cycle started the moment he closed that distance between our bodies. While he was so close, I could feel his body heat in intoxicating pulses. I'd agree to anything he wanted right now. I knew it. He knew it. And the bastard played dirty to get what he wanted.

And yes, somewhere way in the recesses of my mind, that turned me on too.

"This isn't fair," I whimpered and tried to increase the space between us.

But Carmen must have predicted my retreat, because his large hand was at the small of my back in an instant, commanding me to stay.

"Life isn't fair, darling. I'm sure someone's told you that one before." He leaned to the side a bit and kissed a featherlight trail across my jaw to that little magical spot just behind my ear. Not sure how he knew it was there, but kisses, licks, bites, to that spot alone, could make me come if done right.

A deep, husky groan worked its way up my throat and encouraged him to keep up the treatment. The man knew what he was doing, I'd give him that. I had a death grip on the material of his shirt, hoping to save myself from collapsing.

"Holy shit...holy...Carmen, oh...ooh my God. Oohhh, shit," I muttered in a long string that was likely unintelligible to my husband, but he understood enough to keep the pace of what he was doing.

Until he abruptly stopped.

I gasped a deep breath, sure I hadn't had oxygen in hours, and my entire body sagged into him.

"Why? Why would you do that to me?" I stammered when I finally could breathe normally enough to produce more than just vowel sounds. Frustration and physical need were center stage, but there was no way in hell I'd let him see what he'd just done to me.

I hung my head until my crown butted against his solid chest. How had this mild-mannered man—who I was sure was the typical mama's boy type I could gobble up in one bite—gain the upper hand so quickly? He must have been playing me all along and was just lying in wait, ready to use these mad skills to take advantage of me when he saw something he wanted.

Finally, he lifted my face with a finger beneath my chin until our eyes locked. My furious glare collided with his mischievous glint, and I seethed hotter.

Then it hit me. My ire was fueling his agenda. The hotter I got under the collar, the more power I handed him in this negotiation. Or whatever the hell was going on here. All I knew was he still clutched my journal in his capable hand, and I was done being the fool.

With the practice of twenty-plus years, I wiped my face clean of all expression and became a blank slate. People thought I was emotionless—hell—I *told* people I was. It was the keenest defense, and I figured the tactic out very young. Emotionless reactions made people uncomfortable. Usually, when I didn't react on the outside in a given situation, my opponent ended the confrontation soon after. And typically in an acquiescent manner.

Now, I calmed my breathing, applied zero tilt to my lips, and with an expressionless yet very alert and focused stare, I waited. I'd wait him out for twenty minutes if that's what it took for him to backpedal. Hell! I could go longer if I had to. My difficult sister, Sheppard, was the one person who could go toe to toe with me in this arena. There was no way Sandoval would come out on top.

No way.

CHAPTER FIVE

CARMEN

My God, the woman was incredible. Smelled incredible. Felt incredible. Tasted incredible. I had her right where I wanted her. Now, all she had to do was give in. Something I didn't think she was too familiar with doing, but we both had a lot of habit changing in our immediate future.

There was no way I would ever violate her privacy and read the interesting little book I held. But the moment I saw the value of the currency, I had to cash it in. Only a fool would have let the opportunity pass by. I might be a lot of things, but I'm not a fool. I played that role in relationships before, and it just wasn't a vibe that suited me. A lot of people made the mistake of thinking I was a pushover based solely on the fact that I had manners and a deep respect for women in general.

Wrong.

After I discovered my ex had been cheating on me, I had an involuntary dating hiatus. I was always angry, and not just at her. I was pissed at myself for being so naïve and so trusting and was pissed at humanity in general. Maybe that sounded a little extreme, and maybe it was, but I was nursing a pretty serious wound.

After a couple of weeks of self-loathing, I made a conscious decision to regain control of my social life. For every night I didn't have a date, I spent it researching, studying, investigating different sexual techniques and philosophies. When I would land a date, I'd experiment with what I'd learned.

I looked at it as the practical portion of the course syllabus. I had always been an excellent student, and now I had a lot of tricks up my sleeve that women never expected.

That actually worked in my favor. That certain moment when something happened that a woman hadn't anticipated because every other guy she'd ever been with failed at delivering so monumentally was thrilling.

I felt Agatha's entire body soften beneath my touch when I found that spot close to her sexy little ear.

Seriously. Every damn feature on this woman was perfection. She was so many different things all at the same time, it was intriguing and exciting. And hot. God . . . so fucking hot. At the moment, I had an erection that was straining to be unleashed from the confines of my clothing. It was something I got over being embarrassed about at an early age.

Truth in advertising, maybe? That sophomoric thought made my grin stretch wider, and of course, Agatha misinterpreted my expression and thought it was because of her. Indirectly, I suppose it was, but my own thoughts were entertaining me currently. But how the hell do you explain that to someone? Especially a storm of a woman whose temper was about to blow.

"Oh, are you pleased with yourself?" she asked.

While her words were biting and confrontational, her facial expression was as smooth as a frozen lake. Calm. Still. Expressionless, actually. What a strange reaction, or nonreaction, really.

My eyes narrowed with suspicion, but I wouldn't give in

to her. I was fairly certain she was trying to manipulate me somehow.

I held my ground.

The old me—the me before class—would have caved and likely apologized. Maybe I upset her? Maybe I said the wrong thing and hurt her feelings? I'd sacrifice anything to keep the peace. Including my dignity. When I looked back on the me of the pre-class era, I was embarrassed. That guy was a damn doormat. No wonder my ex cheated on me. My behavior told her I had little or no respect for myself. Why the hell should she?

Using my boss's signature move, I tilted my head in question and simply said, "Explain."

My wife's face twisted like she just sucked a lemon. "What is with this posse and that stupid saying?"

"What's stupid about it? It expresses that I'm curious about what you just said in one simple word." I shrugged and waited for her to go on.

We were both silent for a bit, and she huffed a heavy breath. "You can't really be that dense, but I will explain it to you anyway." She hitched a thumb over her shoulder, referencing a space in time rather than the room. "You ramped me up back there and then left me hanging. What's that about?"

She struck this sexy little pose with one hip jutted out and her dainty, feminine hand propped atop it. Her face was still blank as the free letter tile in Scrabble, though. Based on her body language, she wanted answers. For someone so small in stature, she was a fierce creature.

"I told you what I want. And I think if you were honest with yourself, you would admit you want it too." I tried to mirror her inanimate features and waited for her response.

"No, what I want is you to give my *priiii-vetttt* property back and then leave." She enunciated the two syllables as if teaching a new word to a toddler.

"When you agree to my terms. One year. One year of genuine effort."

"Now you're changing it!" For a brief millisecond, her frustration surfaced in knitted eyebrows. But when she paused to inhale and gather momentum for her next accusation or declaration or exclamation—Christ, whatever it was going to be—the outward sign of her feelings was gone.

Yeah, she is definitely trying to work me over.

Clever girl—had to give her that.

"Not necessarily. More like expounding on the original." I tapped off my comment with a quick wink, and I heard her suck in a breath. My grin was back because it felt so good knowing I was getting to her. And in the best kind of ways.

We were going to have so much fun together, I just knew it. Over time, I'd get better at predicting her actions and reactions and would be able to head them off before there was ever an issue. She was smarter than a lot of women I'd dated recently. Or hell, that I even knew. So the challenge would be a little greater, but the reward so much sweeter. I wanted to calm this feisty, lively little storm more than I could remember wanting anything else.

"I'll tell you what, wife," I began.

Before she'd started this mask game she was currently playing, I watched her react every time I called her that. The battle going on in her mind over that one banal title was fascinating. And entertaining. And so endearing all at the same time. It was exactly why the storm comparison kept popping up. She was tumultuous and unpredictable, yet powerful and essential at the same time.

No wonder Elijah came up with the bomb nickname. Of course, I barely knew Agatha. I knew Hannah and the other sisters even less. But based on what I was familiar with, these five women were formidable forces for sure. What they brought to your life was up to you completely. Chaos, destruction, and upheaval, or a lush, peaceful landscape where you could live and thrive in their presence. Your choice to make.

"Stop calling me that. I've said that how many times now?" Then she muttered to herself, but clearly loud enough for me to hear, "Shit, maybe you *are* that dense?"

"Not going to get me going that way either, Storm. You'll have to do better if you want to scare me off," I said through a growing smile. "But for now, I'm going to call for a ride and take off. Please spend the evening packing so you're ready when I stop by after work tomorrow."

I held her journal down at her eye level so she clearly saw I still had it. "I'm going to take this with me," I stated matter-of-factly. "An insurance policy of sorts."

"No. Please." She grabbed my forearm with impressive strength. She didn't hide her bone-deep fear and early-stage panic at the notion. "Carmen, no. Please don't take it with you. How will I know you won't read it?"

And believe it or not, in those few moments, I had thought this through. "This is our first lesson in trust. I'm sure you would agree that a good relationship is built on a foundation of trust and communication, yes?"

She pegged me with an impassive stare once more, and I had to remind myself this was some sort of game she was playing and not let it frustrate me. I'd just witnessed genuine and intense emotion on her angelic face, so I knew she was in control of what she was doing. However, I also knew a solid relationship was built on good, two-way conversation. Her paralyzed mime routine was already wearing on my nerves.

"Answer me, please. There's no need to be rude because you don't like what's going on." When delivered, the words sounded as though I were speaking to a preschooler, and it wasn't my original intent. But when I saw her chest rise with her heavy inhalation, I knew she was preparing to launch one of her acidic rebuttals my way. The previous moment's regret disappeared instantly.

Additionally, I was completely distracted with the way that deep breath pushed out her fabulous tits against the thin cotton T-shirt she wore.

Fuck me, I could not wait to get this woman horizontal again.

"Up here, husband," she bit while angrily pointing toward her face. I was totally busted for staring at her chest, but what about it? I was only human.

I grinned shamelessly when I met her bright-blue eyes. "You're magnificent, woman. Do you have a clue about how fucking beautiful you are?"

She shrugged. *Wait.* Shrugged? Then said, "Yeah. I've heard it all a million times, Carmen. It loses its impact, you know?" She deployed the head tilt this time and looked sexier than ever.

Silence stood sentry between us.

Clearly, she needed to express herself, so I waited for her to regroup and go for it. She was much calmer after the moments passed between my comments and now hers than she was right after she'd caught me ogling her tits. I wish I could say I had planned that, but honestly, it was just dumb luck it had worked in my favor.

"You want communication? You want trust? Let's add respect to the list. And a whole fucking boatload of it. Because I deserve nothing less. Speaking to me like a child is irritating and disrespectful of my intelligence. I would like you to *not* do that again. There," she said with her regular tone of defiance. "How was that for communication?"

"Perfect, actually. I'm completely clear on your needs and expectations regarding this topic," I answered a bit smugly.

She was spoiling for a fight, and I refused to be the one to serve it up. The air thickened between us as we held each other's gaze. I was calm and mature in the face of one of her tantrums, and it completely threw her off.

That fact didn't surprise me at all. I'd known people in my life who acted like this. Even as an adolescent, I had very little patience or understanding of it. Nothing was ever gained, and depending on the tantrumee, tons of energy could be expended on it.

I decided to prompt her a bit by restating the main points of my comments. "You will see that you can trust me to keep your journal and not violate your privacy and read it. Eventually, you will know that you can trust me in all things. But for right now, we start here."

I gave her one of those winks again and went on.

"Rome wasn't built in a day. Agatha, when I give you my word, it's as good as done. I am telling you I will not read this." I lifted the journal between us again. "I'm just keeping it to ensure you don't ghost me. When you get it back, you will know I didn't touch it. In fact, I invite you to put a marker on a page or something that would be disturbed if I opened it. That way you will know unequivocally that I kept my promise to you. As I will always will."

I wasn't foolish enough to hand her the journal. Together we crossed her room to a small writing desk, where I maintained hold along the top of the book while she carefully placed a dried flower she pulled out of some bit of décor on the windowsill between two pages.

She stepped back from the desk very carefully. It was as if she were traversing a minefield. She maintained a distressed stare on the book while doing so. Through lips pressed together nervously, a soft whistle escaped when she pushed out the air she had been holding inside.

She nodded slightly at first and then a more confident dip of her head while muttering, "Okay. Okay, there." Finally, she lifted her stormy eyes and searched mine for reassurance. At least that was my take on what I just witnessed. This was a big step for her, and what started out as a ploy to get my way turned into an exercise of conquering a fear of hers. If nothing else, I would prove to her she could lean on me for strength when she was feeling vulnerable.

Not gonna lie, I was pretty damn impressed with myself and how the situation worked out.

I leaned closer and planted a slow but chaste kiss to her forehead. "Sleep well, Storm. See you tomorrow."

CHAPTER SIX

AGATHA

Carmen left after making small talk with my dad near the front door. I shot him every version of a glare I was capable of while he charmed the hell out of my father.

I totally had to draw the line when my mom joined the conversation and started asking things like, "So, will we see you soon?"

Back in my room, I was a whirlwind of pent-up sexual frustration, exhaustion, and indecisiveness. I couldn't make up my mind if I'd be better working on the article I had due in the morning, unpacking, or calling my sister and pouring my guts out to her.

I was on my hands and knees with my upper body halfway in my closet when there was a knock on my bedroom door. If I ignored it, they'd go away and assume I fell asleep early again.

"Where the fuck is it?" I muttered to the pairs of sensible flats lined up across the floor of the space.

"Dah? You sleeping?" came through the door.

Well, if I were, I'd be awake now, I thought bitterly. It was my youngest, most precious sister, Clemson. She was still in high school and often came into my room just to hang out. She didn't relate to the twins very well but couldn't be faulted for it. The age gap was just big enough to put them at different stages of their lives.

Honestly, no one in the house spoke the same hissing and cussing mashup as Sheppard. Something was deeply wrong with that girl, and it broke my heart watching her become a shadow of the person she used to be.

Time and time again, one of us would risk our own life and approach her to try to start a conversation. Every time, whoever the brave soul of the day was would reemerge from the room way worse for the wear. The only person she didn't really open fire on was our father. Probably because he was the one with the power to kick her ass out on the street once and for all.

"Yes!" I said excitedly to the back wall of my closet. Fingers wrapped comfortably around the neck, I pulled a bottle of vodka from where I stored it last. I only kept it in here for last-minute pregaming before nights out with my friends or Hannah. A nagging voice in the back of my mind—that sounded way too much like my husband—issued an accusation.

"And exactly when was the last time you went out with friends? Or Hannah, for that matter?"

"Shut the fuck up," I told my imagined spouse and unscrewed the top. I just needed better sleep than I'd been getting. A swig or two would knock me right out, and I could get up early to finish the article with a fresh brain.

"See? Perfect plan," I wheezed between slugs.

The knock came on my door again.

Goddammit.

"Go away, Clemmie. I'm sleeping," I mumbled from behind the back of my hand to make it sound authentic. Took a swipe across my lips while I was at it to remove any residual liquor. Not sure if I was selling it or not, but hey, A for effort, right?

"It's your father." A deep voice had replaced the young female one I expected, and I bolted upright.

Whoa, easy there, room. No need to toss me about like that.

"Daddy, I'm beat. Can we talk in the morning?" I went with the hand-over-mouth trick again.

"I'll just be a minute, honey. I'm coming in," he announced while simultaneously twisting the doorknob.

Fuck me. Thank God I locked my door every time I walked in here. I loved my family with every cell in my body. They were amazing humans, and we had always been a very close crew. But couldn't a girl just have some privacy? They barged in here at all hours of the night, no care for my work schedule—or sleep schedule, for that matter.

I glanced at the clock and winced when I saw the time. My body would've sworn it was coming up on midnight.

Nope. Seven p.m.

After a quick assessment of my room's condition, I went to unlock the damn door. The vodka bottle was shoved under the quilt my grandmother made for me the year I started kindergarten. I slept with it almost every night because it kept me grounded and connected to the things that mattered. Or at least that was the woo-woo shit she told me when gifting it to me.

I hadn't felt grounded in a long time.

Subdued considerably from the vodka, I poured it on heavier and mumbled, "Hey."

My father strolled into the center of my room, hands in pockets, and made no attempt at hiding the visual inspection he was conducting.

"Are you looking for something in particular?" I accused impatiently. I was so not in the mood for this. My standards were a far cry from the rest of the family's, except Clemson. She was as much of a slob as I was. Maybe worse.

"I just don't understand how you can live like this, Dah." He turned in slow circles, surveying my room. "I'm one hundred percent positive your mother taught all you girls how to clean up after yourselves. How can you be productive in an environment like this?" With perfect timing to his comments, he stopped turning when he was facing me just as he finished talking.

"Dad, I'm so tired. I have an article due in the morning and haven't finished it yet." I rubbed both temples with two fingers and finished telling him my plan before I got a lecture about that too.

"Here's the thing, honey. Your mother shouldn't still have to clean your room for you."

"She doesn't have to, you're right—"

"You see, this is our house. Our investment. We hate to see any part of it looking so shabby. On top of that, it feels disrespectful to us as individuals because separately, we've both asked you to keep after your own space."

"I've just been super busy, Daddy. And then the unexpected trip to Vegas." I waved my hand in the air in some random pattern. "I'm sorry. I'll clean it up when I get home from the office tomorrow."

"You said that last week. And the week before. At this point, I'm done requesting politely. If you can't do what's expected, you can go find your own place to disrespect and trash."

"This isn't trashed." My immediate thought slipped right through any filter I should've had in place. By his body language, I could tell he didn't care for the reply at all. My father held my stare until it became uncomfortable for us both. My stupid mouth operated on its own accord again, and I spurted out, "I've been looking for a place on my lunch breaks anyway. The commute is getting ridiculous, and gas prices are so high..."

One brow raised, he finally said, "All right, that's good. Let me know if you need any help or want me to look at anything with you." We were both quiet until he finally said, "I'll let you get some sleep, then." He leaned close and kissed the top of my head. "Bit early, no?" he asked on his way to the door.

"We partied pretty hard the past few days. I'm wiped out," I offered as an excuse. Well, it wasn't really a lie. I was genuinely exhausted.

He turned back one last time while going through my door. With his nose scrunched, he said, "I thought I smelled vodka. Must still be coming out of your pores." He chuckled then and gave his head a little shake. Probably mentally reminiscing about his younger, wilder days. Thankfully, instead of launching into a story from his college days, he just continued to grin while closing my door.

I slapped the wall light switch off and flopped backward onto my bed. Forgetting that bottle was under the covers, I knocked the back of my head on the thick glass.

"Fuck." I gritted my teeth, trying to muffle the volume of my reaction. "Good one, Dah," I muttered to myself and rubbed the spot where surely a lump would form.

Up again, I trudged back to the light switch and turned it on. With my current headspace, I'd break a toe too if I kept it off. I fished the bottle from beneath the blanket and inspected it. I would've sworn that bottle was at least half full. I'd only taken a couple swigs from it, and now it was nearly gone.

Clemson was probably sneaking into my room while I wasn't here and helping herself. Made the most sense at least. Whatever. I set the bottle on my desk and vowed to throw it away in the morning when I got up. The last thing I needed was another lecture—from either my parents or my new spouse.

Lights out, covers up to my chin, I let sleep engulf me. I didn't dream very often the way I used to. I loved dreaming and escaping back through them the next day. There seemed to be so many hidden meanings and messages in the movies our subconscious minds played for us.

I wondered if Carmen was a frequent dreamer. I'd have to ask him when I saw him next.

I fell asleep with a stupid smile on my face, thinking about the man I'd irresponsibly tied myself to.

★ ★ ★

"You're gonna be late, Dah!" Maye called through my bedroom door. At least I thought it was the gentle twin's voice that woke me.

"Huh?" I grumbled into my pillow.

Facedown in the squishy paradise of the thing, I was sure whoever it was couldn't hear my reply. If it had been Maye, why the hell was she up so late? I'd set my alarm before going to sleep so I could get up and work on the assignment the newsroom editor sent to my email. She would expect a proofed copy in her basket the moment my feet were in the downtown building.

Digging through the blankets, I located my phone and squinted with one eye open and one closed to see the time.

8:48 a.m.

Wait, that couldn't be right. Turning toward my nightstand, I zeroed in on the clock there and confirmed the horrifying truth. I'd overslept and would never get to work on time. At this point, I'd be better off calling in sick.

But I'd just used my last official days off for the Vegas trip. My boss bitched and moaned routinely about people extending their vacations by using sick days before or after the vacation itself. It was a big no-no in her book, and I was already on thin ice with the woman.

From day one, the shrew didn't like me. There wasn't a particular incident that I could think of or any one specific reason I could put my finger on. It seemed to be a matter of personalities not gelling. And in most work environments, that should be fine. You don't care for someone? Stay away from them. Boom! Problem solved.

But Marla Bines, newsroom editor extraordinaire, was my direct supervisor, and we crossed paths many times a day. She was a plain-Jane woman in her late fifties. Bitter about all the wrongs her ex-husband did to her, she was cranky and mean. The woman had a countdown calendar on her office wall that showed a daily reminder of how many days she had until retirement.

The number was five digits long.

Other than Ms. Bines, as she insisted we call her, I got along with everyone. I tried to just keep my head down and do my job and not call extra attention to myself. That was a great plan for staying out of trouble, but not so great for my career path's upward trajectory. What was even worse was this growing habit of showing up late.

Damn it, I was in for an ass chewing.

Really, I should probably quit and find something else, but

now that my father had threatened that I'd have to shape up or ship out, I needed the income. The luxury of taking weeks to find the perfect job somewhere else was gone.

Getting depressed this early in the morning didn't bode well for the rest of the day. Plus, it was Monday. The rest of the week would follow this one right down the toilet if it was bad. I had to snap myself out of this self-induced funk and get my ass in the shower.

After calling and leaving a message on Marla's voicemail that I had car trouble, I sent up a quick one to the big guy that she bought that bullshit. I couldn't be sure, but I think I used the same excuse last week.

Well, some cars were known to have recurring problems. It could totally be true!

While I rinsed my hair under the glorious hot water spray, I remembered the unfinished assignment. It crossed my mind when I first woke up, but then I started spinning about being late and despising my boss and pushed that fuck-up to the side. Nausea rolled through my entire body, starting with my stomach and pounding out a bass drum beat through my ears.

Maybe I really was coming down with something? As far as karma went, it had to be bad juju to wish for illness. So instead of calling out sick, I sped down the 405 like the CHP was chasing me. My poor, road-worn, commuter car was rattling from every possible nut and bolt. My hair was still wet, and to top it all off, I needed gas in a bad way and didn't have the money for a fill-up. If I made it to my office, it would be a miracle. I'd have to call one of my sisters during my break and ask to borrow money.

Could this day get any worse?

Here's the thing about that saying . . . It's an open invitation for things to get worse.

From the moment I hustled into the huge open space partitioned off with stormy sky-colored cubicles, I zeroed in on my desk. Marla's office was clear across the office in the back corner, so I wouldn't have to pass her fishbowl to get to my spot. She said she liked having an all-glass-walled space. That way she could keep track of what we were doing at all times.

A banker's box with the lid askew sat on the top of my desk. My personal belongings overflowed between the top of the box and its crooked lid. On top of the lid was a pink half sheet of paper.

Fired. She fucking fired me for being late. I was livid but refused to make a scene for everyone to whisper about after I left. I knew how these people behaved, and I wouldn't be their next hot topic.

Like unset color rinsing through fabric, the expression left my face. My whole body, really. I was a robot moving through the necessary tasks to get to the goal.

Empty the drawers of my desk, check.

Log out of the company computer, check.

Grab any personal files I had here, check.

It was all done without a single word to my coworkers who hovered nearby, even when they tried to offer sympathy. The box was so heavy, but I hefted it onto a hip, grabbed my purse, and walked out with my head held high. No one got the better of me. Ever.

Still idling in the parking lot, I pressed my forehead to the steering wheel and exhaled. A normal person would break down at that point, but nothing came. There were two reasons I could identify easily: I hated that fucking job and wasn't really sad to be leaving. The second was the more mature reason. I deserved to be fired. I was a shit employee with shit attendance habits and very little field experience to offer the team. I'd fire me too.

The drive home went by in a blur, and I made the turn into our long driveway before I could register where I was. The dangerousness of my actions only got a moment of airtime before I dismissed the thought. I'd had enough of a beating today already to add to it myself.

After reading the comments Marla had left on the pink slip, I'd be lucky to get another job in journalism. I certainly wouldn't be using the past two years as a professional reference, and then I'd have to explain the gap in employment. It was a screw-over no matter which way I dealt with it.

The house was quiet and empty. My mom went to Pilates religiously, and she would probably run errands after her class. Some people loved routine like that—my sister Hannah was the same way.

Not me, though. I loved surprises and spontaneity. Sure, we all had responsibilities to handle, but why not have fun in between? I was sure a person could be both responsible and exciting. I just had to figure out how to accomplish both, keep my parents off my back, deal with Carmen and this ridiculous marriage mistake, and not call too much attention to myself.

That's when people started offering opinions I never asked for. About my career choice, about my job—well, my former job—about my love life. Hell, even about my clothing and eating habits. How did my family become self-appointed experts on my life? On my likes and dislikes? On my needs and wants? Did I come off as the lost soul who needed their expert guidance? Well... there might be something to that theory, but I wasn't in the mood to hate myself today.

From the moment I declared a major in college, my parents disapproved of the decision. They weren't very good at hiding their disappointment, either. Especially my dad, and that one stung more than I cared to think about. He had his hopes set on my following in his accounting footsteps. Early on, I showed a natural gift with numbers, but I didn't enjoy it the way I did writing.

"There's no money in journalism, darling," he'd said in his official fatherly voice. He had his heart set on me doing an internship at his accounting firm and one day taking over the reins. I had zero interest in any of it.

"Don't you want to be an independent woman?" my mother had questioned when no one else was around. Obviously that was her lost dream, and she was trying to pin it on me now. It didn't take Freud to explain that one.

My parents fell in love and married in a whirlwind of a few months. Within a year, she was pregnant with Hannah and spent the next three decades raising children. I didn't mind kids. They were okay. If that was the path to happiness at some point, then I'd be open to having a family. It just wasn't on my radar now, and my mom wanted grandbabies to coo over and spoil more than anything.

At least with Hannah already knocked up, that weighty sack was lifted off my wagon. My parents didn't pin many expectations on my oldest sister because they were consumed with guilt from an incident that was decades old. At the precious age of five, she was the victim of an attempted kidnapping. My parents never forgave themselves for it happening, especially my mother. One hour out of a lifetime changed everything for our entire family. The rest of us girls were barely affected because we were so young. But Hannah had dealt with residual mental health problems ever since.

My phone dinged in my bag, and I knew the sound meant I had a text message. Since no one else was home, I flopped down on the sofa and carelessly tossed my bag onto the coffee table. I grabbed my phone and situated the three hundred and sixty-one throw pillows to make a comfortable nest. Half landed on the floor, but I was too busy with my phone to fuss about it.

*How is the day treating you? Can't wait
to see you later.*

The message was from Carmen, and my body turned traitor in a second. No one was around to hide my true reaction from, so I let the giddy smile loose. The damn thing spread from one side to the other until I subconsciously raised my hand to protect myself from being exposed.

But then I dropped it again and tossed my head back farther into the pillow pile and giggled. I had no idea how badly I needed someone to care about me right then, but it felt like a wonderful hug when I read those two sentences.

He was probably waiting for a reply while I had this prolonged moment of discovery, so I tapped as quickly as I could.

Like a redheaded stepchild. You?

Carmen's reply came quickly.

Do you need to talk?

No.

Thanks, though. You're sweet.

Was that corny to say that? I didn't know the guy well enough to trust how he'd take it. My eyes bugged when I read his next message. It came almost simultaneously with an incoming call.

I'm calling.

The smile was back, and I fought the urge to cover my mouth with my fingertips.

"Hello?" I didn't have my husband built into my contacts, so the number wasn't identified as his.

"Hi," he said in a voice that was both smooth and rough at the same time. Just beneath the surface, blood rushed to my cheeks, increasing my body temperature to an unbearable degree.

What the hell was this guy doing to me?

"Hi," I repeated his greeting, and my own voice sounded like a sexy night shift deejay for the local jazz station.

"Are you okay? Tell me what's going on," he issued. Though his voice was quiet and calm, a note of authority underlined each word.

Maybe he was in training with his boss. Now that dude was seriously in control of everything he did in a day. I'd venture to say very few people fucked with him.

"I'm fine, really. You didn't have to make a call."

"It's the least I can do. Plus, now I get to talk with you a bit before I see you after work. It's really quiet at your office. I don't know . . ." He paused for a few beats, as if really listening to the background of my end of the call. "I just assumed it would be noisy and bustling in a newsroom."

Oh, here we go.

We didn't even make it into the conversation four minutes, and he was grilling me about random things. My immediate reaction was something acidic, but I paused a second to breathe. Reminding myself that he reached out to me calmed my rising temper. I could try to get away with not telling him what had happened, but it would come out eventually and we'd have another argument on our hands.

"I'm at home," I admitted.

"Are you ill? Still hungover?" He paused a moment between one accusation and another. "Or did you drink last night after I left?"

"No," I sighed. "None of the above." If he didn't drop this bullshit nagging, we would never survive to see our first anniversary.

"Then—"

"I was fired." I couldn't take his guessing game, so I let that lie between us in the conversation like a pile of cat vomit everyone saw but no one dealt with.

He didn't say anything.

I didn't say anything.

We both just sat there quietly and listened to each other breathe.

"Oh . . . well . . . I'm sorry that happened. Do you want to tell me what straw broke the camel's back?"

I tried to make sense of his wording choice. Was he insinuating there were so many things I did wrong that it was inevitable? Was I projecting my own guilty thoughts onto him?

"What's that supposed to mean?" I bit into the phone. It only took two seconds of contemplation until his comment really pissed me off.

"Settle down, Storm. Usually when a person is let go, there are incidents leading up to the big bang. There's no way your HR department would sign off on a termination because you were late one time. Or whatever... That was just my example."

I sighed in resignation. Of course, he wasn't wrong. I just didn't want to admit what a fuck-up I was at my chosen career path.

"Well, I overslept this morning, but I called and told my supervisor I had car trouble and I would be there as soon as possible. But you're right." Christ, how I hated having to admit that. "There have been other things. She just doesn't like me."

"Do you think you were targeted? Wrongfully terminated? Those shitty things still happen even though they could result in huge lawsuits," Carmen went on like the subject expert.

"I thought you were a PA?" I asked.

"Yes, that's right."

"You seem to know a lot about human resources."

"It was my major in school. Just landed this job first before I got something in that field. So here I am." I could picture his easy shrug after he spoke.

Another tick in the plus column for the man. His easy temperament soothed my fiery one. Just talking with him for a few minutes helped calm my nerves more than anything else I tried.

"Okay, my wife, I have to go. I'll see you after work. I get off at five, and I think it should only take thirty minutes to get to your place."

I spurted a cackle at his naïvety. When he didn't comment, I asked, "How long have you lived in Los Angeles, man?"

"My entire life. Why?" He sounded genuinely confused.

"And you think you can make it from downtown to Brentwood in under an hour during quitting time?" I shook my head at the nonsense. "The freeway will be a parking lot."

"Who said anything about the freeway? There are a few surface streets you can take. We'll see who knows what when I get there." I could hear the smile in his tone, and a matching one crossed my lips too.

"Can we do this later in the week?" I suggested. I hadn't packed a single thing yet, nor had I told my parents I was moving in with a man I didn't know but was married to.

"No," he said definitively, and I pulled the phone away from my ear and gave the device a skeptical look in his place. I put it back to my ear in time to hear him say, "There's no point in putting it off. Plus, now that you don't have a job, you can unpack and get organized in no time at all."

"Hmmm," I sounded through pressed lips.

"What? What does that noise mean in Agatha-speak?"

"It means you seem to have it all figured out, don't you?"

"No. Not really. I've definitely thought about some things since yesterday, but I can honestly say supporting us both hadn't crossed my mind." Then, in an intentionally brighter voice he said, "We'll make it work."

If he was always this upbeat and positive, we'd be going to the mat by the end of the week. There was positive, and then there was annoying. Overly optimistic people were suspicious creatures. Because I didn't buy into the attitude fully, it was hard to believe the authenticity of a person who did.

But I already knew this guy was the real deal.

Regardless, bad shit happened to good people all the time. And good things came to really bad people just in equal measure. Acting like everything was status quo when it really wasn't was basically lying. Lying to yourself, at the very least. Projecting that sunshine-and-rainbow crap out to the world was just as dishonest. I tried to live authentically. My friends and family knew I'd always give it to them straight.

It was good to be counted on for something.

My husband's deep voice shook me from the mental lashing I was about to start on myself.

"All right, Storm, I'll see you in a few hours. Try to get packed so we have time to make two trips if we have to."

This guy... I just shook my head. He was in for a big eye-opener once we were roommates.

Playing house was cute when we were kids, but this was real shit.

And I already knew it was going to be a disaster.

CHAPTER SEVEN

CARMEN

Getting anything done after that phone call was hopeless.

Elijah stalked past my desk in a huff about something, and I was too stressed about my own predicament to go handhold him too.

Normally I tried to be a sounding board for my boss if he needed to bounce ideas around or just vent about an office frustration, but I was too wrapped up in my own brood to knock on his door and offer to help like I normally would.

Impressively, he was back in front of my desk after just ten minutes. I really thought he was a great guy, if a bit egocentric. When he took the time to come back out and initiate a conversation simply because he sensed something was off—well, I was genuinely touched.

"How are things going, man? We haven't really had time to shoot the shit since we've been back. I mean, I knew I'd be behind the eight ball from taking four days off, but it's way worse than I predicted." His sleeves were rolled to the elbow, and his tan skin was a striking contrast to the white cotton.

"Sorry. I'm not on top of things today like I usually am. At least I think I normally am. A lot going on." I tapped my temple to indicate the mental chaos I was dealing with.

He chuckled. "You know, I just realized, we're brothers-in-law now. That doesn't make it different around here, though. Cool? I've come to depend too much on you at this spot right here"—he stabbed an index finger down to my desk—"to let an intoxicated screw-up ruin things."

"We're going to try to make it work," I said plainly, and my comment rendered him speechless. And maybe it was cruel, but I sat back in my chair and enjoyed the look of shock until he formed a response.

"Whoa. Really?" He laughed and asked, "Does your wife know this?"

Everyone who knew her knew what a force of nature Agatha Christine Farsey was. The woman was a tiny little package, just five feet one or two, I'd guess. But what she didn't have in height, she had in balls. The traits that most people didn't know about were the ones that kept reeling me in... closer and closer. I wanted to learn everything there was to know about her.

I shrugged and then told him, "We've committed to one year. A solid effort for twelve months, and then we will decide where we go from there." I held his gaze for a longer moment than conversation usually permitted. I needed him to shift out of boss mode and into friend or brother-in-law or whatever the hell we were now.

"There's something about her, man," I said with a deeper level of seriousness. He and I didn't usually talk about personal relationships like this. "I haven't quite figured out what, but I want this to work. She's . . . " I shook my head slowly, grinning the whole time. "I don't know, she's so many things. So many I haven't even discovered yet."

If we were drawn in cartoon cells, hearts would be shooting from my eyes. His too, when I finally refocused on the guy.

My boss smiled wide like me. "I get it, man. I do," he assured me. "They're very special women, these Brentwood bombshells."

We both barked out laughs at the term, and that release of tension felt really good. Exactly what I needed to screw my head back on straight.

Elijah leaned a shoulder against the doorjamb of his office. "Those two are pretty tight. I'd say of all her sisters, Agatha is the one Hannah talks about and relates to the most. I guess their closeness in age has something to do with it, but I think their personalities are similar too."

I listened and cataloged every scrap of history or inside scoop he offered. It was a regular conversation. I wasn't grilling him for details, but I knew very little about my wife, and knowledge was power, no matter the situation.

Apparently, he wasn't done with his thought track. After thinking for a few beats, he continued. "So I wonder why she hasn't called Hannah and told her about this agreement." He waved his hand through the air, maybe trying to come up with an appropriate tag for what we were planning. "You know, whatever you want to call it? A yearlong trial?" His voice rose at the end of the statement, turning it into a question.

"Why put a label on it, you know? When you do that, expectations associated with the term in a generic sense will weigh us down. I want to just live every day and see where life together takes us."

"You're a brave man. I'll say that," he said while running his hand through his hair.

"How am I any braver than you? Or any other guy who commits to a woman by marriage? I'm just curious what you mean," I added when I heard how confrontational my words sounded.

"Dude..." He grinned. "You're doing it ass-backward, that's why. Normally you get to know the woman, ensure you're compatible and all that." Another wave of his hand punctuated the comment.

"Well, I'm not going to pretend we weren't completely irresponsible and foolish for doing what we did, but I was raised in a strict Catholic house. Marriage is permanent. It's a vow you make in front of and to God. It's not just undone the next day." He was thoughtful while I explained the primary and initial reason I decided to make the marriage work.

"On top of all that old-school stuff, I like her. A lot. I was really bored dating these days, you know?"

He nodded thoughtfully. I was on a roll anyway, so even if he checked out of the conversation completely, I'd finish my thought.

"She is the first girl to really intrigue me in a long time. There's so much more to her than that loud, disrespectful mouth."

And why was I grinning like an idiot again? Those weren't traits of a girl you'd take home to your uptight, God-fearing parents.

"As far as her confiding in her sister, I'm sure she will if she hasn't already. We just made the decision late last night. Today, of course, things became a little more complicated, but—"

Elijah interrupted with a raised hand. "What happened? How much more complicated do you mean?" He attempted to laugh through the questions, but the sound that came out was awkward and forced.

I thought for a moment. How much did I want to tell him? If Agatha hadn't spoken to her sister by the time he got home, surely he would tell her the latest. That's what I would do with my wife at least.

Fuck it. I needed a sounding board too. God knew it wouldn't be my sister or any of the coworkers I had from this place.

"Agatha was fired this morning. She's moving in with me tonight. I'm going there after I leave here." I looked at my watch and jolted out of my chair. "Right now, as a matter of fact. Perfect timing."

Maybe if I looked really busy now, he wouldn't ask follow-up questions, and I could get on my way across town.

His loud laugh startled me, so I stopped shuffling the papers on my desk to check on his well-being.

"You okay, man?"

"Shit, my brother. You're not kidding about things getting more complicated. No offense, but how are two of you going to live on your paycheck?" he asked, eyebrows hiked high near his hairline.

From anyone else, the question would've been rude and intrusive. But he knew what my take-home pay was, and he was also a lifelong Angeleno. It didn't take a math genius to understand the shortfall between my earnings and expenses.

"You know what the leading cause of divorce is?" Banks asked.

I crossed my arms over my chest and answered, "Meddling employers?"

"Ha! You're funny. It's money, man. No surprise, right?"

"Not at all." I had a hundred memories of my parents bickering about each other's spending habits and how to stretch every dollar my father brought home.

The situation had me feeling defensive, though, so I added, "She's going to get another job. I'm pretty sure she has a college education." Just admitting that out loud made me wince. Confessing how little I knew about my own wife was embarrassing.

In the future, I'd have to measure my thoughts before blurting them out. We were going to be under the scrutiny of everyone who cared about us. Family, friends, and what do you know? Even bosses. The peanut gallery would be full of advice on how to make our relationship work. Whether we invited the input or not, we had to gear up for a heap of it.

"We'll figure it out," I muttered and shut down my computer. "You working late?" I asked him, hoping the subject change would stick.

"Nah, not tonight. Hannah has some kids' culinary class she's teaching. I told her I'd go along and be her TA," he said through an enormous, genuine smile while closing his office door. "I'll walk down with you if you're ready."

We parted ways out front when he ducked into the same SUV that drove us home from the airport.

Christ, was that just yesterday?

I gave the driver, Lorenzo, a quick wave and hustled to my own car in the parking structure. I figured I could text Agatha while the engine warmed up on my road-worn car.

Leaving downtown now. See you in 30.

It'll take at least 90 this time of day.

Want to make a wager? What do I get when I win?

Hmmm, let me think about it. Don't you mean if you win?

Traffic already looked horrendous when I made the first turn onto a freeway frontage road. If there had been an accident earlier in the afternoon, every artery leaving the hub of the city going west toward Brentwood would be clogged. I flipped on the podcast I started last week and tried to finish the episode. My brain protested any sort of concentration when thoughts of the woman at the end of my commute took center stage instead.

It had been a year since I had someone to look forward to going home to. Even then, the fire in my relationship with Kate had fizzled out long before. Most days, when I walked in the door, she either wasn't home or couldn't be bothered to even look up from her nonstop texting to say hello. Looking back on it now, we stayed together out of habit. Nothing more. It was easier to be miserable in routine than to be brave and move on.

With that as my only comparison, these feelings I had for the golden-haired storm were puzzling. Intense and exciting but confusing at the same time. How could I be so into her already? Maybe it was the newness of the relationship? Maybe the challenge of making our marriage mistake work was the exciting part and not my feelings for the woman herself. That would be completely out of character for me, though. I was a planner. I liked things to happen in a prescribed order and at the expected time. Surprises weren't my thing. Basically, I was a by-the-book kind of guy.

And boring. So fucking boring, I put myself to sleep when I thought about my day to day. Lately, I'd been especially unmotivated regarding my future. Before meeting Agatha, at least. Now, I couldn't wait to see where this crazy adventure would take us. I just had to get her to buy in on making the effort too. With the amount of energy the woman possessed, we could really turn things upside down. We could have tons of fun doing it, too.

I turned into the Farsey driveway exactly eighty-two minutes later. Damn traffic wouldn't cut me a break no matter how many side streets I wove through. I probably added to my commute time with all the zigzagging I did to get to her place, but whatever. I just wanted to move on with this whole ordeal and get her settled at my place.

From outside the front door, I could hear the doorbell chime through the house. Her folks were probably stuck in the same gridlock I just endured, because Agatha's car was the only one parked in the driveway. If I weren't completely opposed to our first time being a quickie, we could probably sneak one in before they came home.

Goddammit. Now my dick was swelling to an obvious bulge, and I'd left my sport coat in the car. Elijah didn't insist I wear a coat and tie every day, but I usually kept one in my car in case he had an appointment with someone important. Similar to what I was wearing currently, a button-down shirt and slacks were my daily norm.

It took the woman forever to answer the damn door. By the time she swung the rustic rectangle open, I had my phone in hand, ready to call her. The door dwarfed her as she inched the enormous hardwood panel open. Through squinted eyes, she recognized me, said nothing, and then turned at once to trudge back into the house.

"What, no kiss for your husband?" I teased after the skulking zombie that was masquerading as Agatha.

There might have been some sort of hand gesture from the woman after my remark, but it was too hard to tell while chasing behind her.

From the hallway outside her room, I thumbed over my shoulder back toward the foyer. "Don't worry about the door. I locked it behind us."

Even though I launched a second snarky comment, I still didn't get a response. She face-planted into her disheveled bed without a single word.

A banker box filled with random office supplies sat at the foot of the mattress, and I grabbed the framed picture off the top. It was my beautiful lady and her sisters in a candid shot from a Christmas celebration. If I had to guess, the photo was a couple of years old, because the youngest of the brood, Clemson, still wore braces in the shot.

Looking around the messy room, I asked, "I thought you spent the day packing. Where are the other boxes?"

Had she been sleeping all day? Since we spoke this morning about her job termination?

"Don't start with me, okay?" a muffled voice came from beneath the covers.

I didn't even see her burrow under the blanket pile, so her soft-though-still-clipped response took me by surprise. But damn if the raspy edge of her bite didn't stoke my arousal.

Clearly I would have to spend some time jerking off before being enclosed in any space with this woman. My only saving distraction was the general state of her bedroom. It looked like a tornado whipped through the place at some point in the past eighteen hours. We were in this room yesterday. Granted, I wouldn't have described the space as tidy then either, but this was next level.

"Did you throw a party in here last night?" I asked while looking at the floor. Cups of all different shapes and sizes were littered about. An open package of Oreos was abandoned on the desk alongside an empty glass still cloudy from the milk it once held.

There was no way in hell we would live this way.

I scanned the foot of the bed to find the edge of the blankets. Using both hands, I whipped the bedding off in one quick yank, leaving Agatha curled on her side on top of the mattress.

And how had I not noticed what she was wearing when she answered the door? Just a T-shirt marked with some university's athletic department's sizing. On the bottom, she wore a simple pair of cotton bikini panties, and I was transfixed as though I'd never seen a woman in just underwear before.

Her feet seemed to move on their own then. I was at the foot of the bed one moment, dropping the bedding in a heap with the rest of the stuff scattered about. In the next beat, I was beside her on the mattress. I had to touch her. Had to feel that tantalizing, warm body. Her skin was lighter than mine, and we looked good together.

She didn't object to my location, and I knew she wasn't sleeping. Otherwise there would be bulldozer sounds coming from her tiny body.

Jesus Christ, her body.

I scooted closer from behind and curled my frame around hers. We exhaled together, and the stress of the past five days beckoned me to sleep.

We had way too much to accomplish for catnapping though. I took one fortifying whiff of her hair and interrupted her pending slumber.

"As much as I would love to do this and similar things for the rest of the evening, we need to get up."

The troublemaker wriggled her ass against my crotch,

and we both groaned from the sensation. My large hand on her hip stopped the delightful torture.

"Are you sure? Feels like you're already up, husband." She snickered at her own joke, and I couldn't help the grin I had just from hearing her happy and playful.

What the hell would the feeling be like to purposefully do something kind for her? I filed that experiment away in the back of my mind. Definitely would be giving it a try sooner rather than later. First and foremost, I needed to learn what she liked and didn't like.

Deciding to leave her comment hang there unaddressed, I changed the topic while getting off the bed.

"Do you drink coffee in the morning? I want to be sure we have all the groceries we need. I can schedule a delivery to arrive when we do."

"Carmen, listen..." She rolled to her back and found me watching her from alongside the bed. We held each other captive in a hungry, needy staredown.

"Go on," I finally urged. My voice was low and promising, but we needed to pack before anything else.

"Two things, actually," she began while sitting up and scooting back to lean against the headboard. "We need to be serious here about this moving in together. How can I afford rent without a job?"

My guess was she thought this would put an end to our agreement, but I'd thought a lot about it last night when I should've been sleeping.

"I'll cover the expenses until you get a new job. What is your chosen career path? Maybe I know someone." My question seemed absurd, but really, I was married to a stranger.

I would not let her sabotage us before we even tried.

Plastering on an extra bright smile, I asked, "What's the second thing?"

"I can't let you do that. I wouldn't feel right," she insisted while searching around the bed.

"What do you need, Storm?" I finally asked after watching her impatience balloon.

First, an icy glare because of the nickname, then a heavy sigh. "Do you see my robe? It's blue with daisy smiley faces on it. I usually put it on the end of my bed for middle-of-the-night walkabouts."

"Middle of the night what?" Now that was a term I hadn't heard used that way.

"Here, in this house, we call it night walking. Most of us have insomnia to some degree, so we are awake throughout the night. Oftentimes, I run into a family member if I go out to the kitchen for a snack or whatever."

I found her robe in the pile of bedding and held it open for her to step into. If she got out of bed, we'd be one step closer to our goal.

I shook the thing by the shoulders. "Come on. I'll help."

She scowled. "I can manage a bathrobe, Carmen."

Like a matador's cape, I waved the blue monstrosity in front of me. "I'm sure you can, but I want to help. Come on."

With a dramatic huff, she crawled off the bed and managed to make that look sexy too. I was transfixed by her creamy skin and felt desire pulsing through my body. I wrapped the robe's belt around her waist and spun her by the shoulders to face me.

I planned on leaving my hands on her until she said otherwise.

"Now, what was the second thing you wanted to address? And then we need to get moving. At this rate, we're going to still be packing at midnight." It took every ounce of restraint not to ask again how she spent her day.

Agatha dropped her eyes to somewhere around my shirt collar. Whatever she was about to mention was uncomfortable to talk about. I could toy with her and make it worse, or I could be the good guy and meet her halfway conversationally.

She was wringing her hands enough that her fingers were flashing from white to pink. White to pink.

"Did you bring my journal? Did you keep your word and not read it?"

I pulled her into my arms to comfort her and hopefully cool her agitation. She resisted at first, but once we made contact, she sagged into my chest.

I planted a kiss on the crown of her head. "Of course I kept my word. That's the kind of man I am, darling. I'm so proud of you for not falling apart worrying about it today, because I saw how difficult that was yesterday when I left with it."

Something about that comment was received sideways, though, because she pulled out of my arms so abruptly she almost tripped over herself.

"What?" I asked, back among the confused.

"What?" she repeated my question in lieu of an answer.

"Why did you pull away like that?"

"I thought you wanted to pack? Make up your mind." The eye roll on the end was unnecessary icing on her sassy cake.

I was back on her so fast, I didn't have time to talk myself out of what I was doing. I wove my fingers through the hair at her nape and cranked her head back to meet my disapproving stare.

"Apologize," I issued.

No missing the rate her breaths increased. Or the glassy,

aroused glare she gave back.

"For what?"

Not one word about releasing her hair or backing away from her either. Just more challenge.

"How does one so small wrangle such a big mouth all day, Storm? I'm surprised you weren't fired sooner."

I added a quick wink after that comment because, in truth, I was teasing her. At the same time, I hoped it was abundantly clear I wouldn't tolerate any sort of disrespect.

"What you should really be wondering about is how one well-placed kick could drop a man of your size so efficiently." Her voice was dark and smoky, with an edge I hadn't heard before. It turned me on that much more.

While she stared up at me, I took stock of her gorgeous features. My wife was a real beauty.

"Tell me, Storm, do you like that?" I increased the grip on her hair just a bit as a clue to what I was asking.

She closed her eyes slowly and gave one dip of her chin. If I hadn't been so close, I would've missed it. Once more, I silently vowed to do whatever was necessary to make this arrangement work. To my fierce little spouse, I showed my gratitude for the answer by covering her mouth with mine.

She opened instantly for my exploring tongue, and I consumed more of her taste, her passion, and her perfection.

Kissing Agatha was easily one of the top three experiences of my life. The incredible energy and chemistry I felt brewing inside was intoxicating. I wanted to strip us both and claim her right then. But instead, I loosened my grasp on her hair and felt the rest of her body relax along with it.

With my lips still pressed against hers, I said, "Let's get you packed so we can go home." Of course she looked like she was about to protest again, so I finished with, "No more arguing. We could've been on the road by now."

Which wasn't true, and we both knew it. There was so much crap and clutter packed into this one room, we'd be lucky to finish boxing it all up in one night, let alone one hour.

Plus, now I had a hard-on to distract me from getting our actual task accomplished. The look on her face wasn't helping our cause either.

She was zeroed in on the front of my slacks, and when she bit into her bottom lip, I was tempted to just throw her down on the bed and do this thing.

"If you keep looking at me like that, we're not going to get much packing done, woman," I warned in a tone so deep, I was surprised it came from my own throat.

Miss Farsey was bringing out traits that I suspected were buried somewhere inside me, but never had I had a woman I felt was worth digging them up for.

The naughty grin that took over her face confirmed she was that woman.

She started toward me, and I held up one hand.

"No, Storm. I'm serious. You don't want to start all that here under your parents' roof. Let's get your essentials packed and go. Speaking of your parents, what did they say when you told them you were moving in with me?"

I watched her face change completely. From seductive and mischievous to guilty, guilty, guilty.

"You didn't tell them?"

"The opportunity just didn't present itself, and with my dad's health," she stammered, but I cut her off.

"Bullshit. That's a bullshit excuse, and you know it. That man is healthy as a horse. You all fall back on that excuse way too often. It's totally overplayed at this point."

Honestly, I didn't even recognize myself in this conversation. I couldn't put my finger on what it was exactly about Agatha, but she brought a side of me into the light.

She was all but begging to be taken care of and, in ways, told what to do. She had so much energy and creativity, but she was lacking direction. My personality naturally responded to those needs, or so it would seem. We were going to be an unstoppable team.

If we could just get her damn shit packed up and get out of here.

"Do you have boxes? I thought you were going to get some today?"

"Well, today went in a different direction than what we discussed yesterday. Stop busting my ass about it, okay?"

She shot me a look along with the declaration, and I raised a brow in response.

"What?" she barked.

"I don't appreciate the tone, miss. I simply asked you a question. You don't have to get so defensive."

"I'm not defensive," she snapped back, proving my point perfectly.

Tilting my head a bit, I didn't have to say anything. She heard the tone of her own voice. I didn't have to annotate it.

"Do you have a few suitcases? Duffel bags? Trash bags? We need something to put your clothes in at the very least. We can come back for the rest tomorrow and bring boxes then. You don't want your valuable things getting damaged," I said, laying out the game plan.

"There's a suitcase on the floor in my closet. I'll get some other things from my sisters' rooms," she said, and I went to the closet and squatted in front of the rows of shoes.

I shined the light from my phone toward the back wall and found the suitcase. When I pulled it toward me, an empty vodka bottle tumbled out of the closet with it.

My wife came back into the room right as I reached for the incriminating evidence of another problem we were going to deal with.

"That's not mine," she said as I turned to face her, gripping the bottle by the slim neck.

"Bullshit. Let's not get in the habit of lying to each other, okay? And while you're at it, stop lying to yourself."

The *thunk* of the empty bottle hitting the bottom of the small trash can beside her desk was louder than a gunshot in the quiet room.

My wife stood with her hands on her hips, madder than a nest of hornets. Instead of taking responsibility for the obvious, she was about to lash out at me. I was already on to her routine.

"Why were you snooping around in my closet?" she asked with a good dose of attitude.

I couldn't hold back my chuckle, and that pissed her off more. "Snooping? Be serious right now. You told me to get the suitcase out of the closet, so that's what I did. The bottle must have been stashed in front of it, because it rolled out when I tugged on the luggage." I shook my head at her absurdity and huffed another disbelieving laugh. This situation wasn't close to funny.

She couldn't formulate a comeback that made sense. She stood there stammering and fuming while trying to think of something.

I strode over to her and pulled her into my arms. With my nose buried in her hair, I said, "This stops here. No more hiding, no more drinking to deal with hard days, none of it. We'll deal with the tough stuff together, and I'll be by your side while you toss this habit like I just did that empty. I'm serious, Storm. You're done as of now."

Agatha tried to pull away, but I easily held her in place. She was so small and feisty.

"You're not in charge of me, Carmen. Get that idea out of your head. I'm not going to be bossed around by a . . . a . . . man!"

My voice was even and matter of fact. "Well, darling, until you can prove you're making better choices for yourself, you most definitely will be. I'm not going to watch you self-destruct."

Her small frame wilted in my embrace, and I felt her body begin to tremble.

Shit, is she crying?

I didn't dare loosen my hold on her, though, and have her bolt from the room like I'd seen her do before. Instead, I leaned back from the waist to get a better look at her face. Okay, so no tears, but her entire body was shaking in my arms.

"Talk to me, baby. Why are you shaking like this?" Every conversation was a learning opportunity at this point in our relationship. I felt like carrying a notepad around to keep track of the hundreds of new things I learned about her hour by hour.

"Frustrated," she mumbled with her face buried in my chest. My dress shirt would surely have makeup battle scars, but the dry-cleaning bill was worth her opening up to me.

"Okay, thank you for naming the emotion. Why are you frustrated?" I asked, and in the back of my mind I could hear Elijah's voice.

I'd heard him talk like this on so many occasions it was rubbing off. I'd never been to a therapist's office, let alone spent money on being counseled by one. But he swore by the service. Couldn't even disagree in the moment that the talk track was useful in getting to the heart of the matter in front of us.

Then, like I'd witnessed before, she took a deep breath and completely erased all expression from her face. Yeah, I definitely wasn't a fan of this parlor trick. Why had she learned how to do it in the first place? Who in her life couldn't handle real feelings that made her think she had to don a mask of complete indifference?

Christ. Did I really want to know? Did I really want to get in deeper with this girl? But I already knew the answers to those questions didn't matter. It was already too late. I was completely into this woman, and I would do whatever it took to make the best of our life together.

CHAPTER EIGHT

AGATHA

Well, if it wasn't clear before, it was glaringly obvious now. I was in deep shit with this man.

Why did I keep going to pieces emotionally around him? All he had to do was wrap those perfect arms around me, and I lost my composure. Yes, our bodies seemed to be built for each other. Yes, I fit perfectly against his chest when he held me close. Yes, he smelled better than anything I could even think of to compare his unique scent to.

It must have been the combination of all those things, plus the other things I hadn't quite put my finger on yet, that made me forget all pretense and simply feel. Just be.

And the fact that he allowed me to just exist while he protectively stood by was the highlight of this whole arrangement.

Because I knew damn well that feeling and surviving in the moment were the two quickest ways to have your heart ripped out and stomped on by a man. Been there, done that bullshit. Had zero interest in repeating the experience.

Each time I forgot myself and expressed feelings around Carmen, he saw the pathway to burrow deeper into my heart. So each time I realized what was happening and quickly schooled my features into an expressionless mask, my husband grew more suspicious. Honestly, the man didn't miss a thing. He was more observant than any man I'd ever dated, and maybe even more so than most people I knew.

Boyfriends of the past would notice a change but shrug and go about their own business. Too much effort was required to dig deeper into my behavior, so it was ignored by most. People didn't really want to get to know me better. Most often, they just wanted to know if I had anything they wanted or if there was something in particular I could do for them that another couldn't.

Figuring out how often I was used made me very jaded when it came to dating. Poor Carmen hadn't tasted that bitter attitude pill yet, but it was just a matter of time until that side of my personality showed itself too. I figured by that time he would be so fed up with my shitty brashness about everything else, it would be the final nudge over the edge and into the abyss of exes.

In my imagination, I saw a bunch of past dates and boyfriends lying at the bottom of a ravine. Broken limbs and bleeding gashes prevented them from doing more than lying there and whimpering as I peered down into the big pit. I laughed maniacally in my daydream and realized I was doing the same thing in truth.

Carmen stared at me with a trace of trepidation. It just made me laugh harder.

Maybe I was losing it? No job, no actual place to live. A man I just met was the only one to take pity on me and insist we move in together.

When I did tell my family the news, I didn't expect them to put up a fuss about the arrangements. Knowing how that was going to hurt made me hesitant to have the conversation.

I'd just be one less kid my parents had to deal with. Two down, three to go.

Maybe they shouldn't have created so many extra humans if they were just going to ignore them in the long run? Just a thought. Nasty, yes. But the truth sometimes was.

"You okay?" he finally asked when my laughing died out.

"Yep. Perfect, as a matter of fact," I said after a solid shoulder shrug, I abruptly changed the subject. "I found these duffels. Should help, right?" I held up the bags with a death grip and tried to get my shit together on the inside. Hopefully he didn't see the way my hands were trembling before I dropped the totes on the bed like hot coals.

"Okay, where do you want me to start?" he asked, opening the suitcase he pulled from my closet and setting it on my bed.

It seemed smarter to pack as though I were going on a trip rather than moving out. I wouldn't be able to fit everything in the few bags we found between us, so I'd take the essentials today and come back for the rest.

"I'll pull stuff out, and you pack it in there. How's that?" I pointed to the open luggage and then looked to him for his input.

"Sounds like a plan. At least we're moving forward," he commented, and I stopped riffling through my jeans to glare at him.

"Storm, just keep going. Not every comment is an invitation for an argument. Stop being so damn defensive and hand me some clothes." He held out his large hand for items to pack, and I shoved a stack his way.

And no, I didn't miss that the green jelly ring was still on his left hand. Exactly where I still had mine.

Eventually we fell into normal conversation while we

packed. He was right—not that I'd admit that to him—but I was very defensive by nature. I was so used to my folks second-guessing every single decision I made or being compared to one of my sisters at every turn, it became my natural reaction to be defensive.

I loved my sisters with every beat of my heart. They were the most important people in my world. But when you looked so similar to four other people and were stacked so closely in age, it was easy to lose your own identity.

It took about an hour to pack the bags we had available. Carmen was loading the last one into the back of my car when my father pulled into the driveway.

"Oh, shit. I was really hoping we could've avoided this," I grumbled.

My husband gave my dad a big friendly wave as he parked his sedan, and I ran through my options on how to handle this.

"Hey, guys, how's it going?" my dad greeted us as he reached into his back seat for his laptop bag.

When he straightened again, leather bag slung over his shoulder, I stepped into his open arms to hug him. My dad was tall like Carmen, and they both dwarfed me by at least a foot.

"What's going on, Dah? You guys going somewhere? Looks like you have a bunch of bags packed there." He motioned to the back seat of my small hatchback with his chin.

"Yeah, kind of. Well, no, it's just . . . "

Great, this is going swell!

The people in my family were used to my unorganized demeanor, so my father patiently waited for me to explain in a coherent way.

Deciding to rip the Band-Aid off, I blurted, "I'm going to stay at Carmen's for a while."

My dad fixed his steady eyes on me for a moment, then gave Carmen the same treatment.

Finally, he said, "I see. How long is awhile? Did something happen here? With one of your sisters? Why the sudden relocation?"

"Well, a couple of things have happened, actually," I started, but Carmen interrupted.

"Maybe we should go inside and talk for a few minutes?"

"Agatha can speak for herself, son. And if she wants to talk to me right here on the driveway, that's fine too."

Well, shit, I'd say that put Carmen in his place, but he was completely unruffled by the mini lecture and politely dipped his chin in agreement.

"All right," he yielded.

"Darling, what were you going to say?" My dad leaned up against my car and gave me his undivided attention. He'd have kittens if someone leaned up against his beloved vehicle.

"I was fired this morning. So, in light of the conversation we just had ... shit, was that last night?" I rubbed my forehead, trying to remember what day it was. After a few beats, I waved my hand through the air. "It doesn't matter when that was, but yeah, Carmen has his own place and asked me to stay there with him."

"How will you contribute financially without a job?" my accountant father asked.

"I'm confident she'll be employed in no time," Carmen interjected. "Until then, I don't mind handling the bills. I'm already used to it, so it won't be any different."

I didn't miss my dad's weight shift. "I don't want you to feel pressured to move in with someone you hardly know."

"I don't, Daddy. Honest. And we've been getting along

great, haven't we?" I looked to my husband with pleading eyes, silently begging him to go along with the talk track.

"Oh, yeah. Absolutely," he said, his voice taking on some strange quality I hadn't heard before.

My dad's alpha dog bit was probably getting to him.

"I'm sure it's going to be great," he continued. "No worries. I mean…"

The man started rambling, and I knew if I didn't interrupt, he'd say something dumb.

"Will you tell Mom I'll call her in the morning? I'll probably have to stop by in a few days for more stuff. We're both anxious to just get going before traffic is unbearable."

Now *I* was rambling.

My dad just volleyed his attention between us, his frown deepening the more we spoke.

"Ready?" I asked my spouse in an overly bright voice. I sounded like a chipmunk after inhaling helium. But I slid my hand into his, and he gave me a reassuring squeeze. My dad zeroed in on our entwined hands, and I realized Carmen's bright-green wedding band was on full display.

Immediately I dropped his hand and gave him a little shove at the small of his back. "I'll follow you."

After a quick peck on my father's cheek, I nearly dived into my car and busied myself with the seat belt.

"Bye!" I shouted through the closed window and then waved and put my little car into reverse and waited for Carmen to start backing out. I gave my dad another wave, and we sped off.

Holy shit, that was a disaster. At least he didn't seem stressed about any of it. Just confused. I didn't need his precarious cardiac condition hanging over my head too.

We merged onto the 405 northbound, and I realized I had no idea where my husband lived. Normally, that should've come up in a conversation at some point, but our relationship was anything but normal.

The control freak in me immediately summoned the Bluetooth assistant in my car to call Carmen while we sped along the surprisingly uncongested freeway. Before the call connected, though, I pressed the End icon on the dashboard display. It was time to show a little faith in the man and just follow him to our destination. I might have a panic attack by the time we arrived, but I was out to prove to myself, if not him too, that I could do this.

Turned out my new address was in Glendale. We turned into a newer complex that was manicured to perfection. Really, the place suited Carmen to a T. He motioned for me to pull alongside him, so I did and put my passenger-side window down.

"There's assigned parking, so ensure you always park in one of our spots or you will be towed. And they don't mess around with that rule above all others, so seriously, Storm, spot 219 right there, or under the covered parking on the other side over there."

"Okay," I said but continued looking around the grounds of the complex.

"Did you hear me?" he repeated, and I swung a glare his way.

"Yes, I heard you," I replied in a very petulant tone. "But if you ever speak to me that way again, I'll drive right back to Brentwood. What do you have against the ocean anyway?"

He looked confused while answering, "Nothing. Love the beach, actually."

"Well, we just logged a lot of eastbound miles, dude."

"It's called affordability, darling. Sorry it's not Malibu, like your sister landed, but I bring in a fraction of what that guy does."

He defended his location and salary, and it looked like I might have ruffled a feather or two. But he gave his head a little shake and was back to the affable guy he usually was.

"You park there"—he pointed to his spot again—"and I'll meet you at that staircase." With the second comment, he indicated an outdoor stairwell that led to two doors off a sizable landing.

I gave him a quick salute and zipped into the parking space. Loaded down with as many bags as I could manage, I lumbered toward the apartment. A very good-looking guy stopped me and slid two of the bags from my shoulder and insisted on helping. When we cleared the stairs, my husband looked ready to blow a gasket.

"Darling, making friends already?" he said in a snarky voice.

Ooooo, someone is jealous, and it looks adorable on his normally serious features.

"Carmen, this is Blake. He insisted on giving me a hand up all those steps. Phew. Good thing too!"

I poured on the helpless-girl routine, and Carmen glared.

"Hey, man." he said to the guy and gave him a casual dip of the chin. But the new neighbor was much friendlier and offered a hand to shake.

"You guys just moving in?" Blake asked with a genuine smile. I liked the guy's vibe, but based on Carmen's glare, he wasn't as impressed.

"My wife is moving in today. I've lived here a few months.

Thanks for the help, man. Looks like we got it from here." He turned his back on our neighbor and strode forward to unlock the door.

The guy just looked at me, and I shrugged. Not sure why Carmen had to be a dick about it, but I could've used a new friend.

"Maybe I'll see you around," Blake said, and I just smiled.

"You coming?" Carmen nearly barked, and I swung my stare his way.

He stood with the door wide open and motioned me inside. With a quick goodbye to the nice neighbor, I stormed past my husband and stood inside the door.

When the panel clapped shut behind me, I sucked in a breath, ready to give my new roomie a piece of my mind.

"Listen, I don't appreciate you flirting with other guys right under my nose," he lectured before I could get a word out. "It's really disrespectful, and you're sending that guy the wrong message."

With hands propped on my hips, I asked, "And what message was I sending him?"

"That you're available. Need I remind you why you're moving in here with me?" He held up his left hand so I could clearly see his green wedding band.

As if I'd lost sight of the damn thing since he put it on. Or I put it on. Still a bit fuzzy on that whole night.

"Let's be completely clear. I don't belong to you. You're not my liege or my warden. Spare me all the caveman shit, too."

When it first seemed like he was a little jealous, it was kind of cute. But once he launched into an actual lecture, I had to draw the line.

"Just act like a married woman, and we shouldn't have

anything to worry about," he spat.

It took me that long, but I realized he was actually hurt by that whole incident.

I stepped forward and closed the space between us. With my hand on his forearm, I said, "Carmen, he was just helping me carry the bags. I mean, look at me. I'm the size of a schoolgirl. Any man with common decency would offer to help. It doesn't automatically mean he wants to get in my pants."

"You can't really be that naïve. Can you?" he asked while looking down to where I held his arm.

"Don't be rude on top of bossy," I warned. "Very unattractive."

He took a few deep breaths, and I just stood there watching the exercise. Was I that infuriating that he had to go through some calming deep-breathing technique?

Jesus, we were never going to make this work.

Trying to get past this nonsense, I asked brightly, "Which room will be mine? Give me the grand tour?" My tone was hopeful and as positive as I could manage after that little spat, and I hoped he wasn't going to pout or storm around all night.

"Why wouldn't we sleep in the same room? We're married—"

But I interrupted at once. "We're practically strangers. You can't expect me to just hop into bed with you because of some stupid paperwork." I looked at him with disbelief, and a slow grin spread across his lips. "What's with the smile?" I barked.

"Do I need to remind you about the one thing we do seem to have going for us?" His voice turned deep and seductive as he crowded into my personal space until I took a few steps back and thumped into the hallway wall.

He kept coming, though, until his very toned body was against mine.

Even though my body liked what was happening, I brought my hands to his shoulders to keep him at least a few inches away. Carmen slowly bent his head toward mine until our lips met.

Do I want this? Yeah, I think I want this.

The kiss was slow and soft, and I considered just how warm his body felt against mine. My stupid brain never stopped, even in intimate moments. Always an internal dialogue, always a personal commentary or debate. I wanted to just shut it all off and feel what was happening. Just enjoy the sensations.

It was a big reason I liked drinking. My brain slowed down then, and if I had the right amount, I could get it to shut up completely and still keep my wits about me to have a good time. It was a precarious sweet spot, and admittedly, I typically overshot the mark more than stuck it. But it was something I was willing to practice until I got it right.

"Where are you right now?" he growled beside my ear and then sank his teeth into the fleshy lobe.

A sly grin stretched my lips, and he saw my reaction before I could school my features.

"You liked that, hmm?" he asked, but I was pretty sure it was a rhetorical type of question based on the tone of his voice.

He bit me again, only this time on my neck, and I might have actually purred. With that vocal encouragement, Carmen made a trail of bites down the length of my neck until I was almost moaning for more.

He stepped back, and the cool apartment air washed over my flushed skin.

"Now, that's more like the welcome home I was fantasizing

about while we drove here." He smiled down at me, and for once, I didn't have a snarky comeback.

Carmen slid his hand down the length of my arm until he reached my hand. With our fingers intertwined, he tugged me deeper into the apartment.

"Come on. I'll show you the place, and then we can get you settled. Are you hungry? I have some groceries here, but we may have to order in until you can get to the store tomorrow."

Well, that stuttered my dreamy steps, and I yanked my hand free of his. "What did you just say?"

"I'll show you the place?" He tilted his head to the side, looking thoroughly confused.

"After that."

"I'll help you unpack?"

"After."

"Dinner?"

At that point, I figured he was intentionally being obtuse, so my hands went to my hips again and I asked, "Why would you think I'm going for groceries tomorrow?"

There were so many things wrong with the statement, I didn't know where to begin bitching him out.

"Because I'll be at work all day and you won't be?" he asked, propping his hands on his hips to mirror my stance. "God, woman. Does everything have to be a damn argument with you?"

"Only when you're acting like a chauvinistic asshole," I snapped.

"The comment had nothing to do with me being a man and you being a woman. It was simple logistics."

He stepped toward me again, and I put my hands up to signal stop. But the persistent man entwined our fingers and pulled my knuckles to his lips.

After kissing each one, he said, "Storm, listen to me." He dropped his chin to his chest like he was gathering every ounce of patience he could rally. "I'm not the enemy. We're in this together, right? You can bank on the fact that every comment out of my mouth is not a personal attack on you, and then hopefully we can avoid all this bickering. Doesn't that sound like a more pleasant existence?"

I huffed in frustration, but he patiently waited. When a few more moments went by without comment from either of us, he dropped my hands and strolled across the kitchen.

"Come on, let's get your stuff unpacked," he called before opening a door at the far side of the room. "This is the bedroom. I'll clear some space in the closet and dresser for you."

Picking up two of the bags I brought in from the car, I followed after him like a lost puppy. The whole scene was so awkward: not my home, not my stuff, I didn't even know where the bathroom was.

The master bedroom was smaller than my bedroom at my parents' home, but I had to remind myself it was pretty typical for apartment living. There was an en suite bathroom at least, so I could work with that. When I saw the size of the postage-stamp closet though, I balked.

"We can't share this closet, man." I stood staring into the open doorway and then let out a laugh. I bet the complex brochure advertised it as a walk-in.

"Dare I ask why not?"

"Carmen, look at it. It's already crowded past a usable limit with your stuff. My things will never fit in here too." I looked between the closet and my husband two or three times before he said more.

"Okay, I know how we can handle this. I'll move my stuff to the closet in the other bedroom. That way you can use the whole thing and won't have to go all the way to the other side of the apartment after you shower."

"All the way, huh?" I chuckled. If the whole place was a thousand square feet, I'd be shocked. Then in a moment of charity I said, "That doesn't make sense. Let me just put my stuff in the other room. Then you don't have to move all yours. It's twice the work to move your stuff."

"Yes, but I think this one is bigger. This is designated as the master, so technically it should be bigger, right?"

"One would think," I replied. "But I don't really have much. And I didn't pack everything I have. Let's just start with me in there"—I thumbed over my shoulder, assuming the other bedroom was in that direction—"and we can see how it works out."

"All right. Fair enough." He smiled and scooped up the bags I had dropped at the opening of the closet and walked out of the room, me following behind him once again.

"I still think it would be better if I slept in here too."

"On what? The floor? I won't have it." He was adamant about his answer.

Why did the solution seem so obvious to me?

"Can't we get more furniture?"

"With what, darling? Our good looks? You don't have a source of income currently, and my paycheck has to cover everything else. Furnishing an entire room just isn't in the budget at the moment."

"Maybe my folks would let me move the furniture from my room at their house," I thought out loud.

"But you were just saying that the twins wouldn't have to

share a room now that you've moved out. Won't they need the furniture?"

My shoulders dropped along with my excitement. "Yeah, you're probably right. I can unpack this stuff. You don't have to help. Like I said, there isn't that much. I'll be done in no time." And to be honest, I was nearing an emotional disturbance. I could feel it churning in my stomach. Some alone time would be much appreciated.

"Why don't I see what I can throw together for dinner while you do this? Is there anything you don't like?"

Oh, this was going to be another debate and lecture. I knew it before I even answered.

"Pretty much vegetables and fish. Other than that, I'm easy."

"You don't eat vegetables? Or you don't like them?" he asked, his good-boy face set in a mask of horror.

I laughed at his expression and said, "I don't eat them because I don't like them."

"Okaaaayy." He dragged the reaction out across more beats than he needed to. "Narrow it down for me. Like, you don't like broccoli?"

"All of them. They're mushy and gross, and you're not going to get me to change my mind, so don't make this our next spat, 'kay?"

Even though he was shaking his head, he replied, "Yes, dear."

Good thing he didn't see the one-finger salute I flipped him as he left the room.

What had I gotten myself into? I flopped back on the floor and used one of the duffel bags as a pillow. I needed to come up with a game plan, because this arrangement was never going to work out. He'd be sick of me by week's end, and then I'd be jobless *and* homeless. The last thing I wanted to do was show up on Hannah's doorstep and beg for a place to crash.

First thing tomorrow, I'd brush up my résumé and start sending it out to the contacts I'd made from my old job. I wouldn't be able to use them as a reference now that I was fired, so I would either have to lie about why I moved on or make up other job experience so I wouldn't have a long gap in employment. That never looked good on an application. But I had to find something. Hell, I'd work at Hot Topic if need be. There was no way I'd be financially dependent on Carmen—or anyone else, for that matter.

I must have been lost in my thoughts, because when my husband poked his head back in the room to let me know dinner was ready, I was still lying on the floor.

"Hey," he said, then saw my position and lack of progress. "Have you been lying there this whole time? Shit, it's been like an hour. You could be finishing up by now."

"Don't start with me again," I snapped but then sighed. "Please. I don't need another lecture of disapproval right now. I had no idea that much time slipped by." I finished off the admission at close to a whisper and hauled myself up off the floor. Changing the subject seemed like a good plan.

"Something smells delicious. What did you make?" I asked, stomach growling with hunger now that I caught a whiff of his cooking.

"Come on, before it gets cold."

He held his hand back for me to grab, and I just looked at it.

"I'm going to freshen up quickly, wash my hands from all this." I waved around to the bags scattered across the floor. I really just needed a moment to breathe, and I'd rather do it without his assessing stare. "Is there a guest bath?"

"Yep, right here." He tapped on the closed door while walking past. "Do you want water with dinner?"

"Wine if you have it, please. Beer works too, depending on what you made."

God, could I be so lucky to catch a buzz to end this day?

CHAPTER NINE

CARMEN

My beautiful wife had us up twice the night before, and I felt like I'd been out all night partying instead of dealing with an insomniac. Of course, she had sleep problems on top of all the other things she dealt with. And, like the majority of her issues, the fitful sleeping was a product of her own bad habits.

I couldn't keep lecturing her or scolding her for her unhealthy behaviors, though. Hell...I was getting on my *own* nerves. I could just imagine how she felt.

But we needed to find a way to stop bickering. It wasn't in my nature to just *Yes, dear* her on everything we didn't see eye to eye on, so that wasn't a viable option. But anyone who witnessed her jump-down-your-throat reaction style to any and every topic would sympathize with me and what I was dealing with.

We both had to want this marriage to work. I couldn't do all the bending all the time. Maybe we needed to go to counseling. My boss was known around the building as a therapy junkie, so maybe I'd pick his brain about the merits of a few sessions.

That conversation could dovetail with another one we needed to have. On my drive in this morning, I rehearsed my talk track regarding a salary increase. It had been a while since I had a raise, and he had to admit I did a really great job keeping him organized and running on time throughout the day. Now that I was financially responsible for two people, more money would definitely be a bonus.

Because she was up half the night, I assumed my wife would sleep in for a few hours after I left. But I definitely planned on calling her on my first break this morning to make sure she was spearheading a legitimate job search. Maybe there was something that suited her at Shark Enterprises. I made a mental note to talk with her about that and that I could put in a good word if she were interested.

Elijah Banks strolled past my desk with a mischievous grin taking up the majority of his facial real estate. He had just pocketed his cell phone, so whoever had been on the other side of the device just then could likely be credited for his affable mood.

Might as well strike while he was chipper. I loathed these types of conversations with an employer, but again, I had more than myself to worry about now. I waited for him to settle in at his desk before I picked up the phone to see if he had a minute to spare for me.

"Hey, Carmen. How can I help you?"

"Hi. Do you have a minute to talk?"

"Sure. Always. Do you want me to come out there?"

"No, frankly, I'd rather talk behind closed doors. I don't know if you know this, but the gossip network in this building is shameless and far-reaching. I don't need everyone in my business. I'll be right in."

After a few deep breaths, I knocked on his door.

"Come in," he shouted from the interior of his office.

In the past, I had confessed to my boss how much I disliked confrontation. Especially with a superior. No matter what I told myself in an effort to calm down, my body wouldn't listen. My stomach already grumbled from skipping breakfast in favor of sleeping a tad more. Now I was also feeling jittery from drinking coffee on an empty stomach and anticipating this conversation.

I closed the door behind me and took the chair in front of Elijah's desk.

"You okay, dude?" he asked with his trademarked head tilt.

Fiddling with the cuff on my sleeve, I said, "Yeah, just a little off this morning."

"What's going on? How can I help you?" he asked, and his friendly vibe was helping me relax a touch. It was ridiculous to get so worked up the way I was, but years and years of conditioning from very strict parents was hard to just undo.

"Agatha moved in with me last night," I rushed ahead and told him.

He and I were now connected in more ways than our original boss and assistant relationship, and once I started talking about the woman who was driving me crazy in every imaginable way, I rambled on for several minutes without a single pause.

Luckily, he was one hundred percent focused on our conversation and caught all the facts I blurted.

"And on top of everything else, she's an insomniac. I think we were up more than we slept last night, and I know I can't survive on that little sleep night after night."

I finally finished and relaxed back into the chair.

Elijah wore a grin, and I scanned everything I just told him to find where he got humor.

"Why are you grinning like that?" I asked and winced

when my defensive tone bounced around the room.

"Dude, I remember those first few weeks with your wife's sister, and listening to you talk is bringing it all right here." He motioned between us like we were staring at a pile of laundry that neither of us wanted to fold.

"Yesterday, just getting her out of that family house was an ordeal. It's like *everything* has to be an ordeal, you know? Even if it wasn't originally, she sabotages herself until it is. I think she has trouble functioning outside of chaos. So she creates her own if necessary."

I thought about what I had just concluded and nodded. It was a solid theory.

"I haven't had a lot of interactions with her, so I don't know one way or the other on that, but I have known people like that throughout my life. My ex was super dramatic." He thought for a moment. "Well, you've had a few run-ins with the she-devil. You know what I'm talking about. The woman never just faded into her surroundings. Always had to be center stage."

I sighed and shifted in my seat. I was about to dig into the important part.

"So, the reason I'm bringing all this up is now that I'm supporting both of us, I was hoping I could get a raise. I feel awkward asking, but it's been a while since I've had a performance review ... " I trailed off there and watched the man for any clues about his feelings on the matter. I willed him to interrupt with a response so I wouldn't have to continue groveling. He was a smart man, and he could connect the dots I just scattered in front of him.

Instead of the friendly, affirmative response I'd hoped for, he screwed his face up in confusion.

"Just curious, and you can tell me to fuck off—not my

business and all that," he said as the lead into what I assumed would be a bigger question. "How did she lose her job? I know she wasn't thrilled with the commute, but something is better than nothing."

My boss's gears were spinning at top speed. I'd seen that look on his face before.

My own exhaustion and frustration seeped out of the cracks in my tone as I scrubbed a palm down my face. I wasn't trying to be coy or evasive in this conversation with my boss, but every time I brought the topic up with Agatha, she changed the subject, so I still didn't have a clear idea about what led to her termination exactly.

"I don't exactly know," I finally admitted.

He reacted after turning my admission over a couple times. "Oh, damn, that's not good."

"No, it's not." I frowned. "The timing couldn't be worse. They just raised my rent, too, so I was looking forward to having someone to share the larger financial obligation with."

After my comment, the quiet just bloated between us. Minute by minute ticked by, and we were both so lost in our own thoughts, we could've been seated at our own desks instead of attempting to have a conversation.

Finally, Elijah gave his head a quick shake and said, "Sorry. Totally spaced out thinking about those bombs we married."

He was grinning, but not in a salacious way. His expression communicated his thoughts had been admiration and affection, and I smiled too.

"Definitely a handful," I muttered.

"I don't think she's told Hannah that she's lost her job. I'm almost positive my wife would've mentioned that. I know you said something yesterday, but I didn't tell Hannah, figuring her sister would've," he said thoughtfully. "Though Hannah's had morning sickness nearly all day, every day, so she's been napping a lot. Maybe she just missed the call."

"And to be fair, I picked her up right after work last night and helped her get some things packed. From Brentwood, she followed me to Glendale since she'd never been to my place."

"Dude . . . Glendale? That's like . . . so far from the beach, man. How can you stand to be so far inland?"

He had no idea how snobby he sounded with that comment, and honestly, it pissed me off a little. I was living the best life I could on the salary I brought home. Not all of us had beachside mansions in Malibu to call home.

"It's what I can afford," I snapped. "And now even Glendale is going to be a stretch." And now I sounded petulant and desperate, and I hated every second of it.

I stood abruptly and planned to bolt to the door before my boss put up a reassuring hand and said, "Okay, settle down. I'll make it happen. You definitely deserve a raise, and I'll push for the company's max, and we can go from there. Don't go freaking out on me."

All I could push up my throat and across my lips was a quiet, "Thank you." The volume had nothing to do with my sincerity or gratitude, and I hoped like hell the man knew it.

He assessed me with a knowing gaze before saying, "Every new relationship is tough, man. You guys have some unique extras added on, to say the least. Hang in there, okay?"

By the time he was finished issuing his advice, he stood in front of me with a kind palm gripping the ball of my shoulder.

"Do the in-laws know about the nuptials yet?" Elijah asked with a chuckle, and all I could do was shake my head. There was still a wad of emotion lodged in my throat preventing words from getting out.

"But they know she's staying with you?"

"Yeah, our new father-in-law came home last night just as we finished loading our cars."

"And how did that go? I don't know about you, but I think he can be damn intimidating for an accountant." Elijah studied his shoes while making the admission.

"He didn't really put up much of a fuss."

Well, that had his head snapping up again. "What? Are you kidding? Shit, if Hannah had pulled that stunt, they would've guilted her about his unhealthy heart and that she was breaking up the family." He rolled his eyes heavenward. "Don't get me wrong. They are some of the nicest people I've ever met, but those parents have the guilt trip mastered where my wife is concerned."

"At least they care. My wife is all but ignored. And it's definitely taken its toll on her over the years. She's made a few comments under her breath about Hannah being the center of their universe and the others get whatever crumbs are left over."

"That's kind of fucked up that her sisters say that."

"What's fucked up is the fact that the other sisters have to."

"Well, there's stuff in her past that you probably don't know about. It will make more sense one day when Agatha shares more with you," he said, and suddenly we were both on the defensive.

Before that kind of bullshit could escalate, I said, "Well, thank you for the forthcoming raise. It'll really help, and I'm beyond grateful."

I extended my hand respectfully, and we shook.

"Guess we should get some work done?" he suggested with a big grin.

Good... No hard feelings for either of us. I'd hate to make my work environment awkward because we married into the same family. While I didn't aspire to be someone else's assistant for the rest of my life, I enjoyed my job and the people I worked with. The company had tons of growth potential, and I was stoked to be in with one of the owner's right-hand men.

Feeling a little embarrassed to have to admit I didn't have Elijah's schedule committed to memory yet, I said, "Yeah, probably an emergency fire somewhere you should be putting out. Let me get back to my desk and check out the calendar."

"I think I'm open until a nine thirty downstairs with HR. It will give me a perfect opportunity to submit your review package, so I'm going to work on that until then. Maybe hold my calls unless it's absolutely necessary?"

"You got it. Thanks again, Elijah." I made sure to hold his gaze so he knew how sincerely grateful I was.

"You deserve every dime, my man." He gave me a solid thump on the back as I walked out.

I quietly closed his door and slid into the chair behind my desk. I really wanted to fire a quick text to Agatha and share the good news, but I didn't want to wake her. Figuring I'd tell her when I got home, I dug into my email inbox and barely looked up until it was time to leave early that evening.

I'd be lying if I said I wasn't a bit disappointed I hadn't heard from my girl all day. She did have a lot on her plate, with unpacking and job hunting, so I decided to surprise her with some takeout. I snagged a pretty bouquet from the few remaining in the white five-gallon bucket the local street vendor always sold her choices from. The kind elderly

Mexican woman had a fresh daily selection at the corner by the market, and they always looked better and lasted longer than the grocery store offerings.

"Honey, I'm home," I called into the dim apartment and tossed my keys into the ceramic bowl on the entryway table. Agatha's keys and handbag were right where they were this morning when I'd left.

I ventured toward the kitchen, figuring I'd find her there, but that room was quiet too. Maybe she'd lain down for a bit? I left the flowers and food on the small countertop and went toward the master bedroom.

"Storm?" I called out but got no response. I didn't want to startle her if she was sleeping, so I opened the door on quiet feet, and there she was.

"Didn't you hear me calling to you?" I asked, wondering why she didn't respond.

And for Christ's sake... are those the same pajamas she had on last night?

She popped a pair of pods out of her ears and said, "Oh, hey. You're home early."

"It's almost six"—then added when she continued wordlessly staring at me—"*in the evening*. Have you been in bed all day?"

"Pretty much," she said with a careless shrug, and I could feel my body temperature climb.

"Agatha..."

"Don't start on me the moment you walk in the door. 'Kay? I deserve a day or two to myself, so don't harsh my mellow here." She glared at me with challenge all over the expression.

On a dime, she changed topics and demeanor and popped out from under the covers.

"What smells so good? Did you bring food?"

She was toe to toe with me and stretched up to hook her arms around my neck. I was still trying to catch up from the mini ass chewing I'd just gotten, so she completely caught me off guard. I leaned into her embrace and wrapped my arms around her tiny waist.

"Yes, I grabbed us some dinner. I don't know what you like, so I took a chance. But no way are you eating in our bed, so come out to the kitchen." I gave her forehead a quick peck and released my embrace.

While we went out to the kitchen, I stretched my neck from side to side. I pulled out a chair for my wife, then released the top two buttons of my shirt.

"You sit, and I'll get plates. You probably don't know where everything is just yet."

Because you've been in bed all day.

My God, what a waste of so many hours that she'd never get back. How does one lie in bed all day and do nothing? I could never understand the concept and was never afforded the opportunity to try while growing up. My parents insisted my sister and I had our chores done before any extracurriculars could happen. On the weekends, especially, the list was long and detailed.

"These are for you," I said sheepishly and handed her the bouquet.

"Carmen...how lovely. And so thoughtful. You really shouldn't have." She buried her nose into the crowns of a few of the larger blooms, but I could still see the corners of her mouth tilted up in a delicate smile. She was arresting like that, and I wanted to freeze time and live in this momentary bubble of tranquility.

Score one for the husband!

"Do I smell garlic bread? I swear, if I do, someone's getting lucky tonight!" She cackled after she saw my expression rise with hopeful excitement. Looked like I discovered a fast and sure way to my girl's good nature. Italian food!

We chatted and ate until we groaned from being so full. The food was from one of my all-time favorite restaurants. They had the best chicken parm on the planet, and apparently Agatha was their newest fan.

"Okay, the least I can do is clean up. Thank you again for getting this." She motioned to the empty containers strewn across the counter.

"I'll help, and we'll be done twice as fast. How's that?" I offered.

Her mood was one of the best I'd ever experienced. I was so into spending time with her, even washing dishes sounded delightful. Because I didn't want to wreck her good mood, I steered clear of the job-hunting topic.

"What did you major in? In college—obviously," I asked, hoping it was a safe topic.

"Biology. If you can believe that," she answered wryly.

"Of course I can believe that. I believe you can do anything you put your mind to," I answered, quickly wondering if I was pouring it on too thick.

Her eye roll confirmed my fear, but still she answered, "You sound like my parents."

"They obviously love you. Aren't parents supposed to be their kids' cheering section?" I slung the dish towel over my shoulder and turned to face her. "How did you get a job in journalism with a biology degree?"

"Why all the questions?" she asked, and just like that, her

words held an edge. I wasn't trying to make her feel defensive and realized I had to step carefully with my follow-up or I'd ruin our whole night. That was the last thing I wanted to do.

With a careless shrug, I said, "I'm just trying to get to know you better."

"Okay." She sighed.

I couldn't really pick up the vibe of her reply, but she continued talking.

"Here's the cold, hard truth. I barely made it through my last year of school. I had completely lost interest in . . . well, everything, I guess. I hated the co-ed life, and I just wanted it to be over. I probably should have switched majors sooner, but by the time I got my act together and looked into what it would take to do that, I was only a few credits away from graduating. My heart has always been in writing. It was my parents' dream to have a scientist in the family. Or an accountant. But I stopped wanting that bullshit before I was out of high school." She sighed with the last part, and her spirit wilted. "But here I am. The scientist."

"Have you ever considered going back to school? Maybe if you were pursuing the right major, you would get more out of the process."

Agatha thought about what I'd said for a few moments while she dried the last dish. "No. I guess I've never considered going back. For one thing, my parents would be so disappointed. For another thing, I don't have the money to live and go to school. And I already know that working and studying at the same time is too much for me mentally. I know that for sure. Once I get overwhelmed with a commitment, I just shut down completely. Then nothing gets done."

"Is that what happened here today?" I asked, knowing I

was really pushing my luck with the question. But I also knew I didn't want to set a precedent that I would tiptoe around her volatile moods.

As predicted, she squinted her eyes and revved up to jump down my throat.

But I shut her down before she launched into whatever she had in mind. I closed the space between us until her lower back was against the countertop's edge. One large hand on either side of her body caged her in place. The woman stared up at me with the biggest, most curious ocean-blue eyes I'd ever seen.

And so alluring. Intoxicating and enthralling.

"Don't get pissy with me because I asked a question you didn't like. You can politely explain why you stayed in bed all day when you had unpacking and job hunting to do. You're not a bratty teenager anymore, so spare me the attitude. We both have to pull our weight around here. Okay?"

"What makes you think I have to answer to you? Account for my time?"

I considered my answer before snapping back with the first thing that came to mind, which would sound something like *Because I'm your husband.* I knew a comment like that would not go over well with my fierce storm, so I gave my reply a little more thought.

Elijah's comment from earlier today about Mom and Dad Farsey using the guilt-as-guidance parenting style rang in the back of my head. I was starting to think that was their method with all the girls. Not just with Hannah.

"I'm sorry. I didn't mean to come across that way, and I can see that I did." I offered the apology sincerely and waited for her acceptance. Instead, I got a fiery stare, little fists balled at her hips, and a proud defiant chin thrust forward, ready for combat.

My God, this girl is a hellcat.

She said nothing.

"Did you hear me apologize?" I asked, getting irritated with this hot-and-cold routine.

"Oh, I heard you." She nodded haughtily. "I'm trying to decide what to do with it."

My screwed-up face gave away my confusion.

"What to do with it?"

"Yes. Accept it or toss it in the trash with the other garbage."

She was infuriating me. I closed the distance between us, and right when I was in front of her, I bent forward and tucked my shoulder into her abdomen. When I stood to my normal height, I had a sexy blond bombshell slung over my shoulder. Her small hands smacked at my backside, and in between her uncontrollable giggles, she tried to sound serious.

"What do you think you're doing? Put me down!" She sucked in a breath, and the air expanded her lungs and crushed her tits against my back. "Right now!"

I smacked her ass with an open palm, and the crack bounced around the confined space of the hallway that led to our bedroom. The pint-sized beauty laughed harder, possessing me in ways I didn't anticipate. Her happiness was becoming my crack, and like a genuine junkie, I imagined I'd go to greater and greater lengths each time to experience it.

But what would be the ultimate price? My patience? My sanity? My dignity?

Maybe all three.

CHAPTER TEN

AGATHA

"What are you doing to me, girl?" Carmen husked in the deepest voice I'd ever heard from a human.

My eyes had to be cartoonishly wide in reaction to both the sound and actually feeling his question vibrate through my body.

He hoisted me over his shoulder in the kitchen and stalked to the bedroom like some sort of Viking on a village raid. Not going to lie, the image totally worked for my pussy and every other hormonally motivated part of my body. When he tossed me on the bed, it was done with so little care, I actually bounced a time or two. I almost rolled right off the other side, causing another maniacal laugh to burst out of me.

And then I heard him issue that question. Now all I could do was stare at him while I skittered back on the mattress. That didn't stop his advance, though. He prowled across the bed and then loomed over me with an intense, lustful stare. I swallowed so hard, it made a sound we both heard.

"Wha—What do you mean what am I doing?" I choked through my own desire.

"My body," he growled. "My body seems to have disconnected from my brain. I want to tear those pretty little pajamas off you and do things married people do."

He leaned closer and pressed his lips to mine. A moan escaped when I opened for his insistent tongue, and the sound only encouraged him. More of his body weight settled on top of me, and we sank deeper into the bedding. It was a down love nest, and my incredibly sexy husband had such hunger in his stare and his kiss, and my God, the way he pressed his hips into me in the same rhythm he stroked my tongue with his own, I could barely catch my breath or organize a thought, forget about any sort of sassy remark, because my brain and body were in complete surrender mode.

I wanted him to make me feel good. Just forget about life's stressors for a while and feel good. The promise of it was right there in the way our bodies moved together. Right there in the way we fit together so perfectly when he unexpectedly flipped me onto my stomach and mounted me from behind.

While he issued his desire to remove my clothes, they still provided a maddening barrier between us. His too. It all had to go—right the fuck now—so I could feel him deep inside my aching, needing core.

"Please," I whimpered into the bedding. "Please."

The man was at my ear again, that dark, rich tone coating his normal voice in a blanket of hot, dirty sex. "I want you so bad, Storm. You have no idea the things I want to do to this tight little body."

"Tell me," I rasped into the sheets. I could be bold if I didn't see his face.

"Tell you what, baby?"

"Tell me what you want to do to me," I panted. My own alto voice took on the scratchy quality it did when I was desperately trying to turn off the circus in my head and follow my body's lead.

"Oh, darling," he rasped in what seemed like a warning. But based on the need in his voice, and the things he proceeded to say in that voice, I was like a kitty with catnip instead.

"Do you want me to say dirty things to get you hot and wet? Tell you the way I fantasize about you throughout the day? About touching you. Tasting you. And God, baby, I'm going to fuck you so good. So deep and rough that you cry and beg me to stop."

"No, no, no," I babbled while he teased me. "Don't stop."

My husband nuzzled his face into my hair while I whimpered my pleas. He found the skin at my nape and bit into my flesh without tenderness or caution. Lightning struck, zapping every coherent thought from the moment I felt his warm breath blanket the back of my neck. Christ, it all felt so good.

"You're making me crazy. I'm so ready, please. Please, fuck me." There. If he was waiting for me to beg, I delivered with earnest effort.

"First, I have to taste you. It's all I can think about."

He shifted his weight off me, and I flipped around so fast, I almost kneed him in the groin. But it wasn't eagerness inspiring me to move so quickly.

"No. No, you can't."

"There's no way you're going to be shy now," he said while tugging at the drawstring of my pajama bottoms.

"No, seriously. I haven't showered today. I don't want—I wouldn't—I mean—"

His sexy grin grew wider as I stammered through my protests. I was too embarrassed to say outright that I'd rather be fresh from the shower if he wanted to spend time down there. I already knew he wouldn't let me off easy. I wouldn't get away without expressing my concerns in words for his entertainment.

Bastard. Incredibly sexy bastard.

"Say what you will, wife, but that just makes me want it more. I can't wait to have your scent in my nose and on my face. I have dreams about your cunt, girl. You have no idea."

Who was this guy? I had him pegged completely wrong this whole time. It turned out my husband was a dirty, dirty man. His declaration made my pussy gush more, but I still batted at his hands that were trying in vain to get my pants untied and off.

"Do I have to restrain you, Storm? I'll fucking do it if you don't put your hands over your head immediately." The voice was layered with an extra threatening edge. The intense stare was present too. My arms betrayed me and lifted high on the pillow. Clearly my body knew what it wanted—no, needed—and wasn't about to let any part of my brain fuck this up for us.

He backed down my body to perch over my knees and pulled my pants down slower than traffic moved on the 405 at quitting time. I threw my head back and sank deeper into the pillow. My chest dipped and heaved with anticipatory breaths.

Finally, when the pants were tossed to the floor, a low, masculine groan came from my man. I sneaked a peek to make sure we were still in the go zone and found him staring with complete fascination at the creamy place between my legs.

"Open for me, baby," he rasped while stroking strong hands from my calves to the inside of my thighs. "So fucking warm here." But he just kept staring. I needed his mouth on me more than my next breath, and I was going insane waiting.

"Carmen, please," I whispered while my hands were on their way down my body to entice him more.

Bad call apparently.

He withdrew his hands from my body and glared. "If I tell you again, it will be while I'm strapping you down to the bed. Got it?"

"But I ... I just wanted—"

He cut my explanation off with his mouth.

The kiss was aggressive and urgent and spiked my arousal even higher. From my mouth, he started his exploration down my body with hard sucking kisses that left a trail of bruises on my pale skin. He got closer and closer to my pussy but then would move back to an earlier mark and put the finishing touch on it with his teeth.

I writhed beneath him without shame. I needed to be satisfied in a way I'd never known and began begging in nonsensical gibberish. Promises fell from my lips easier than ever, knowing when I finally did come, it was going to be earth-shattering.

I felt the tight coil of my abdominal muscles and the giddy buzz of endorphins through my entire body. My head swam with pleasure, and my skin burned with desire and need. This man was unraveling me thread by thread, and for whatever reason, I felt completely fine about it. I knew he wasn't using me, and I'd be completely stunned if he intentionally hurt me. Knowing I was safe with him allowed my mind to quiet and my body to rejoice.

Carmen did amazing things with his mouth. He wasn't exaggerating when he said he was a little obsessed with my lady parts. He spent more time lavishing my sex with his unbelievable attention than my last three partners spent combined. By the time he was working me up to a third climax with his knowing tongue and fingers, I was on the verge of real tears.

"Please. Please … Carmen … " I gasped between moans of pleasure.

"What do you need, Storm? I can't get enough of your cunt. I knew it would be the best, baby."

"I can't come again," I pleaded, and the fucker actually chuckled. "Don't laugh. I'm serious. If I go off again, I'm going to pass out."

"No, my love, you won't. Relax. Let me make you fly. It's so good, right?"

"I can't even … I don't know what … Oh shit, I'm serious. Please."

"Come for me again, Storm. Then I'm going to finally sink into this heaven."

He issued the instructions while doing something with the three fingers that were buried deep inside my body, and my soul splintered into pieces. My shout was silent because I couldn't gulp enough air to supply it and every muscle in my body as I convulsed.

I gripped both sides of his head with the little strength I had left and held him a few inches above my throbbing core.

"What the fuck are you doing to me?" I accused, but the goofy, sated grin that split my face gave the man all the accolades he needed. If I had an ounce of energy left, I'd roll over and repay the oral favor. God and all the angels knew my husband deserved my very best effort in gratitude.

But my limbs weighed a hundred pounds each, and I was exhausted. He wrang that last orgasm from my soul, no lie. If that wasn't a chakra cleansing of the best kind, I couldn't imagine what would be.

Wordlessly, I held my arms out to him, and blessed be the man between my thighs, he came to me. He kissed me passionately and held me so close with his strong arms, I wanted to fall asleep right there. The safety that blanketed my normally chaotic mind was overwhelming and frightening while being serene and magnificent at the same time.

Tears were suddenly choking off my breath, and I rolled my eyes back, trying to stave off the emotion. I'd only had this happen one time before after having sex, and with that dude, it was so embarrassing because it was a one-night stand. For a guy, what could be worse? The chick you took home and nailed to the twin bed in your childhood bedroom of your parents' house goes stage-five basket case on your ass?

He never called for a second date.

But my husband arranged our bodies so we were lying on our sides, and he fit his perfectly behind mine. His need was still a hot, pulsing demand nestled in the crack of my ass, and no way was he getting in there. Not tonight at least. But I would still gladly welcome him inside my pussy if he made the attempt.

"Condom?" I asked about ten minutes later when the dry humping grew feverish again.

I didn't think we'd ever get enough at this rate, and especially if it was always this good. A girl could get spoiled really quick with a man who's this good in bed. It would be easy to forget about all the embarrassingly bad bedmates who came before him—literally.

It was probably like all bad experiences in life, though. You quickly discharged the negativity from your brain for self-preservation. Lord knew I'd had so many bad lovers in recent months. If I'd dwelled on those experiences, I wouldn't have been in bed with my husband now. I would've missed out on all this glory.

His deep voice snapped me back to the moment instead of getting lost even deeper in my thoughts.

"No," he said simply, and because he scrambled my brain by running the tips of his fingers through my sex, it took me a moment to understand what he was refusing with that answer.

"Fuck, baby, you're so wet for me," he said, stating the obvious.

"I know," I panted. "Come on. Suit up and give it to me," I insisted.

"No," he repeated. "No condom."

"Stop fucking around. Do you not have one?" I turned my head as far as possible to meet his hungry stare. "I might have one in my purse."

"I have one. I just don't want to use one. You are my wife. I'm clean. I'm assuming you are as well?"

While this conversation was complete shit, Carmen continued stimulating my pussy while we debated protection. I didn't know how to respond. It seemed irresponsible—I mean, it had been drilled into our heads that you always used protection until you're ready to take on the responsibility of having a child. I almost laughed out loud at that notion but harnessed my giggles to salvage the sexed-up atmosphere.

Carmen knelt behind me and lifted my hips off the mattress. I felt him line the head of his dick up in preparation to invade. It already felt so good. I pushed my ass toward him in a tempting invitation.

"Please," I whimpered into the sheets.

"You didn't answer. Tell me we're good to go here," he gritted out.

He leaned over me and bit my nape again right where he had earlier. The spot was so tender, it shot exquisite, pleasurable pain through my whole body. The sensation caused a moan to rocket out of me like a plea of its own.

"Yes. Yes. Yes . . . " I rolled my head from side to side using my forehead as the pivot point. "I just had testing done before we went to Vegas."

The moment I completed that sentence, he thrust into me until his hips met my ass. Every molecule of air was sucked from my body. I couldn't shower him with praise. I couldn't shout joyful declarations into the air. Fuck, I couldn't even breathe.

And, oh my God, he was bare. The sensations were so much more intense without that barrier between our bodies. Just the heat was enough to make me stutter.

"You good, wife?" he asked with his next slow stroke. "Talk to me, Storm. Tell me what you need more of, less of. I want to know all the ways I can please you."

"Harder. Do it harder."

He dug his fingers into my hips and held on while he slammed into me. Over and over again, causing us to travel toward the headboard. At that point, I had nowhere else to go, and my neck was bent at an uncomfortable and probably dangerous angle.

Of course, Carmen noticed my predicament and scooted back down the bed. The man noticed everything, it seemed. With one strong forearm banded beneath my abdomen, he dragged me with him. I felt like a little doll the way he handled me. Moving me to suit his needs. Just his plaything.

And it was so fucking hot.

"Get there again, baby," he encouraged. He spread my ass cheeks with his two large palms, and just the thought of him taking me there—I exploded. For the fourth fucking time in one night, I came with a guttural moan.

"My God. My God, woman. This cunt. I will never get my fill of this hot, tight heaven."

I looked back over my shoulder in time to see him loll his head back between his shoulder blades and moan. "Feel me come, baby. Feel me fill you up," he instructed while he climaxed deep inside my channel.

So many things started running a mad-dash loop in my brain. If I could pluck one or two out of the jumble, I'd be on steadier mental footing.

One. There was nothing responsible about letting this man ejaculate inside my body. Not one thing.

Even though I was on birth control pills, I'd have to dash out for a morning-after pill and pray for the best. Married or not, there was no way we were ready to be parents, and I knew I hadn't been taking my birth control pills regularly this month.

Two. Where the hell had this version of Carmen Sandoval been hiding? Dominant, bossy, strong-willed men were my preferred type. If I had known this was underneath Mr. Kind and Considerate all this time, I might have been nicer to him in the off-sex periods.

Maybe.

Three. How soon could we do all that again?

Four. There was a strong possibility I was catching feelings for this guy. I told myself I could stick it out for a year, if for no other reason, it was a place to live that wasn't my family's home. But also, he had my journal. And to be one hundred percent clear on that point, there were things—so many things—written in that one linen-covered book that could destroy every relationship in my life. Including the bonds I had with my sisters and the respect and love I had for my parents. Sordid details of my sexual and emotional romps with others were commented on in great detail on those pages, too. Confessions regarding unethical things I'd done in my life up to that point could be found in my own handwritten words.

No exaggeration. My entire life would be ruined.

And that's how I found myself in this position. Well, not the exact physical position I was in at the moment, but the general predicament with Carmen. If he hadn't snatched that little notebook off my desk and bargained for a year of my life, I would probably already have a divorce or annulment in the works.

Every other time I thought about his blackmailing scheme, I became furious all over again. But my body was buzzing with so many happy chemicals thanks to his mad, mad bedroom skills, I barely raised an eyebrow about it.

Shit, if this was a snapshot of my life for the upcoming year, I'd be glad to stay.

"Jesus Christ, girl," he said from beside me. He flopped onto the bed after emptying himself inside me.

I watched as he lay with his eyes closed and came down from the sex high. Ebony lashes rested high on his sharply defined cheeks as he slowly regained control of his breathing.

After observing him for a few moments, I said, "Thank you for . . . for all that." The words were issued quietly in case he'd fallen asleep. He really gave one hundred and ten percent, and it was almost insulting to thank him in such a banal way.

He slung his forearm across his face and said, "Give me a few minutes and we can finish up."

I snapped my head in his direction so fast my neck cracked. "What do you mean, 'finish up?'"

I watched his grin grow wider before asking, "You haven't

had enough?" In my mind, I was high-fiving myself because I'd never been this lucky with a lover in my life and felt like it was damn time someone treated me right. And of all the people, my husband! Maybe karma wasn't as pissed at me as I previously thought.

"We definitely need to get some condoms in this house," I declared and braced for his resistance.

He uncovered his face and rolled his head in my direction. "I told you I was clean."

"Yes, but are you also sterile? Because I don't want to get knocked up like my big sister, you know?"

He propped up on an elbow and looked down at me and asked, "Wouldn't you like to raise your children together? I thought that was something sisters did."

I never actually gave the concept a thought, so I just stared back at him.

"You're so beautiful, wife." He tucked a chunk of unruly hair behind my ear while complimenting me. The gesture was so tender and sincere, I nearly choked on it.

"I think you lost some brain cells in that huge load you blew," I teased to minimize the moment.

"No, just stating the truth. Do you really not know you're stunning? I mean, come on...you have a mirror. You have eyes. You've seen what other people look like, and you know you receive tons of attention."

"I just don't think like that, though. I think I'm a pretty woman, sure. But I don't stand in front of the mirror thinking, *Damn, now that's a smoke show.*"

"Well, you should. Because you are. How are you feeling, by the way?"

"Feeling? What do you mean? I feel fine. Please don't

start in on me again about not job hunting today."

I tried to sit up, and he pushed me flat to my back and moved on top of me in one smooth motion.

"Settle down, Storm. That's not what I meant. I was asking you—not very clearly, apparently—if you're hurting. You took a pretty good pounding, lady."

"Are you seriously hard again? Did you take Viagra?"

He tossed his head back and laughed, and the sound enthralled me. From my body's reaction, I realized I'd never heard him laugh before. Because never had I heard something so sexy and pure from another human. I knew I was staring up at him with gigantic, intrigued eyes, but I couldn't stop. This man was really starting to crawl into my mind and shit... maybe my heart.

My smile was wide and genuine when he finally asked me, "What is this look?"

Cocking my whole head to the side, I chuffed, "A smile? It's not really *that* rare of an occurrence from me."

"Let me rephrase, *what* are you smiling so beautifully about?" he amended and sifted his fingers back through my hair.

"Never mind," I said, feeling self-conscious. Instead of admitting what I was thinking, I went with my usual tactic and tried to distract with a sassy remark. "I thought you were going to fuck me again?"

Carmen circled his hips so I could feel his fully erect cock.

Instantly I wanted more. Needed more. The way he was gazing into my soul while he did it was ramping up the heat to an unbearable degree.

"Fuck, man. Do you have some magic spell on me? I've never felt like this before," I admitted and immediately wanted to take it back.

Mentally, I flogged myself for allowing such vulnerability to be exposed. I had to be careful around him, or this whole situation would get really messy. And I didn't do messy. I usually ran in the opposite direction from messy.

"Woman, you're so fucking hot. But before I fuck you again, because this time I'm sure you're going to pass out afterward, I want to settle this condom talk. Take the pill, or whatever. Or don't. Either way, I'm good. But I'm not going to have a barrier between my body and yours." He finished the decree with a passionate kiss that ended with a sharp bite to my bottom lip.

"Say *Yes, dear*," he instructed after licking the stinging pad.

I glared at him. If I didn't want his amazing dick so badly, I'd knee him in the thing. "Don't push me, Sandoval."

His eyes glittered with promise. "Oh, baby. I'm going to push you. Over and over again. Right to the edge and leave you hanging there until you beg me to let you fly. Or you can do what I asked and get what you need right now."

He reached between our bodies to circle his thumb over my clit. I moaned unabashedly and gyrated my hips in sync with his hand's movement.

Carmen kissed his way back along my jaw while his fingers stayed busy.

When he got to my ear, he whispered, "Two words, Storm. Say them for me."

I considered supplying two of my favorite words in place of what he wanted, but out of fear of him stopping, I whined instead. "Why are you torturing me like this?"

"Feel how hard I am. Taunting you turns me on. I could do it for hours just to watch the flush that creeps across your skin.

Your pale glow is warming to a sexy rose. Do you feel how wet you are again?"

He pushed just one finger inside, and it wasn't close to enough. When he didn't move any more, I whimpered.

"You want me to fill you, girl?"

"Yes. I want it so bad. Please, Carmen."

With my hands locked behind his head, I held him to me so we could kiss and kiss some more. When he tried to pull back, I held on, and he lifted my shoulders off the bed.

"Give me what I want," I growled through clenched teeth.

"You're not going to be able to walk when I'm done with you, baby," he promised and slammed into me.

"Fuck yes," I shouted and wondered briefly if the neighbors had heard it. Then, like before, he erased my terrible habit of getting lost in thought while in the throes of ecstasy. The man held good to his promise, because by the time we both came, I thought my left hip might actually be dislocated.

Carmen crumpled to an exhausted heap beside me and pulled my back into his front in a full-body cuddle. Our skin was slick with perspiration, and I had to fight every urge to sneak a little taste of his flesh. I knew he'd taste salty and musky, and I squeezed my eyes closed and tried to stop the obsessive thoughts.

We were in big, dangerous trouble here. I felt it through every breath I took in rhythm with his, and in every overheated pore that rejoiced when the ceiling fan clicked on above us. I turned my head to look up at the thing, realizing I hadn't even noticed it had been there before it started turning.

Carmen tossed a little remote to the mattress beside his pillow and mumbled, "Just for a few minutes. If it's too cold for you to sleep, I'll click it off when I cool down."

"'Kay," I mumbled because I was crashing fast. Two more minutes, and I'd be gone for the night. Maybe, just maybe, I'd make it through the entire night.

"Thank you. Again." I chuckled lightly after that one but added, "Night."

"Night, Storm. Sleep well," my husband replied, and we were fast asleep moments later.

CHAPTER ELEVEN

CARMEN

Despite the interrupted sleep throughout the night, the morning was already off to an exceptional start. When the little woman stirred in my embrace, I was disappointed to have to untangle from her.

My morning wood wanted to blaze in the woman's fireplace with painful urgency. I trudged to the bathroom and cranked the water in the shower to the fully hot position. It only took a couple of minutes to warm up, so I leaned against the wall and thought about last night.

I knew I had it bad for Agatha before we fucked, but now that we finally had? Man, there was no way I would let her leave when our year was up. So many times I'd been tempted to open that journal I swiped, but the long-range win would well be worth my unsatisfied curiosity. By far. Plus, it was the only bargaining chip I had. If I negated its value by going back on my word, I'd really be screwed.

We were only a few days into our arrangement, and I was head over heels for the girl. And sure, we had a few dates before we got married, but I felt like I saw some new, fascinating, and glorious parts of her the night before.

My wife didn't handle emotions well. That was one major takeaway from the mind-blowing sex we had. She thought I didn't see the mini breakdown after I pulled three back-to-back orgasms out of her. But I expected the waterworks to switch on from past experiences with my ex.

Whenever we had intense sex, she would cry. And our sex was nothing like what I experienced with Agatha. Most of the time, I was positive my ex was fantasizing about someone else fucking her, and toward the end of our relationship, it didn't even matter or hurt the way it once had.

Agatha was a pro at stuffing down emotions, though. She had those tears retreating in no time. At most only two escaped before she regained control and masked the feelings. Now, I couldn't help but wonder what had been going through her mind when she broke down. I doubted she'd tell me if I asked.

Another small victory in our short time together was that she hadn't been drinking. Well, that I knew of, at least. Between yesterday morning and the morning before, I'd sneaked all the liquor I had in the apartment out with me when I went to work. The bottles found a cozy new home in the complex's dumpster.

Now, if she wanted a drink, she'd have to source alcohol from somewhere else. The plus side of that was that she had very limited funds, and that shit wasn't cheap.

Yes, the tactic was a bit underhanded, but I was willing to do what it took to preserve the beautiful, vibrant, smart, and funny woman I married. I would not sit by and watch her waste her life.

I was also overjoyed how well she responded to my dominant side. It wasn't a persona I displayed to the everyday world, but I couldn't be any other way in the bedroom at this point. Once I got a taste of that dynamic, I knew it was what had been missing in my previous encounters.

Maybe if I had taken charge of Kate early on, she would've

respected me enough to have been faithful. Infidelity would never be tolerated again in my world. I was much better at reading people now than I was then.

When I got to my desk, the first thing I did was send my sister an email. We were long overdue for a lunch date, and I was excited to tell her about Agatha.

The jury was still out if I would go into the whole marriage-by-intoxication aspect of our relationship, though. There was so much more going on between us, and I knew that fact could be a huge red flag for people. I just wanted my family to be happy for me. My sister generally was, but my parents were another story all together.

Over recent years, both my mother and father had become very bitter. I was still trying to figure out why, exactly, but it made them unpleasant to be around. No matter what good news I shared, one of them would point out a negative. Would it be so hard to just be happy because I was happy? When I brought up the problem to my sister, she echoed my experience with our folks as well as her general dislike for their negativity.

Gray shared a few incidents she recently had with our mother in particular, and I was appalled. While my father had become my harsh critic, our mother was hers. When you considered our same-sex parent was our biggest influence in life, their behavior and attitudes sucked even more.

My inbox chimed when a response came back from my sibling. Elijah still wasn't in, so I opened the personal email and couldn't help the broad smile while I read her note.

> *Well, hello there! I was starting to worry because I haven't heard from you in more days than I'd prefer. Guess I could've reached out sooner too, though. I would love to*

meet for lunch but can't until Wednesday of next week. I
have a giant project due, and if I impress the client, I think
I may get a promotion! Does that work for you?

Let me know and love you!

XO Gray

I wrote her back and teased her about becoming way too important for her lowly brother but glad she could find time for me in her busy schedule. As I was adding the appointment to my calendar, my boss came past my desk.

"Morning," I said with a warm smile.

"How are you today?" he asked and lingered by his office door.

"Good. Damn good, actually. Did I miss a meeting this morning? I haven't looked at your calendar, but it's a little later than normal for you to just be getting here."

I wasn't giving the man guff. I was legitimately worried I missed something on his calendar. I always asked if he needed anything prepared for his appointments, and in general, I tried to keep track of where he was if he wasn't in the office.

"No, you didn't miss anything. We had an unscheduled visit with the obstetrician this morning. Hannah had some spotting last night and was completely freaking out. I knew she wouldn't calm down until she heard it from her doctor, even though I showed her two different testimonials online that said it was normal."

"Oh, I see. And everything checked out? Baby's good? Hannah?" The concern in my voice was heartfelt. I knew how excited my boss and his new wife were to be expecting, and it would devastate them if something happened.

"Yep!" he said with more enthusiasm. "Right as rain. Baby looks good. Growing so fast, it's incredible." His proud-papa smile could still be seen behind the coffee mug he lifted to his lips.

"Good to hear, man. I know Agatha is excited too," I replied but quickly added, "Excited about her sister's pregnancy." The last thing I wanted to deal with was the pool of gossip sharks that worked in this building. If word got out that I got married in Vegas and didn't remember it, I'd never be able to walk through the corridors again. If rumors started that she was also pregnant . . . I physically shuddered while thinking of that nightmare.

"Does Agatha want to be a mother?" my boss asked as if plucking the subject directly from my mind.

"Not one hundred percent sure, but I think so. Maybe just not anytime soon. I think we have enough to figure out without throwing an infant in the mix, you know?"

"How were things last night? I think yesterday you said she was job hunting. Anything look promising?"

I started to feel a bit protective of my wife. I appreciated that he cared about my life and my relationship, but I also had a weird feeling that he might be asking me things so he could report back to Hannah.

Thinking it best to answer in general terms, I said, "Yeah, good. Things are good. I think she mostly unpacked and worked on updating her résumé yesterday, and the real search begins today. I think . . ." I trailed off with uncertainty, knowing damn well I was lying and not liking the way it lodged like a sideways pill in my throat.

Once my wife and I had more time under our relationship belt and I had a better understanding of her relationship with her sisters, I would be more comfortable talking to Elijah in greater detail. At the moment, though, it felt like I would be selling her out if I said more.

"Well, I guess we should get some work done."

"Probably a good idea." I grinned. "Let me know if you need anything."

"You know I will." He laughed and closed the door between us.

After checking the time, I decided it was still too early to check in with my fierce little storm, but I could already tell I was going to have a hard time concentrating on work. Hopefully I'd get involved in some big project for the boss man and wouldn't have time to piss, let alone daydream about my wife.

Craig, Sebastian's assistant, invited me to have lunch, so that broke up the monotony of the day. Being cooped up in a high-rise building all day, knowing the sun was shining just beyond the thick walls, was torture. Getting out for a noontime break was exactly what my scattered brain needed.

Before I knew it, I was packing up to leave for the weekend. I tried calling Agatha twice throughout the workday and got her voicemail both times. My temper flared thinking about her blowing off her responsibilities again, but rationally, I knew I wasn't being fair. She could be busy and couldn't have gotten to her phone.

She wasn't the type of girl who had her cell phone in hand all day. In fact, I never saw her goof off on social media or even text message.

What if she was feeling abandoned sitting there alone all day? It was the last thing I wanted, so I called her a third time when I got situated in my car for the commute home.

The phone rang several times before she picked up, and I

truly thought I was about to hear her voicemail greeting again.

"Hello?" she said in her tempting alto. Not sure if it was possible, but her voice sounded even sexier over the phone.

"Hi. Just warming up my car for the drive home."

There was quiet between us for a few seconds, and finally I asked, "How was your day? I tried calling a couple of times, but it went to voicemail."

"Oh," was her initial reply. Thankfully she decided to add more. "Sorry. My phone was dead for a bit before I realized it. I normally plug it in overnight, but I haven't settled into a routine here yet, you know?"

I was relieved she didn't get defensive or bite my head off for just trying to make conversation.

"Sure, that makes perfect sense," I replied, trying to keep my cool about it. She didn't need a lecture right out of the gate on how she should be more responsible. Instead, I went for a reminder of what we had been doing instead of worrying about power levels of electronics.

"Are you sore today?"

"Umm, no? I'm not that out of shape that carrying a few bags and suitcases would send me to the emergency room." Her husky laugh vibrated through my entire body.

"That's not what I meant, darling." My voice naturally dropped into the lower register she seemed to respond to.

"I'm not following then, I guess." A few beats went by, and my smart girl caught on. "Oooohh, you mean from that thorough fucking you gave me?"

"Indeed I do," I answered smugly.

There was an audible inhale before she replied. "A bit, yes. But I wouldn't turn down a repeat of that performance, Mr. Sandoval."

"I'll be home by five thirty, then!" I teased but meant every word of the vow.

And then the strangest thing I never expected erupted from Agatha Christine Farsey—a giggle. An actual schoolgirl-style shy and carefree giggle erupted from my wife, and it was so musical and, of course . . . arousing. I had to close my eyes and take a deep breath before putting my car in gear to get on my way.

"Let's go out for dinner tonight," she proposed then. "It's Friday after all."

Where the hell had this week gone? I didn't think we should be spending the money, but she sounded so hopeful when offering the suggestion, I didn't want to be the bad guy all the time.

"Okay. That sounds fun. Anything sound good? And nothing too fancy since we're watching our cash." Being the designated wet blanket sucked for so many reasons.

"I'm not really familiar with your neighborhood. Is—"

I interrupted with a correction. "It's *our* neighborhood now."

Agatha sighed. "Yes, fine. Our neighborhood. I like pretty much everything."

I merged onto the freeway and spoke up over the traffic noise. "There's a really great Indian place."

"Eww, no. Not that. I don't like Indian."

I smiled at her contradiction. "You just said you like everything."

"Okay, everything but Indian. Oh, and not a big fan of Thai, but I love Japanese and Chinese."

This was the most animated she'd been in days, so I just sat there listening with a big grin on my face.

"What about Mexican?" she asked.

"Nah, not Mexican. I had that for lunch. But there are two really good places close to the apartment when we do want that."

"Well, I better go get in the shower so I don't keep us waiting too long. I'll see you when you get home," she said cheerfully, and I bit into my cheek until I swore I tasted my own blood.

"Okay. See you soon." I disconnected the call before I said something that launched an argument. If she'd spent the whole day in bed again, I wasn't sure I could hold my tongue. Why was she just getting into the shower at five in the fucking afternoon?

The commute took longer than usual, but I was grateful for the extra time to work through all the thoughts and emotions running through my mind. I didn't want to bicker every conversation. Who would?

I reminded myself repeatedly that being in a relationship meant compromising from time to time. She wouldn't always do things the way I liked, or the way I would do them. Just like I wouldn't do everything to her liking. But I had to dig deep and find the ability to look the other way when something bothered me, regardless of the fact that it went against my nature.

It wouldn't be fair, though, for me to expect Agatha to do all the changing and giving in while I didn't do the same.

It was closer to seven than six when I finally walked through the door.

"Hi!" Agatha called from the bedroom and turned down the music she'd been listening to.

The air evacuated every cell in my body when she walked into the living room. She looked like a fucking goddess, and I was dumbstruck by her beauty.

My feet took charge of my whole body and walked to meet her halfway through the room. I bent low to wrap my weary arms around her waist and breathed in her sexy, sinful scent.

"My God, woman. You're simply stunning this evening. And you smell good enough to eat." I leaned back and gave her a head-to-toe eye fuck and said, "As a matter of fact . . . "

She laughed and put a straight arm's distance between our bodies. "Easy, killer. You'll mess up my hair and makeup, and we have a date, remember?"

I used the hand she had thrust toward me and yanked her body against mine. Directly into her ear, I growled, "If I want to eat my wife's pussy for dinner, that's what I'll do."

She giggled again, and the joy spread to my face too. "Sooooo . . . " She dragged out the word while doing a little twirl, and the short skirt flared out at the hem. "You like this outfit?"

"I do. You're an absolute vision." I dropped all my features to a very serious and disappointed presentation and said woefully, "I don't think I can take you out in public like this, though."

"What? Why?" Of course Agatha was instantly outraged at my disappointing declaration. She rushed to the long mirror in the hallway and looked at her outfit while I stood right behind her. She turned to the left, then to the right before demanding to my reflection, "What's wrong with my outfit? You just said I was a vision!"

The girl was so easy to rile up it was unfair. Zero effort put into my tease, and she was near hysterics. I could probably talk her into something completely outrageous if I put effort behind the ruse.

I wrapped my arms around her from behind and explained, "If you're seen in public looking this incredible, it would be so unfair to every other woman in the place. Every pair of eyes will be on you, darling. A lot of couples are going to be fighting on the way home tonight." I bit her playfully, and she smacked at the top of my head since my face was buried in her perfect neck.

"Don't leave a mark!" she insisted between giggles.

And I had to admit that now that she had brought it up, the idea had merit.

"You love the marks I leave on your body. We both know you do," I teased, but really I meant it. I'd watched her just that morning checking out a few in the mirror when she didn't know I was looking.

But I had to derail that thought track, or we really wouldn't make it to dinner. Even in this suburb of LA, reservations were a must on Friday night. Your table was promptly filled by the next waiting party if you were more than ten minutes late.

Stepping back from my sexy little bomb, I said, "Let me grab a different jacket, and we can go."

I strolled into our bedroom with the biggest smile, and then I saw it. The path of destruction she'd left while getting ready. My—no, *our*—entire bedroom was in shambles.

Clothing was tossed everywhere...from the floor to the bed and beyond. There was even a bra hanging off the doorknob. In the bathroom, hair and makeup products and contraptions littered the countertop and even the ledge of the bathtub. Every inch of usable surface had shit spread atop it.

Well, I could call her back into the room and demand she clean up after herself.

I refused to live like an animal, and I already knew this

was her norm from seeing the state of her room at her parents' house. But if I did that, not only would we argue and ruin both our good moods, but we would miss our dinner reservation. She was so excited to be going out, it was palpable in the air. The selfish part of me was enjoying basking in that glow of happiness. I didn't want to ruin all of that.

From the Choose Your Battles chapter of my imagined *How to Have a Happy Marriage* primer, I sucked in a deep, calming breath through my nose and let my frustration go with the exhale. It took two more cycles of the exercise to stop the heart palpitations, but by the time I was back in the crowded entry of the apartment, I was once again on level mental ground.

At least that's what I told myself as I locked the front door and offered Agatha my arm to grip as we descended to the parking lot.

She leaned into me while we walked and said, "You look very handsome, husband. I like that leather jacket with the button-down. Casual and still put together." She gave me a thoughtful nod. "Yeah, looks good."

I did all the things I normally did for a date I wanted to impress. Opened the car door for her and made sure she was situated before closing it and hustling around to the driver's side. I even let her choose what we listened to on the radio. I held the door for her to walk ahead of me as we entered the restaurant and stood possessively with a hand at the small of her back while we waited to be shown to our table.

Men never hid their ogling as well as they thought they did, and I strutted like a proud peacock through the crowded dining room.

That's right, fuckers. She's all mine. Signed, sealed, delivered. Mine.

One of the greatest things about Agatha was her humility. There was no doubt the woman was a smoke show. But she was kind to the staff and polite to another patron who blocked our path at one point. She wasn't conceited or smug, and it added to her attractiveness.

By the time we were looking over the menu, I couldn't take my eyes off her. Any ire over the wreckage she left in our bedroom faded into the ether. It also helped that I fantasized about punishing her for the disaster the entire drive to the restaurant. There were at least three ways I could ensure she sat uncomfortably tomorrow, and if my great mood kept up, I might even let her choose the one I administered.

Because she would definitely learn a lesson by the end of the night.

I selected a bottle of wine from the extensive list and sampled it like a pro when it was brought to the table. Agatha seemed a little too eager to down the first glass, though, so I took my time offering her a refill. But the attentive server was on the task to sabotage my effort before I could decline for us both until the meal arrived. She tossed that glass back like a frat boy too.

"You know, this is very good wine. Maybe if you slowed down a bit, you'd enjoy it. Or taste it even," I commented and instantly knew I should've held my tongue.

The glare she shot me from across the intimate table was meant to be lethal.

"Please don't ruin a lovely night with your nagging. Okay?" she snapped through clenched jaws.

"A single comment is hardly nagging, darling," I replied with a sugar-sweet tone. Neither of us wanted the night to crash and burn. We agreed on that point at least. "What looks good? Do you want to share an appetizer?" I asked, trying to steer her back into friendly territory.

"You pick. The appetizer, I mean." And then she snorted a laugh.

The sound made me laugh too while I widened my eyes to encourage her to explain what was so funny.

"Could you imagine ordering my dinner? You don't even know if I'm allergic to anything, or if I'm vegan." She shook her head with a big grin. "How funny would that be?"

"I could totally order for you, and it would be something you'd love," I said with complete confidence.

"No way," she said, still perusing the menu. "I don't think I'd take that chance."

"Don't you trust me, Storm?"

She sat back in her seat before saying, "I don't think it has anything to do with trust. Just facts."

Smugly, I wagered, "I would bet I know a lot more about you than you think. Definitely more than you know about me."

Well, that shut her up. She picked up her wineglass before remembering she'd drained the thing.

"Hit me," she said and thrust her glass toward me.

"No," I told my date, and she responded with that glare again. "With your meal. I don't want you shitfaced when we leave here."

"Why are you such a grampa? Do you ever just cut loose and have fun?" she challenged, and I saw right through her game. She thought by insulting me she could get me to take the bait and prove I know how to let go. Such an amateur tactic.

Fortunately, our waiter arrived to take our order. I bit my tongue and let my queen order for herself. I really wanted to prove my point but also didn't want her to cause a scene. The wine she chugged was giving her a combative edge, and it was the last fire I wanted to stoke.

After we were alone again, I started a new conversation. "So, on Sunday, we'll be expected at seven-thirty mass. I can help you pick a dress from your closet tomorrow so you aren't frazzled from running late when you meet my family."

I launched that grenade without any sort of warning and kicked myself for not having my phone out to capture the resulting look on her face.

After a long stare, she gave her head a little shake. "Do what now?"

I shrugged like it was no big deal. And really, for me, it wasn't. I'd done the same thing every Sunday morning for my entire life. Now she would too.

"Sunday?"

"Yep, got that." She nodded and watched me cautiously.

"Mass. As in church? You've been, I'm assuming? I mean, you don't get to be our age without ever stepping foot in a house of God of some sort at some point, right?"

And why was antagonizing her so much fun? I knew it was bordering on cruel and definitely playing with fire regarding her temper. But the woman had to understand that I wasn't a doormat, and I wouldn't tiptoe around her volatile personality all the time.

"You can't be fucking serious," she said at a volume much too loud for our surroundings. At least two parties looked our way after that F-bomb dropped.

"Please modulate your voice in this establishment," I said calmly and took a slow drink.

"Carmen, seriously. No. I'm not going to church with your family. Enough is enough."

Uh-oh. She was legitimately pissed. Made evident by the way she balled her napkin before slam-dunking it to the place setting in front of her.

Quickly, I covered her hand with mine to hold her in place because I was fairly certain she was about to bolt.

"Look, calm down. We can talk about this more later. Or tomorrow." I tried to smooth the mood, but she wasn't having it.

"There's nothing to talk about. I'm. Not. Going." She crossed her arms defiantly over her chest, and I was transfixed by the way her breasts were heaving with her anger.

I leaned toward her and said very quietly and calmly, "You are. And that's the last I want to hear about it." I straightened back into my chair, and by the grace of God, our server showed up with our food.

As I took my fork in hand, I looked across the table at my petulant, immature queen. She was pouting monumentally, and I'd had enough. Very carefully, I set my fork beside my dinner and held her gaze. I leaned across the table so the neighboring tables weren't part of our conversation.

"Stop acting like a bratty child. Eat your dinner."

"No. I've lost my appetite. Give me the keys. I'll wait in the car."

"You'll do no such thing. Pick up your fork and eat immediately, or I swear, woman . . . "

"Are you threatening me right now?"

"Yes. It would appear that way, wouldn't it? Eat."

"I said no."

"Fine. But you're not leaving this table until I'm finished. So either sit there and have a tantrum like a child and earn even more of a punishment than the one you already have coming..." I paused and took a big gulp from my water glass.

I didn't miss the way the side of her mouth ticked up after I issued that one, but she quickly masked her excitement and went back to pouting.

"Unless you want to eat that cold, I suggest you dig in. I also won't tolerate you being so wasteful."

"You know what? You really need to check yourself right now," she hissed across the small table. "I don't know who you think you're talking to, but I'm a grown woman, Carmen."

"Then fucking act like one," I said through gritted teeth and dropped my fork with a clatter.

The same nosy bastards who looked when the last outburst came from our table turned their heads once more.

"Goddammit, woman," I seethed.

CHAPTER TWELVE

AGATHA

"This is ridiculous," I muttered at the same time he growled something.

Once again, the man brought out more emotion than I could contain, and I felt impending tears stinging the backs of my eyes. I'd be damned if I'd let a man reduce me to tears, especially in public. I closed my eyes and took a couple of calming breaths. I could get through this rationally. I knew I could.

In an effort to salvage the evening, I picked up my fork. Carmen visibly relaxed when I did, even if by the slightest degree. He watched me steadily until I actually took a bite of the dinner in front of me. My appetite was completely gone now, but I was trying here. I really was.

After chewing, I asked very calmly, "Why would you force me to do something I don't want to do? I don't understand that."

"They're not going to care if you eat the meal or not, Storm. They're still going to charge us for it. You may as well enjoy it. I don't enjoy wasting money."

"That's not what I'm talking about." I set my utensil down and entwined my fingers in my lap. "I'm not a religious person, Carmen. It's an institution I don't support at all, as a matter of fact. I will embarrass us both, and that's not the impression I want to first make on your family."

All of that was true. It was the next part that would be difficult to say without getting angry all over again.

"Also, I don't care for the way you think you can tell me what to do." I leaned toward him now that we had the unwanted attention of several other parties in the room. "I mean, it's hot in bed, but not all the time. I can't live like that. I *won't* live like that."

There. Got all that out without raising my voice or even using profanity. Look at me maturing.

"I've met your parents. Hell, we spent an entire long weekend with your whole family."

"What does that have to do with anything?" I asked, my face twisted in confusion.

"I want you to meet my family. What is so hard to understand here?" He was as frustrated as I was at that point, and I was glad. Why should I be the only one who got worked up over things?

"That's different, and you know it. I mean, shit . . . " I took a quick look to the man in particular at the neighboring table. He was the one who seemed most interested in our conversation. When I looked in his direction, he was staring right at me. Didn't bother to look away or even appear embarrassed to be caught eavesdropping.

"What the fuck are you looking at? Maybe if your own date was a bit more exciting, you wouldn't be so invested in ours. Hmmm?" I bugged my eyes out as a prompt for him to defend himself.

But the guy was a total pussy and finally had the sense to look away. When I refocused on Carmen, he was grinning.

He just shook his head. I had no idea what the smile or the gesture meant, but at least he didn't seem mad about my outburst.

"My God, people can be so rude," I muttered and took a bite of my meal. And promptly groaned in delight now that I allowed myself to taste it. "Dude, you weren't kidding. This is fabulous," I commented, stabbing my fork downward toward my dinner.

"Thank you for eating. I hate wasting food, or money for that matter. And I'm not trying to ruin our evening. I seriously thought it would be better to give you some warning on the expectation rather than spring it on you Sunday morning."

I really didn't know how to proceed. I didn't like being railroaded into doing things I didn't want to do, and the whole situation was giving me déjà vu. Deciding to just lay my cards on the table, I took a deep breath and attempted to explain to my man why I got so riled up. Marriage was all about compromise, after all. Right?

"I'm just going to be straight with you here, okay?" I waited for him to assent in one way or another and then just blurted what came to mind before I lost my nerve. "I feel cornered when you try to make me do things I don't want to do. And I'm not referring to sex in this statement at all because that's a whole different conversation. But I feel minimized as a person and as a partner in our relationship when you treat me that way."

Wow. I impressed the hell out of myself with how articulate that was. He had to give me points for the honest communication if nothing else.

Then I couldn't seem to stop myself from explaining further. "My parents treated me that way my entire life. Even as an adult. *Oh, flighty Agatha can't make her own decisions. We better tell her what to do.*" I held his stare with my own for a few beats, then finished with, "I don't want to feel that way with you too."

Carmen was thoughtful for a bit, and I got very nervous in his quiet. He took a couple bites of his meal, thoughtfully chewing over my words along with his food.

When he spoke, I expected praise for my articulate expression or a comment about the context, at least. Instead, he said, "This is the best steak I've had in a long time. I think they have a new chef here."

I stared at him with a blank expression. And not the manufactured one I slid on when I was hiding my true feelings. This was legitimate, dumfounded confusion. *Really?* We were going to talk about beef and the current employee roster of the restaurant? I was just more vulnerable than I had been with anyone—or cared to be—and that was the feedback he gave me?

"Darling, listen to me. It's two hours out of your life." He lifted a brow and continued. "Can you just do this for me?"

When I didn't immediately reply, he added, "Please?"

"That's a dirty tactic, and you know it." Yeah, another thing that reminded me of my parents, but did I share that with him? What good would it do other than make me more vulnerable, and I'd already had my share of that for the evening.

"I'm not trying to play dirty. I'm not playing at all. Why do you feel that way?"

"Because it feels like you're guilting me into doing what you want! How don't you hear that in what you're asking?" My volume grew much louder than appropriate for a restaurant, but the frustration strangling me dictated the level.

I needed to calm down, so I slid my wineglass toward him by the round base. Of course, he had an opinion about that too.

He looked at the glass like he had never seen such an object and then raised his eyes to meet mine. "I'd prefer if you ate more food first, Storm."

Through clenched teeth, I hissed, "Right now I don't give two fucks what you prefer. Either fill my glass, or I'll stand up and do it myself. I've had enough of your controlling bullshit for one evening." I raised a finger before saying, "No, strike that—for the rest of time."

Begrudgingly, he filled my glass halfway and slid it back toward me. I snatched the thing so aggressively, some of the liquid sloshed over the rim and onto my hand.

"Goddammit," I muttered. Even after wiping with my napkin, my skin was still sticky. "I need to go wash my hands," I said in explanation as I stood. "He can wrap this to go if he comes by." I waved toward my barely eaten dinner.

I stood in front of the mirror in the restroom and just stared at my reflection. I really could use a sit-down with my sister to try to straighten out all these mixed-up emotions I was having.

There was a constant battle going on inside my brain and, if I were honest with myself, in my heart too. This whole damn situation I'd gotten myself into had so many facets, I couldn't settle on one feeling and stick with it. First, I thought the whole thing was ridiculous, and I needed to get myself out of it just like I'd gotten myself in. No one would be coming around to fix this for me.

But then he would do something sweet or kind and considerate, and I'd go to mush inside. And what the hell was that all about? I wasn't the mushy kind of girl typically. This man had me turned backward and sideways and every other way possible. I couldn't even take the physical attraction into consideration because I'd throw away all my common sense and vow to spend the rest of my life with the man. It was that intense... it was that good.

On the other hand, we bickered so much it was exhausting. But what did I expect would happen when I moved in with a man I barely knew? The parts of him I did know, though, I liked. A lot, as a matter of fact.

Carmen had a clever sense of humor, and once we settled into a groove financially, I had a feeling we'd have a lot of fun doing everyday things and special things too. But we had to figure out how to stop arguing.

I'd already lived through years and years with people judging me for every move I made. I wouldn't choose a partner with the same propensity. No way. I thought talking to him openly and maturely would be the way to find our even ground. But when I'd just tried that at the dinner table, it was a huge backfire.

My God, I was so confused. And if I didn't get my ass back to the table, he'd probably break down the ladies' room door to make sure I wasn't in here throwing back shots.

Though I could really go for a round or two.

We finished our meal and drove home in near silence. Other than common courtesy exchanges, we didn't speak. I was hurt, pissed, confused, and frustrated. I couldn't isolate one weighing in heavier than the others either, so I said nothing. Just sat in the passenger seat and stewed.

Maybe I should move out. If I was reading the guy right, he was feeling the same things I was, and neither of us wanted to touch the powder keg of our emotions.

Carmen pulled into the parking space at the condo complex and turned off the engine. Rather than get out, he just sat there staring out the windshield.

"You okay?" I asked with my hand on the door handle. I didn't need him to open it for me, but the new treatment had been nice. That one thought rushed forth a revelation, and my stomach turned over at the notion.

Was I so desperate to be treated well that I'd put up with a slew of other things I wouldn't normally stand for? Was he breadcrumbing me with gestures of kindness I wasn't used to getting? I was so needy to be genuinely loved and cared for that I'd sacrifice other things I thought were important?

How much of a loser could I possibly be? Worse yet, knowing that was what was happening and staying dead center anyway.

I nearly dived from the car, slamming the door behind me before I took off toward the apartment. In hindsight, it was probably a stupid move because in essence, I was trapping myself. Once we were both inside that place, he'd never allow me to storm out.

And that was the exact mood I was in. I'd always chosen flight over fight when it came to that. I did so much better when I could escape for some solitude to gather my thoughts and typically calm my temper. If Carmen decided to corner me once we were inside, I'd probably turn feral.

Feeling bad about myself wasn't a new thing. Didn't mean I liked it or wanted to explain the habit to my husband either. I rushed through the apartment to the spare room where my clothes hung in the closet. Without waiting to see what he had planned for the rest of the evening, I whipped off my top and threw it on the floor. My mood was completely shot, so if he wanted to still go out, he could go by himself.

I shimmied out of the cute skirt I'd been so excited to wear. When I put it on, I knew it looked good on my short frame and was something he would appreciate. Whatever good any of those thoughts were now. I wanted to crawl under the bed—with a bottle of vodka, if I was living right—and forget all the doubt and disgust in my head.

I heard him sharply inhale from the doorway and looked up. Standing there in a white thong and matching bra, I felt more naked than my state of undress.

"Do you knock?" I clipped and looked around for something to cover with.

The hunger in his stare couldn't be missed, and if he kept it up much longer, we'd be on the floor like two animals mating in the wild. We would yield to instinct only and not our better sense.

"On what? The door was wide open." He took a couple of steps toward me.

"Just need some pajamas," I muttered while riffling through my clothes. Now that my back was to him and he saw the full effect of the skimpy panties, a low groan vibrated from deep in his throat.

"Jesus, woman. Are you trying to kill me?"

I swung my head around to glare at him and was immediately stalled by the look on his face. The protruding crotch of his slacks just added to my dry mouth.

"Get out!" I shouted with a pair of lounge pants balled in front of me.

Slowly, he shook his head. Left to right and then again.

"I'm serious. Leave this room. I want to be alone."

"Don't think I can do that, Storm."

Fine. He could stand there alone, because I was bolting. Well, he'd be there with that hard-on that was so big, my eyes kept shooting to it and then back up to his face. His chuckle told me he knew exactly what kind of war I was waging at the moment. Instead of having the common decency to give a person in the throes of a mental and emotional breakdown the space she requested, he took another step closer.

And then another.

I put a stiff arm out in front of me to keep distance between us. But he was undeterred. With warm hands, he gripped my hips and yanked me against his body. His erection felt exquisite between us, crumbling my resolve to not get physical with the man again. It just confused my feelings more when we fucked, and I was already so damn confused.

"Carmen . . ." I gasped as he sank his teeth into my neck. Fuck, why did it have to feel so good?

Bastard. He knew it, too, and he would use the same weapon over and over if I kept giving in.

"Let me make you feel good, baby," he rumbled beside my ear.

"You're not being very fair," I whimpered while tilting my head farther to the side so he could continue the trail of nips and kisses he started beneath my ear.

"Fair about what? I want to pleasure you all day and all night. I can't think of anything else when we're apart. I want to worship every inch of this mighty little body. How is that not fair? I can't get enough of you, Agatha Christine." He finished his declaration with a hard bite to the juncture of my neck and shoulder.

My moan was out and about the room before I could straighten my thoughts enough to control it. I whispered,

"More. Fuck, more . . ." And I thought there was a good chance I'd said that to myself, but then he swept me right off my feet and cradled me into his chest while he took off across the apartment to our bedroom.

I would hate myself in the morning for this. I knew it with one hundred percent accuracy. But damn, I'd feel so good getting to that miserable point again. If I couldn't drown my unhappiness in alcohol, I could mask it with all the endorphins he would skitter through my system.

This is the last time, I swore to myself.

If I made that silent vow, I could be at peace enough mentally to enjoy fucking him. Then, on Sunday morning, while he went to church with his family—without me—I'd pack up my stuff and leave.

It was so obvious now that I couldn't stay with the man. He was dangerous for my already precarious stability. Becoming any more dependent on him, in any way, would end in catastrophe. I'd get out now before either of us really got hurt. If I stuck around and tried this arrangement for the whole year, I'd be a shell of myself. I was already giving in to him whenever he came near me with an erection, and over time the cost would be way too steep.

He laid me on the bed like a gentle lover. Not the toss and bounce treatment I got the last time. Yet this careful, loving handling was far more unnerving. My eyes were wide and attentive as I tried to figure out his game plan. Why the change in demeanor? I definitely made it abundantly clear I liked the rougher handling.

"Wha-What are you—why are you—" I couldn't figure out what to ask, so instead I sounded as nervous as I felt.

"Spit it out, girl." He chuckled and slid onto the mattress

alongside me. He rolled a bit so he hovered over me, and the intense look on his face was in direct opposition to his gentle touch. "Why what, baby?"

"Why are you being so—" I waved my hand between us, which basically signaled nothing.

So he caught my fingers, entwined them with his, and rested them on my abdomen.

"So what? It's not like you to search for words, Storm. Maybe I should be asking you what's gotten into you instead of the other way around." He closed the space between us so slowly, I had time to worry about several things before our lips met.

Was there garlic in my food?

Should I really be allowing this physical interaction? It would just continue to confuse what's happening between us.

What the hell is happening between us?

Carmen ran his fingers through my hair and spread the mass of it out on the pillow behind me.

"Look how stunning you are." He shook his head while his eyes darted between the features of my face. From my wide, wild blue eyes to my eager, sometimes spiteful mouth, he studied me as though I were the rarest treasure he'd ever seen. He made me feel beautiful and sorrowful at the same time.

But I'd had enough of the emotional circus for one night. I wanted to get lost in carnal pleasure and drown in the endorphin tidal wave this man could conjure with the slightest move of his hips.

"Please. Please, Carme—" My voice cut off when he gripped a fistful of my hair just at my nape. "Aahhh ... " I sighed into the dimly lit room. The pain was exquisite and centering, and I guessed he knew both those things when he gave a second tug.

"Beautiful Storm," he whispered into my neck. "Tiny, powerful queen," he groaned along the other side.

Uninvited tears were threatening to come if he didn't stop with the lovely words of praise. I wasn't used to being spoken to with such reverence or, hell, at times, even respect. He was filtering through my stability and threatening to collapse me like a California hillside after an unexpected deluge.

"Please," I croaked one last time, and the bastard grinned down at me.

"Please what? Tell me what you want, baby. What you need," he said in that sexy, demanding way when in the bedroom.

So, instead of words, I wriggled the best I could beneath his body weight.

"Aahh, I see. My storm wants to be fucked. Is that it?"

"Yes. Please, yes." Those words escaped before I pressed my lips together in an effort to preserve at least some of my dignity. Because so many more thoughts were zipping around in my busy mind.

Take me away. Make me forget everything else. Punish me. Hurt me. Love me...

"Oh, baby, we're definitely going to fuck. But I want to take my time with all this perfection. I want to savor your body, explore every inch of your silky skin. Kiss this pouty mouth," he explained before lowering his lips closer to mine.

I closed the final space separating us and kissed him. Softly at first, getting onboard with the slow burn. I delighted in the masculine smell of his skin and the rough feel of his late-in-the-day stubble. When I swiped across his lower lip with my tongue, his groan vibrated through both our bodies.

"Mmmm, you like that?" I teased and gave his lips another taste.

"All I can picture is you doing that to my cock. It's making me so fucking hard," he answered and pressed his erection into my hip.

"I think that can be arranged," I offered while staring at his eager expression.

But when he quickly backed off the bed and stood, I was confused. Until he pointed to the floor in front of him. Then it made sense.

I scampered off the bed and sank to my knees while reaching for his belt buckle.

Carmen swatted my hands away and gave me a playful but stern look. "Sit back on your heels," he instructed, and I was quick to comply.

The room air was cool on my exposed skin, and my nipples perked up behind the lacy bra. Impatiently, I watched him palm the erection still tucked behind his slacks. He ran his hand up and down, up and down, and I was hypnotized by the motion.

"Show me," I whispered and looked up the length of his body to find his hooded stare fixed on me.

"Quiet now. You'll take what I give you. Won't you?" he taunted. Good Christ, the man was so alluring in his dominant stance above me.

I just nodded, trying to follow the rules as they were issued.

"See? You can be a good girl when you want something." He slowly unfastened his belt.

I shifted my weight from one side to the other, and he grinned.

"Anxious, Storm?"

I just nodded again but added a slow lick of my lips in anticipation.

"Kneel up and finish opening my pants," Carmen instructed, and I immediately complied. I was going to blow this man's mind when I finally got to work as punishment for all this bossy torture. The slickness of my pussy gave away how much I truly enjoyed the scene, though.

Careful not to make contact with his dick, I unfastened his waistband and tugged down the zipper. His breaths were labored from the excitement, and I gave myself a mental pat on the back. Two could play at this hurry-up-and-wait game. With my flat hands, I spread the material open wide on each side. My guy actually moaned when I smoothed over his erection and it jerked beneath my palm.

With big, curious eyes, I looked up to him. As much as I wanted to dive in, I waited for his permission.

"Fucking hell, girl. Dying to feel that wet mouth." He shimmied his pants and boxers down to his hips and freed his balls from the confinement too. He gave himself a tight pull, and my mouth watered as I watched the motion.

"It's all yours, baby," he growled. "Suck me."

And did I ever. I gave my husband the best blow job I'd ever given. His shaft was slick and incredibly hard from my efforts. He had to drag me away when he wanted me to stop.

"Let me finish you," I said—or asked, I guess. But he was already shaking his head when I focused on his face.

"No way. Not this time. I need to fuck you after that. Damn, girl, that was incredible. On the bed. Hands and knees."

I still had my thong and bra on, and my husband's attention went right to the fabric sinking between my ass cheeks. He ran one finger beneath the material starting at my tailbone and slowly inched toward my soaked opening. I should've predicted the muttered curse words when he felt just how wet

I was, but we both seemed perversely proud of the situation when he got there.

"Agatha...my God..."

Did he really think I wouldn't be primed after all that? He teased my pussy with knowing fingers before dragging the panties down to my knees. When I started to shimmy them off completely, he gave me a solid smack on the ass.

"Who said take them off?" he snapped.

"I just thought—" But my explanation was choked off when he spanked me a second time.

"Quiet!" he demanded, and I whimpered. Why ask a question if you didn't want an answer?

"Your job isn't to think right now. It's to feel. Stay out of your head and *feel* with me," he lectured.

I let my head hang loosely between my arms and got lost in the moment. How had he figured out that my busy brain sabotaged my pleasure in the bedroom? I knew for certain we hadn't discussed it before. However, it was a fairly common problem for women, and clearly the man paid attention to the details here.

Carmen thrust into me without any further discussion, and a loud cry of pleasure and gratitude came from deep inside me.

"Neighbors definitely heard that one," he said, and I could hear the grin in his voice.

"A little warning next time," I gasped as he thrust in again, "unless you want the female population of the complex waiting outside our door."

He grabbed a handful of my hair and cranked my head back until we could see each other. "Who said speak?"

I rolled my eyes, and he shifted his grip to my throat. He

didn't squeeze or hurt me in any way, but the possessiveness of the hold was thrilling.

"I think you're a sexy"—thrust—"sassy"—thrust—"troublemaker, Mrs. Sandoval," he growled between exquisite lunges of his hips.

"Shit," I gasped. "Hell yes, I am, if this is my punishment," I teased through the fucking as we took turns groaning and taunting.

"Do you need my dick back in your mouth to stay quiet?"

"I wouldn't say no," I teased, but something snapped in the man, and he released his hold on my throat and gripped both hips when I tumbled back to my forearms.

Carmen pounded into me over and over again. His hips shuttled in and out like they were running on a separate power supply. Not sure I'd be able to walk or even move when we were done, but I didn't issue a single word of complaint.

How could I, when I loved every minute of the treatment? The only problem was Carmen was ruining me for all other men. If I wasn't careful, I could really fall for the man, and then I'd be completely wrecked when this was over.

"Come for me, Storm," my lover panted from behind me.

But I was nowhere near getting off. Because I'd let my thoughts run away from me, I had lost the connection with the physical feelings I was being treated to. Honestly, I didn't think I had the energy to start all over again, and he'd been working so hard, there was no way I'd tell him the truth about what happened.

Time to employ my acting skills and give the man the award-winning performance I was so used to giving in this situation. Bummer too, because so far with Carmen, all my orgasms had been legitimate. This would be the first one I faked my way through with him. I had an adult lifetime of practice faking it, though, so I knew he'd never know.

"Yeessss…" I drew out the word, just on the edge of a whimper. "I'm so close. So close." I squeezed the muscles inside my channel that would naturally tense during climax.

He kept up a steady pace like the excellent lover he was.

It was the absolute worst when you told a guy you were about to come and they switched up whatever they were doing that got you to that point. It was the surefire come killer. Every single time. And for some reason, almost every dude I'd ever slept with did it.

"I'm right there with you," he exhaled and leaned over my body to sink his teeth into my shoulder.

"Fuck! Yes, Carmen." I pretended to gasp, and when I let the deep breath out, I announced, "I'm coming. Fuck. So good," I said through fake ragged breaths. I continued to flex and release the muscles I had control of inside my body, attempting to sell the completion to my partner.

He stilled with his cock deep inside me, and our mixed breaths sounded like feral animals on the prowl. His hard shaft pulsed and jumped within my walls and seemed to go on for an eternity.

When he finally withdrew, I could feel his warm, thick semen trickle down the inside of my thigh. When I looked back over my shoulder, Carmen was watching the mess drip from my pussy, completely transfixed by the sight.

"Fuck, that's so hot," he finally said and collapsed to the bed beside me.

I snuggled into him with my back to his front, and he wrapped me in his embrace. I felt him burrowing through my messy hair with the tip of his nose and was blanketed by his warm breath each time he exhaled.

"Thank you," I finally whispered. Even if I didn't get off, the experience was amazing. He worked hard and deserved my praise and gratitude. "You're really a great lay, in case no one has told you before." I chuckled softly and added, "Amazing, really."

Carmen kissed the back of my head and was unusually quiet. I told myself he was probably exhausted and closed my eyes and tried to fall asleep.

But my spouse was restless behind me. Finally, I gave in and asked, "What's going on? You should've passed out after that."

"I'm wrestling with the right way to ask you why you faked getting off. I don't want to argue with you because you're right, I'm exhausted. It's probably best to revisit the conversation after we've both had some sleep. Night."

And with that announcement, he pulled away from my body and turned onto his other side, leaving me to stare at his defined, muscled back.

CHAPTER THIRTEEN

CARMEN

I was lacing my running shoes when she sat up in bed.

"What time is it? It's not even light out." She rubbed her eyes while she spoke.

Her blond hair was in a tangled cloud around her face, and she looked completely fuckable. Well, if I wasn't still in a foul mood because of last night. I knotted the lace with a huff and looked over my shoulder in time to watch her flop back on the mattress.

Yeah, I could totally mount her right now. I had always loved morning sex, but again, still a bit annoyed from our last romp.

"Go back to sleep. I'm going for a run. I'll probably be back before you wake up." My comment was delivered devoid of emotion, and she rolled to her side to watch me.

"Hey," she said in the gentlest tone I'd ever heard from her. But I pretended not to hear her and continued searching for my keys on top of the dresser. She had so much crap spread around the room, I couldn't find anything I looked for this morning.

"Carmen?" This time she was a little louder but still careful in tone.

I swung around to meet her stare and couldn't identify

what I saw there. Maybe it was an apology, but that was one I definitely hadn't seen from her before to reference. I knew it wasn't surrender, but it wasn't confrontation either. So I waited for her to add to the conversation first. I just wanted to go for a run and try to clear my head. Unlike her, I'd slept like shit. Funny, because she slept like the dead for the first time since moving in, and I lay there most of the night and watched her.

She finally gathered the courage to ask, "Do you want to talk? About last night, I mean?"

"Later, okay? I really want to get a run in before the sun comes up and it gets too hot." And yes, I was kicking the can down the road by putting off the conversation we definitely needed to have, but it was way too early to battle with my darling wife.

I must have mapped out the conversation four different ways throughout the sleepless night, but no matter the approach I thought best to take, we were going to end up bickering.

Out the front door, I made sure it was locked behind me. I jogged down the concrete staircase and hit the pavement with heavy feet. I definitely didn't have the energy for a run this morning but knew it was the best way to clear my head. So I took off through the complex to pick up the jogging at the trailhead the city maintained. The sun was just a pinpoint of light on the horizon, and the early morning air was crisp.

Most of my life I'd been a runner. The feel of the ground was solid beneath me as my feet fell into a familiar pace. After the first mile, my muscles were warm, and my breathing rate was barely above normal. Yeah, this was a good call. Over the next two miles, my body was on autopilot, and my mind really started to wander.

The star of most of my thoughts these days was Agatha. Never had I met such a confusing little package as the one currently fast asleep in my bed. She was delightfully infuriating and frustratingly enthralling. How was one woman so many contradictory things? Moreover, would our relationship always be that way, or was it another byproduct of marrying someone you hardly knew?

But I simply refused to give up on her. On us. Because when we were good, we were so good. She was smart and witty as hell and possibly the bright spot in life I'd been missing. I knew I had been digging myself into a rut before I met her, and life had been anything but boring since.

Agatha made me laugh, even when she wasn't trying to. She had an innocence about her underneath all that tough-girl bluster, and it shined through in the most curious ways. The careful consideration she had for the people she cared about was one of her most inspiring qualities. I listened to her chatting with her younger sisters, and she was always thoughtful in the advice she gave them and attentive when they just needed an ear.

I found myself daydreaming about the mother she'd be one day and had a goofy grin on my face as I marked the third mile on my route. Parenthood was far off in our future, for obvious reasons, but she was definitely the kind of woman who would be a naturally great mother. I suspected that had a lot to do with her own parents, and that thought led me to another one I didn't like admitting.

Would I be a shitty parent because mine had become so bitter and emotionally destructive? Were they always that negative, at least to some degree, and it just took Gray and me this long to see the truth of it? It seemed like a check in the plus column that I recognized their shortcomings and could identify how their toxicity affected us. Maybe by having that degree of awareness, I wouldn't repeat their mistakes.

Maybe it was easier to think all these things not having walked in their shoes. Every person I knew who was a parent said it was the toughest job they did every day. Another reason to wait to jump in that pool . . . I wanted to give the task my one hundred percent so my child—or children—would know they were my priority.

My thoughts came back around to Agatha. I'd bet she never gave parenting this much head time. That's what I meant by her seeming to have a natural inclination for raising children. She accessed her patience and tenderness when appropriate but could be a total ballbuster when she had to be, too.

The running trail looped around to make a big circle, and I neared the end strong. The endorphins from the exercise would energize me for most of the day. Back at my front door, I was rummaging through my pack to find the key when the door *whooshed* open.

My wife was awake, showered, dressed, and ready for the day. Her skin was fresh and free from makeup, and her blue eyes shimmered when the morning sun danced in them with promise.

"Hello, sexy," she said with a sultry grin while scanning my body from head to toe.

"Hey yourself," I said with a matching smile of my own.

Agatha just stood in the doorway and seemed to be in a daze after inspecting me so thoroughly.

Stepping closer to her, I asked, "Are you on your way out?"

"I was going to go check the mail," she explained. "I should be getting my final paycheck since it wasn't ready the other day. They said they would mail it."

"Do you know where the mailbox is? I can walk with you if you'd like some company. Although I'm a bit sweaty," I offered.

"I like this sweaty thing you've got going on," she admitted, and a little pink blush colored her cheeks. "Sexy."

After giving her a sideways smirk, I said, "Is that so?"

"Indeed," she purred back. But when I reached for her waist, she smacked at my seeking hands.

"No, no more. My vagina needs a day to recover from your mad skills." She laughed.

"Fine." I manufactured a forlorn face. "Fine." I didn't waste her agreeable mood, though, and scooped her hand into mine to entwine our fingers.

She sneaked a glance or two at the image our two hands presented. My silly green wedding ring on top where my hand completely engulfed hers. I didn't tease her about the visual sweep, though, because I knew how often I looked at the one on her delicate left ring finger.

"Do you want a real ring? Like a diamond or whatever?" I blurted without giving it any consideration. Seriously, where the hell would I get money for a diamond?

Agatha splayed her free hand out in front of us while we walked as though she were showing me the most treasured heirloom piece of jewelry. "No, I actually like this one. It suits me, and it's my favorite color, so there's that." She gave a little shrug while we both continued to admire her jelly band and then added, "I don't know. It seems perfect for this whole thing." She made some sort of lassoing gesture above us, and I guessed she was indicating our entire relationship thus far.

I chuckled then too. "Yeah, I guess it does."

Her check was waiting in the mailbox like she'd hoped,

along with the electric bill and an offer for a credit card I certainly didn't need or want.

But my wife was uncharacteristically quiet, so I looped around the complex to where the greenbelt offered a few tables and benches along with a couple of public grills.

"Want to kick back here for a bit?" I asked, thinking if we got this talk out of the way now, we could enjoy the rest of the day. Maybe if we had the talk out in the open, she wouldn't get so hostile.

"Sure, if you want to."

"You seem a bit off this morning. Did something happen I don't know about? Have you spoken to your family?" I said as a way to kick off the conversation.

"I think I'm just tired. I slept so well last night, but sometimes, because my sleep debt is so big, when I get quality sleep, I feel worse. Like I was just teasing my system with what it needs so much more of." My gorgeous girl ducked her head sheepishly, and I was sure I'd never seen that gesture from her before.

"I don't know if that makes sense, but that's my theory," she explained further.

"No, I get it. It actually makes perfect sense. If you want to sleep the whole day, baby, go for it. It's the weekend after all. And other than tomorrow morning, we don't have anything planned."

Yes, that was a minor shot across her bow to remind her she wasn't getting out of the commitment I made for us to join my family for Sunday mass. She didn't even know that I had to just about sell my soul to keep the family dinner afterward an uncommitted invitation.

Beside me on the bench, she sighed and drew her knees

up to her chest and sat there huddled in a little ball. She looked so young and small and, fine, I'd admit it ... unhappy.

"Storm, I'm sorry it feels like I'm forcing you to do something you don't want to do," I said so she would at least hear me acknowledge that I knew what this engagement tomorrow was costing her. It still didn't mean I'd relent, though.

Quietly she asked, "Then why are you doing exactly that?"

I angled my body toward her and wrapped my hands over her knees. "My family goes to church every Sunday morning. It's a tradition in our household, and even though I no longer live in the same house, I'm expected to attend. Not just by my parents, but by the entire parish. It's noticed immediately when someone's missing, and then the hens start clucking. I won't cause my mom that sort of grief. She doesn't need it, especially when it's something I can easily do for her. For the whole family."

"So it's not at all about the unity or spirituality of the gathering. It's about the gossip and saving face. Do you hear how fucked up that is?" she challenged but remained calm.

"Of course I do. I've been complaining about the hypocrisy of modern religion since I've been able to organize my own thoughts. But tradition is tradition in the Sandoval household, and if you want to keep the peace, you don't rock the boat." I paused there, and she didn't add anything more. I concluded by saying, "It's not the hill I want to die on. You know?"

"But how does that involve me?" she fired back and dropped her feet back to the ground.

"Because you are my wife. Do I really have to spell that out?"

"No one even knows you have a wife, Carmen. Unless ... " She looked at me skeptically. "Have you been telling people?"

"Not a single person. To this day, the only two people who know are your sister and my boss. That's it. But if I'm being honest with you, Storm, I don't want to hide it. I'm very proud you're mine."

And I really was. If she needed a list of reasons why, I had at least a dozen. I also didn't miss the little grin she had because of my declaration—even though she was doing her best to hide it. I was starting to pay very close attention to that type of reaction from her. The natural ones she tried to keep under wraps. She was a lonely girl inside that brash shell, and it seemed like a little genuine love went a long way with her.

Fine by me, because I had a ton to give. And a ton to shower her with, specifically. She deserved to be loved and to freely love whomever she chose. Each time I learned one of these little secrets she guarded so carefully, I felt like I completed another piece of the Agatha puzzle. Eventually, I'd have the complete image figured out, and then we could really start enjoying building our life together.

There was something about me I hadn't successfully gotten through her stubborn little head. When I cared about a person, making them happy and caring for them in all the ways imaginable genuinely made me happy. My sister always commented that when it came to love languages, I spoke them all. She pretty much hit the nail on the head with that assessment, but I wasn't surprised. Gray knew me better than anyone else in my life. She understood what made me tick, and we both wanted the other to be happy.

"So let's move on to the events of last night," I suggested. At that point, we'd pretty much beaten the church attendance thing to death. We were going, period. If I had to carry her into the sanctuary kicking and screaming, I'd do it.

But my God, I hope it doesn't come to that.

Agatha rubbed wearily at her brow and wouldn't meet my gaze.

"Please know that I'm not being so insistent we have this conversation to embarrass you or make you uncomfortable."

"Carmen." She sighed. "You should know by this point, that topic doesn't embarrass me."

"Good. Me neither. So we should be able to discuss this like adults and just speak our true feelings." I waited for her to add more, but she was unusually quiet. So I dived into the heart of the matter but couched it with some information about myself first. Maybe if I showed a little vulnerability first, she wouldn't feel so defensive.

"It makes me happy on a bunch of levels to make you happy. Whether it's with kind words, little gifts, or giving you pleasure with my body. When you're happy, I'm happy."

With a smile, she said, "You've been very good to me. I appreciate the efforts you make because I know they are premeditated. That says a lot about the kind of human you are."

"Thank you, darling," I said sincerely.

"But I want to try to explain something about me. About what goes on in here." She tapped on her temple with her index finger, and her bright-green wedding band made me smile.

I took her hand and kissed her fourth finger and continued holding it while we talked. It was hard to be near her and not touch her in one way or another.

"Okay, I'm all ears," I encouraged.

"Inside my head . . . " She huffed. "It's pretty chaotic. Like, all the time. It's probably the biggest reason I don't sleep well. I have trouble turning off the inner dialogue." She held up her hand to stop me from interjecting, but honestly, I wasn't considering doing so. I could be patient and hear her out.

"Unfortunately, it's no different while we're having sex. Okay, that's not completely true with you, but for the most part…in my experience so far…the running commentary continues no matter what I'm doing physically."

"Can you explain what you mean when you said it's different with me?"

"Isn't that self-explanatory? You've been the only lover I've ever had who can manage to pull me from the mental distraction. But then last night, I slipped back into that comfort zone," she explained, but then she started talking so fast, I wasn't sure I caught everything she said.

"And I felt really bad about it. About losing my concentration. I was right there, right about to come, and something sneaked through the cracks, and my mind took off in twelve different directions. I know from experience there's no way to come back from that point, so I gave you an out."

I tilted my head to one side because I wasn't sure I heard that right. "Gave me an out?" I repeated her words in hopes she would hear how lame they were.

Instead, she gave a firm nod, completely standing by the statement. "Yes. You'd already worked so hard at…at what was going on, and I thought you'd be disappointed if I didn't climax. It's not fair to you, for one thing, and sometimes a woman's body can only take so much before it becomes not enjoyable. You know?"

"Okay, fair enough—the part about your body, at least. But I'm telling you right here and now, to make it my official stance on the matter. I would rather you tell me the truth than fake it. That's harder on a guy's psyche than an honest conversation.

And my beautiful storm..." I couldn't resist reaching out and tugging on a lock of her blond waves. "A man worth your time in bed can totally tell when you're faking. So don't think you'll do it again."

"But..." she began but slouched down on the seat, looking completely defeated.

"But what?"

"Never mind."

"Please. Tell me what you were going to say. I'm not mad, and you're not mad—we're just two people sitting here having a conversation. About a very important topic, no doubt, but there's no reason not to say what you want to say."

"I was going to explain why I did it, but it will just sound like I'm making lame excuses. That's so not me."

"All right. I'm one hundred percent clear you're being genuine. Please finish your thought."

She sighed long and heavy and thought for a few moments. I was just about to get growly and demanding when she spoke.

"My brain is a very busy place."

"Yes." I couldn't stop the grin that spread across my lips. "I would agree with that assessment. It's one of the things I love about you." And yes, I heard the words that just slipped past my lips but had no intention of recalling them.

"Like I just said, it's really easy for me to get distracted—like, all the time. So I end up thinking about fourteen other things when I should be concentrating on what I'm participating in."

"This will seem like it's coming from left field, but do you like pain with sex? So far, you seem to like what we've done in bed, but I think I have a few other ideas to keep you present in the moment. I wouldn't do something more intense without your consent first."

The question was a legitimate one, and a little pain during sex had been proved to keep a person grounded and focused. We might have stumbled into a really fun solution to the problem.

If she agreed to it, of course.

For the first time... well, ever, I saw what the shy, embarrassed version of my wife looked like. She seemed to regress by years from her actual age, and the sheepish, bashful woman before me was so alluring, I felt my dick twitch.

"I-I-I'm not really sure. Like, what are we talking about? I don't want to be whipped or given electrical shocks, I know that much," she answered while studiously inspecting her twisted hands in her lap.

"Why don't you leave *what* and *how* up to me? You just have to tell me it would be okay. You have to trust me that I will know when and what to try." I definitely had an erection now. I unabashedly adjusted myself in my running shorts, but messing with it only made it worse.

"Fuck me," I muttered while shifting my weight on the hard seat.

"You okay there?" She laughed, and I just gave her a serious stare. Immediately, she clapped her mouth shut and widened her eyes.

We both relaxed over the next few minutes, and Agatha was first to break the silence. "So when do you want to test this theory?" She looked me over from head to toe, and a beautiful rosy tint colored her cheeks.

"I'll worry about the details, darling. You just have to say yes." I paused a few beats and then pressed for the answer I was now painfully waiting for. "Are you saying yes?"

Instead of words, she gave a quick dip of her chin. I was

shocked. For all her bold, mouthy comebacks and brash attitude, this was the topic that was making her squirm. At the same time, I loved uncovering new things about her. Each time I did, it felt like we became a little bit closer.

I slid closer to her on the bench so there was no chance anyone passing by would hear our conversation. Dropping my voice to the most seductive yet commanding tone I could, I told her, "Say the words, Storm. Out loud. Tell me to hurt you, baby." I leaned closer to her and bit the lobe of her ear, increasing the pressure until she moaned.

"Oh God, that feels so good," she said and sounded like she just finished the five-mile run I had this morning.

"Tell me," I said again.

Boldly, she met my stare straight on. "I want you to hurt me, Carmen," she whispered, and that was more than good enough for me.

I stood abruptly and tugged her to stand too. She yelped in surprise, and it was a delightful little sound.

"You can trust me. I won't push you further than you can handle," I vowed while looking down to her upturned face. "Thank you for your consent. You're not going to regret it," I said through a devilish grin. When she tilted her head, probably ready to ask about my expression, I continued. "You're also never going to fake coming again. Understand?"

She nodded eagerly, and we were both breathing a bit faster with excitement. I wanted to yank down the white jeans she wore and mount her right there on the complex's greenbelt, but I used some restraint.

Once we were inside the apartment, though... all bets were off.

CHAPTER FOURTEEN

AGATHA

Every dress I owned was off the hanger and strewn about the room. I hated every single one I tried on and found myself biting a hole through my cheek so I didn't launch into another tirade about having to go to church this morning.

Me! In church! The whole idea was ludicrous, but my bossy husband wouldn't budge on me attending. He peeked into the spare bedroom from the doorway, eyebrows up at his hairline when he took in the condition of the space.

A threatening growl rumbled in my chest. If he dared to utter one single word, I'd throat punch him.

"That one looks lovely. Why don't you wear that?" he asked very carefully.

"You don't think it's too snug on my ass? I mean, for church? And look at the front. Is this too much cleavage?" I pointed out the details of the current piece that were preventing me from considering wearing it.

"No, honestly, darling. You look beautiful. Please don't stress this much, okay? These days people show up in jeans and T-shirts. You're making too much of an issue out of this." He waited patiently while I glared his way, and he finally added another, "Okay?"

"No, actually it's not okay. I don't want to go in the first place and you're forcing me to. I'll tell you one thing, *husband*." That word got a heavy coating of venom today. "You're going to owe me for this. Big time," I threatened, and even though I'd promised myself we wouldn't argue before doing this, his mere presence was a reminder of the situation I was being railroaded into.

"I think you look beautiful. I hope you keep on what you're wearing. We need to leave in fifteen minutes, so I'll let you finish up." He cautiously backed out of the doorway and into the hall. When he was clear of the room, he turned and quickly went to the living room. I heard him flip on the television, probably to kill some time until I was ready.

"Okay, girl. Breathe. We're not going to be late on top of everything else. Dress looks good, get your hair and makeup done, and this will be fine. It's going to be fine." I coached myself in from the ledge and finished getting ready.

I took a few minutes to shoot a text to my sister Hannah. It had been more than a week since we spoke, and that was unusual. I could really use her support right now, so I was missing chatting with her more than normal.

After one last look in the mirror, I decided it was as good as it was going to get. My nerves were really getting the best of me still, so I dug through the contents of the medicine cabinet in hopes of finding anything that might take the edge off.

There was a full, unopened bottle of nighttime cold medicine beneath the sink, and I eyed it cautiously. Before I was of legal drinking age, my high school friends and I used to chug this stuff before class. I knew it would be good to at least smooth out the wrinkles. The shit was disgusting, though, and after the first swig, my stomach turned over on itself.

"One more should do it," I muttered to myself and took

another healthy gulp of syrupy, green decongestant. A shudder racked my whole body after the second dose went down, so I chased it with some water straight from the tap. Digging through the mess on the bed, I found my handbag and then went to find Carmen.

He stood when he saw me and reached for my hands. I was more comfortable with his frequent touching now and placed mine in his. Unexpectedly, he lifted one hand high above our heads and twirled me around like a dance partner. The surprise move and the cold medicine I just ingested made me topple off balance and right into his embrace.

With steadying arms around me, he nuzzled his face into my neck. "You look gorgeous. Thank you for doing this. I know it hasn't been easy."

My voice was a child's when I bashfully thanked him for the compliment. Not liking the vulnerability, I quickly said, "We should probably go."

I hooked my arm in his to traverse the staircase outside. That damn medicine went straight to my brain, and the ground swayed beneath every step I took. I tried blinking slowly several times to clear the staticky edges from my vision, but it didn't help.

My handsome date secured me in the passenger seat and strolled around the hood to take the wheel. He looked so dapper in an open sport coat and button-down shirt. Matching slacks were tailored to his lean body, and I instantly recalled images of him after his run yesterday. Hot and sweaty with muscles stretched tight from exertion, the memory was vivid and arousing. A groan slipped past my lips and filled the silence of the car and caught the close attention of my partner.

"You okay?" he asked with more concern than confidence,

so I played it off the best I could.

"My stomach is doing a number on me because of my nerves," I explained as he backed out of the parking space and drove out of the complex. It wasn't far from the truth.

That crap I'd chugged probably wasn't the smartest decision, because I truly felt nauseous from it. But the last thing I wanted was his attentive caretaking, so I added, "But what I was really thinking was how handsome you look in your Sunday best, Mr. Sandoval. I'm surprised there aren't a bunch of unattached parishioners saving you a spot in their pew each week."

"Cute." He grinned, and a smile spread across my lips too.

"Is it far?" I asked, getting a little concerned about the way my insides were gurgling.

"Nah, less than thirty. Traffic is usually light on Sunday mornings."

"Yes, because all the sane people are still sleeping, not getting dressed up to be judged and gossiped about," I said in a pleasant tone.

His sideways glance let me know I probably shouldn't try to sneak in another little zinger like that.

We arrived about twenty minutes later, and groupings of people milled around outside the building. After a quick observation, everyone seemed familiar with each other, and lots of friendly hugs and greetings were being exchanged.

Carmen had a possessive hand at my lower back, and the reassurance I was getting from that small gesture should've unnerved me. I continually lectured myself about not becoming dependent on this man so I could keep up some sort of wall between us where those dangerous feelings were concerned.

It was all fine and good to sleep with the man. Hell, I was all for that one, actually. But the confusing things like gaining confidence from his kind words or feeling secure because of his physical presence? Well, I didn't want to rely on anyone for those things. I wanted to be independent and know I was capable of giving myself those positive reassurances.

My husband steered us through the crowd and stopped in front of his family. I assumed these people were his family, at least. There was an older man and woman and a young lady about my age. The woman wrapped Carmen in a fierce hug while the man looked me over from head to toe. It wasn't a creepy leer, but the assessment of a curious stranger. I gave him an easy smile, and he returned the expression.

"Carmen, my boy." The man took his turn hugging his son, and then my husband stood back and held out his hand to me.

"Mom, Dad, this is Agatha. Agatha, my parents, Hector and Manuella Sandoval."

I sensed he was nervous, but damn, did he look handsome with the pride that was glowing all over his face. The bright morning sun created delicious shadows beneath his cheekbones, and I was momentarily lost in admiring his good looks.

Carmen's parents were cordial and shook my hand while he and his sister whispered along the edge of our little group.

"And this troublemaker is my sister, Gray," he said with a chuckle, and the girl swept me into a hug that nearly knocked the wind from my lungs.

When we separated, she took a playful swipe at her brother and said, "Well, now I know why I haven't heard from you much lately. Been busy, huh?"

"Graziella, mind your manners," Mrs. Sandoval chided.

"We've just met the young lady."

Her daughter simply rolled her eyes at the woman's comment.

"Shall we go in before all the good seats are taken?" Mr. Sandoval suggested, but I wanted to run back to the car and hide. If I survived the next few hours, the members of this congregation would witness an actual miracle in their house of worship.

Carmen's hand was at the base of my spine again, this time attempting to steer me toward the church's front doors. But I stopped in my tracks and braced to resist his urging forward.

He looked across his shoulder to where I was rooted to the pavement and asked, "You okay? You're very pale." He pivoted to shield me from the front and ducked down to be at my eye level. "What's up, baby? You really don't look so good."

"I feel like I'm going to be sick," I whimpered. "I told you my stomach was bothering me."

"I figured it was just nerves and you'd calm down once we got that initial introduction out of the way." Giving little credence to my situation, he prattled on. "See? They're not so bad, right?" he asked hopefully, and I couldn't even fake a smile. One false move, and the contents of my stomach would be making an encore appearance.

"I don't want to go in there, Carmen. Please. If I get sick in front of all those people, I'll be mortified. Please," I begged with the sincerest intent. I should've never guzzled that cold medicine on an already precarious stomach, but I couldn't explain that to him either. Oh my God, he'd lose his freaking mind. Not to mention adding to his self-righteous opinion about my drinking habits.

He tilted his head to the side and eyed me skeptically.

Instantly I felt defensive just from the look on his face. The bastard didn't believe me.

"Storm, is this some elaborate ruse to get out of doing something you don't want to do? Kind of childish, wouldn't you say?"

Now I was livid on top of nauseated. How dare he accuse me of faking?

"Fine. Let's go on in. If I barf all over your family and judgmental friends, so be it. You'll be as embarrassed as me, and we can call it even. But..." I sucked in a breath through my nose as a tidal wave of queasiness rolled through my body. When it passed, I picked up with my comment exactly where I left off. "You should know I will never forgive you for accusing me of faking. That's so completely shitty..." I stammered for the right words to complete the thought but came up empty. "Yeah, just so shitty. Thanks for the support."

"Okay, let's calm down. You're actually looking green. We can stay out here until the first hymn starts, but then we're going inside. Walk it off"—he waved a hand toward the sidewalk that bordered the street—"or do whatever you need to do until then."

"You're an asshole," I leveled through gritted teeth. I knew my eyes were clouding with unshed tears, but I'd be damned if he'd have the satisfaction of hurting me on top of accusing me of lying.

"And you're an immature drama queen who is so used to getting her way, you're willing to make yourself physically sick rather than do something someone asked of you." He widened his eyes as if giving me my cue to respond.

"Fuck you, *husband*." I spun on my heels and headed for the parking lot. I was so mad, I couldn't even see which direction I was rushing. What I didn't fail to register, however, was the fact that his mother had walked up just as I was spewing that last little bit his way.

Her audible gasp confirmed that she heard exactly what I'd said.

Good. Let him deal with the mess he insisted we try to make work. Mr. Calm Down. Mr. Walk It Off. He could seriously go fuck himself. I was done.

Completely finished.

CHAPTER FIFTEEN

CARMEN

As I registered my mother's presence, my wife disappeared around the far side of the building. I warred with going after her or trying to explain to my mother what she'd just overheard. And there was no way in hell the woman hadn't heard my lovely wife's vitriol. She had the sharpest hearing of anyone I'd ever met and had for my entire life. Even if it was whispered, she could repeat word for word the conversation she'd heard from across the house.

Imagine what a nightmare that was as a teenage boy. Not only did one of my bedroom walls divide my room and Gray's, but with my mom's superhuman hearing ability, there wasn't a moment of privacy to be had.

At about sixteen, I gave up worrying about it and figured if they wanted to be creepy enough to listen to me masturbate, that was on them. Funny how Gray seemed to increase the volume on her TV or stereo at the exact same time I needed to rub one out.

"Son? What did that woman just call you?" My mother's face was nearly as pale as Agatha's.

"I'm not sure, Mom. We were arguing, and I'm sorry you had to witness it. A lot of things were just said that weren't meant." The response was lame and I knew it, but I was hoping for a little break somewhere.

The woman strode over to where I paced and grabbed my left hand. After inspecting the green jelly band, she thrust my hand in my face.

"What on earth is this?" she demanded.

"It's a cheap green ring I picked up in Vegas."

Her gasp could've stopped traffic.

"Carmen. Sandoval. What have you done?"

I wasn't in the mood for any of this. Especially on the street in front of our family's church. Especially when I should be in pursuit of my wife to ensure she was okay.

"I need to go after her, Mom. We can talk later."

"You'll miss mass!" she proclaimed as if it were the worst thing happening in that moment.

"Well, I'll repent next time I'm in the confessional. As you've witnessed, I've got bigger problems at the moment." Most of the glib remark was thrown back over my shoulder as I set off to find my woman.

As I rounded the back side of the church that opened to the parking lot and play yard for the Sunday School classes, Agatha was across the lawn, bent over at the waist. I picked up my pace to a quick jog and was beside her in a flash.

I swept her hair back from her face and held it at her nape while the poor thing barfed neon-green fluid with alarming force. Good Christ, did she have an alien smoothie for breakfast? What the hell was that?

"Oh, baby, you poor girl," I crooned as she gave a shuddering dry heave. I continued to assist with her hair until I was certain she was done and quickly supported her around the waist when she finally stood up.

"Tell me how to help you. You want some water? There's a

fountain just inside the play yard gate," I offered, at a complete loss on what to do for her.

"Leave me alone," she groaned. "Seriously, Carmen, just go. You'll be late for church, and what will they all say?" she bit as she attempted to wipe her lips and chin with the hem of her dress. I stopped her before she ruined the pretty outfit and dug for my handkerchief in the pocket of my slacks.

"Here. Don't ruin your dress, baby." I held out the cloth, and she glared at it and then at me like she'd like both to spontaneously combust. But fluid was dripping down her chin that she swiped at with her hand.

After looking at the gross streak now on her fingers, she begrudgingly snagged my offering.

"Thanks," she muttered and turned her back to me as she cleaned up. She hung her head, and her whole body shook.

It took me a few seconds longer than it probably should have to realize she was crying. I couldn't just stand there and watch her fall apart, because I truly cared about the woman. Not to mention, she had told me she never cried. Was this a turning point... or her breaking point?

"Come on, I'll help you to the car," I offered and put my arm around her trembling body. At once, she wriggled free from my assistance and whirled on me with an expression that was downright frightening.

"I said leave me alone. We're done as far as I'm concerned." She angrily pointed back and forth between us and said, "This isn't going to work between us. I may have been trying to convince myself that maybe there was some snowball's chance in hell that it could, but now I know."

The disheveled woman shook her head ruefully. "That"— she stabbed the air in the direction of the church, and it wasn't until she continued chewing me out that I realized she was referring to the conversation we'd just had in front of the building—"that was unforgivable and a real eye-opener. You can't take shit like that back. So don't even try."

"What are you talking about?" I asked, because a lot was said in a short period of time, and we were both pretty pissed off. Honestly, I couldn't even recall what I had said.

"You don't trust me. You accused me of faking being sick. Did that look fake?" She thumbed over her shoulder so forcefully, I thought she might have dislocated the ball and socket.

"No, that looked like alien stomach bile, if I'm being honest. What the hell did you eat?" Yes, it was a stupid remark, especially given how pissed and hurt she was, but unfortunately, it was the first thing that came out of my mouth.

I deserved the glare I got that time. I'd be the first to admit it.

"Sorry. I'm not trivializing anything you just said. I've just never seen anything like that." I chuckled, trying to lighten the air between us, but she wasn't having it.

"I'm glad this is all a big joke to you, Carmen. I want my journal back first thing when we get home, and then I'm packing my stuff and leaving." She scanned the parking lot for what I assumed was my car and then set off in the wrong direction.

"Where are you going?" I called while jogging to catch up to her as she stomped across the uneven grass in her high heels. I was in position beside her just in time to catch her small frame as she nearly overturned her ankle on top of everything else.

Even though she didn't return the embrace, I stood with my arms snuggly around her until she calmed down and was breathing evenly.

I ducked down so I was staring right into her glassy blue eyes. In the sunlight, I noticed strands of gold through the blue iris that I hadn't seen before. Instinctually I pressed a kiss to her clammy forehead and said against her skin, "I'm so sorry I hurt you."

She looked up to hold my gaze but said nothing. Tears were back, and she squeezed her eyes shut as if doing so would hold them in.

"Let's get you home and tucked into bed. I think you must have picked up a bug somewhere." With my arm firmly around her shoulders, I turned us in the opposite direction and started off toward the other side of the parking lot.

"I thought we parked over there?" she said weakly.

"No, we're this way, just a few rows in. You okay to walk? I could carry you," I suggested and had every intention of making good on the offer if she needed me to.

"Don't you dare. I've already embarrassed myself enough for one decade. Just take me home, and I'll be out of your way in an hour or so," she rambled as we made it to my car.

After situating her in the passenger seat, securing her seat belt, and adjusting the vents so cool air would wash over her, I went around to the driver's side. Behind the wheel, I looked over at my wife and felt deep sadness at the thought of her leaving.

"I can't let you leave, Storm. I won't do it." I quietly but resolutely made the declaration and started the ignition. She could argue and protest all she liked, but she wouldn't be moving out today.

Or tomorrow, for that matter.

We drove home in silence. My thoughts were all over the place, and I couldn't settle on one in particular that seemed like a good jumping-off point to a productive conversation. At a red light, I looked over and saw she had dozed off. My beautiful storm was finally calm, peaceful in the first stages of rest.

The jackass behind us laid on his horn when the light changed and I didn't immediately take off. I was too transfixed by the woman sleeping in my passenger seat.

Asshole, I mouthed to the guy via my rearview mirror and slowly pulled out. Agatha slept the rest of the drive home even though traffic ensured the journey took a bit longer. When I pulled into my parking space, I debated if I should wake her or attempt carrying her.

When I released her seat belt, she opened her groggy eyes and tried to focus on my face.

"I'm going to carry you inside, okay? Stay asleep," I issued in my more assertive tone, but she sat forward and tried to push me out of the way.

"No, I can walk. I'm fine." She shoved at my hip a second time, and I growled without thinking. Her stubbornness could really be infuriating.

"Why are you so resistant to help? You just barfed your guts out. You're going to be weak," I lectured as she bolted upright from the car.

And instantly wobbled on her legs and then plopped right back down into the car. She cradled her face in her hands and slowly shook her head.

"What the hell is going on? I've thrown up more times than I care to admit. And I'm usually better for it. This is ridiculous."

"Darling, I saw what just came out of your body. I think you're actually ill and not vomiting from a bender like you're used to."

That was apparently the wrong thing to say, because she defiantly stood again but held on to the door to ensure she was steady first. She must have been satisfied with her balancing ability because she abruptly slammed the car door and headed for the apartment. By the time she was midway up the stairs, though, she slowed to a full stop.

Thankfully I was right behind her to support her, or I thought she might have tumbled backward down the flight. I tucked my shoulder into her abdomen and hoisted her up and over it. Not the graceful, caring hold I had in mind initially, but in the middle of a concrete staircase, there weren't many options. I just wanted her back on solid ground as quickly as possible. I already had my keys in hand, so we were inside in a snap.

"Put me down. This is making me queasy," she said from where she hung over my back.

I slid her down to her own feet immediately and held her by the waist until she looked steady.

"All right, let's get you in bed. No arguing. You need to sleep and drink something so you don't get dehydrated. Your poor lips already look dry."

With my comment, her tongue swiped out over the bottom lip, and she groaned.

"Okay," she finally acquiesced.

Internally I cheered in gratitude and led her to our bedroom.

Beside the bed I instructed, "Arms up, baby."

"Huh?"

"You can't sleep in this dress. You'll ruin it. Arms up, and I'll help you get changed." I internally battled for some patience. Why did everything have to be a damn debate?

"You don't have to do all this... this caretaking. I'm an adult. I can change my own clothes."

I bent forward again to grab the hem of her dress and explained, as I pulled it up over her body, "I know I don't have to, but I want to. Do you not understand that I genuinely care about you?"

She puffed out a breath, and because we were standing so close, I caught a very intense whiff of medicine. Odd...

But then the color of her emesis flashed through my mind again. I combined that particular green color with the odor of medicine, and the pieces clicked together. I narrowed my eyes and debated speaking my theory.

I mean, no way was she that bad that she'd be drinking cold medicine for a buzz. Was she? That was adolescent bullshit I definitely wouldn't tolerate. I just wasn't prepared for the confrontation that would come after the accusation. We still had to address the things that happened this morning in front of the church.

Agatha sat on the edge of the bed in her bra and tiny panties. Even in her ailing state, she robbed the air straight from my lungs. Before my dick got any stupid ideas, I hustled to my dresser to grab a T-shirt for her. She flopped back on the mattress with her arms extended above her head, and her silky hair spread across the blankets.

Don't, I silently warned myself. This was not an invitation to mount her, even though every healthy young male cell in my body tried to convince me otherwise. When I tried to ask her to sit up so we could get the shirt on, my voice was unrecognizable. After clearing my throat, I tried a second time.

"All right, gorgeous. Let's get this on so you're warm and I'm not tempted to fuck you. My God, woman. You're like a siren lying there like that."

A devilish smile crossed her lips for a brief moment, but by the time she sat up, all traces of the expression were gone. I bunched the shirt up and slid the neck opening over her head, and she handled the rest. I watched with typical male fascination as she unhooked her bra and pulled it through one of the arm holes like some sort of magic trick.

She pulled the covers back and got beneath them, but not before tossing the simple white bra on the floor. I bent to pick it up in the same second and laid it delicately on top of her dress on the armchair near the window. Once she was settled in, I'd hang it up properly.

"I'm going to get you a nice big water. Do you want ice?"

"Yes, please," she mumbled into the pillow as she got comfortable on her side. I tucked the covers in around her body and closed the blinds so she could rest.

"What about some Tylenol or something?" I asked from the doorway. "What hurts?"

"Carmen, I'm fine. You've done more than enough," she replied from the nest of blankets. "I'll be good to go after a little nap. I'm sure of it."

By the time I came back with the water, she was softly snoring in the middle of our bed. So I left the glass and two pain relievers on the nightstand, grabbed her dress and bra, and headed to the spare bedroom to hang it up.

I should've never even opened that door. It looked like we had been burglarized while we were gone, because the room was ransacked. I thought it was bad the night we went out to dinner, but this was next level.

All but two of the hangers in the closet were empty. The ones that remained on the bar were turned in every possible direction, and a few on the floor were actually tangled together.

One by one, I took my time rehanging her clothes. She didn't have a ton, but while strewn about the room, it looked like there was enough to fill the women's department at Saks. I lined up her shoes along the bottom of the closet. The pairs that no longer had a box, I paired together and put there too.

An audible groan escaped when I saw the en suite bathroom. Like the other night, products were strewn about the countertop. One of the doors to the cabinet beneath the sink was wedged open by the cord to her curling iron, but at least the damn thing wasn't left on. After wrapping the cord around the barrel, I bent down to put it beneath the sink.

"What's this?" I asked aloud and pulled a half-empty bottle of nighttime cold medicine from the cupboard. My suspicions were confirmed when I poured a little into the sticky measuring cup that rested on top. The same green color I couldn't shake from my memory of my wife's vomit, and the same hideous smell I thought I detected on her breath. I set the bottle on the countertop and finished putting all her shit away.

I had to broach the subject with her. Maybe not right when she woke up, but I refused to let this go on. I'd check her ass into rehab myself if it meant saving her from self-destructing. That bottle was untouched before this morning. I remembered buying it after the last time I was sick to replace the one I'd emptied. That way it would be on hand next time I was under the weather.

That meant she downed half the bottle this morning. For recreation. Christ, no wonder she threw up the way she had. Even her body was trying to tell her to chill out. The more I thought about it, the angrier I grew. Why would she do something so foolish? She had to know guzzling that stuff was dangerous. How many assemblies did we all sit through in junior high that beat that message into our brains?

★ ★ ★

She slept most of the day. While I considered waking her several times to ensure she was drinking enough and didn't end up feeling worse from dehydration, I never went through with the notion. Every time I went into the room to check on her, I lost another half hour simply watching her sleep.

The woman was so beautiful, it hurt inside my chest. She'd spent a lot of time on her hair before church this morning, so it cascaded over the pillow like a silky veil. The urge to run my fingers through it—or better yet, bury my nose in it—was almost too much to resist.

Agatha was a restless sleeper, even when exhausted. Her brows went from furrowed to raised to drawn together, as if she were deep in concentration or maybe participating in a spirited conversation. She mumbled and sighed and flip-flopped from one side to the other. Watching all the activities her body engaged in while it was supposed to be recharging explained a lot about her daily low energy.

I also understood the situation better now because my own sleep quality had sharply declined since she'd moved in. The number of times we'd been wide awake through the night was ridiculous. If I weren't so stubborn, I could admit that fact alone would be enough for me to break up with any other person.

But Agatha Christine Farsey had some sort of magic spell cast over me. When I thought about her following through with her threat from earlier—her packing her things and moving out after she rested a bit—a wave of panic washed over me.

In the short time we'd been together, she'd brought more excitement to my daily grind than anything or anyone else. When I was at the office, I'd count the hours until I'd be home. When I was at home, I wanted to follow her around the apartment like a pesky little puppy demanding attention.

There was no way I would return her journal, either. This morning I was pretty sure that was the only thing keeping her from leaving me. She had to know by now that I hadn't read the thing. If she gave that fact the props it deserved, she would realize I could be trusted and genuinely cared for her.

In the wildest fantasy in my mind, she'd come to me and ask for help ditching the drinking habit, and her goals would become our goals, and we'd get through it together.

Maybe if I articulated those same sentiments and caught her in a receptive mood, we'd really make some progress. Inside my pocket, my cell phone vibrated, so I hustled out of the bedroom to take the call and not disturb my peaceful storm.

I put the phone to my ear once I was in the kitchen. "Hello?"

The display told me it was my sister, and for the most part, I welcomed the call. I just wasn't up for the ribbing and prying into my life I would have to endure. After the way I spoke to my mother this morning, I was probably lucky any of my blood relatives were speaking to me.

"Hey, Carmen. Just calling to make sure you're okay," Gray said casually.

"Yeah, I'm good. How was mass?" I asked. Might as well just rip the Band-Aid off instead of tap dancing around what she really wanted to know.

"Oh, you know, same gospel, different Sunday."

"Ha! Good one," I said dryly. "Seriously, how's Mom?"

"She'll get over it. Not after milking it for every bit of attention she can first. But yeah . . . she'll get over it."

"I'll apologize in a day or two. I just felt like so many things were falling apart all at once, and I guess I panicked. Doesn't give me the right to be disrespectful," I told my sister, sounding more mature and responsible than I felt about the situation.

My sister's voice was gentle when she responded. "Hey, listen. You don't have to do that for me. You know that. I know firsthand what a bitch that woman can be. I wouldn't judge you for anything you said to her."

"I appreciate that, Gray. I really do."

The air between our two phones charged with her mischief then, and I figured it wouldn't take her too long to get on my case about Agatha.

"So, tell me more about your friend. She's very pretty. All-American beauty queen." She likely meant what she was saying, but it was also serving as the warm-up stretch before the wind sprints. The spoonful of sugar to help her medicine go down.

So I made her work for any details I shared. "Thank you. She's definitely a beauty."

And I left it at that. If she wanted more, she'd have to ask.

"Where did you meet?" my sister asked immediately. I'd be shocked if she'd even heard my gratitude because she was busy deciding what to ask next.

"My boss, Elijah Banks, is married to her sister. We met at his wife's birthday party."

"And what does she do for a living?"

"She's currently looking for something new. You guys hiring?" I teased, but if she said yes, I'd definitely steer Agatha in that direction.

"Hmm, not sure. If you're serious, I can find out. What does she do?"

"She's a journalist," I answered flatly.

"Why are you making me pull every crumb of information from you like this? Based on the way you were so googly-eyed over the girl, I kind of figured I wouldn't be able to shut you up about her," she said with a forced laugh. It was her way of letting me know she wasn't trying to start an argument.

"I was not googly-eyed," I insisted. "I'm just exhausted, I guess." I heard how lame that sounded. It wasn't untrue, even if it wasn't the actual reason I was hesitant to offer up too many details about my wife. "She got very sick in the parking lot before we left, and it's been a bit dicey here since this morning."

"Oh no, what's wrong? Do you think it's a bug or something? A couple of coworkers were out this week with a stomach thing. Must be going around." Gray was genuinely concerned. She was one of the most compassionate and empathetic people I knew.

"Honestly, I think it was a combo of things. She was very nervous about meeting the family, plus something she ate this morning didn't agree with her." Okay, so it was a tiny fib. Just stretching the truth, really.

Before we got into the marriage conversation, or debate, depending on if my sibling was going to support me on the topic or not, I tried to end the conversation.

"I think I hear her stirring, Gray. I'm gonna get going. I appreciate the call. Love you, sister."

But her disappointment came through in her tone. "Oh. Okay, I guess. We really need to have lunch, though. I feel like we haven't talked in so long, and I also want you to know you can speak freely to me. I mean, you know that, right?"

"Yeah, of course I do."

"Then why do I get the feeling you're giving me the brush-off here? You know I'm very open-minded, Carmen. I'm not going to criticize or judge."

The solemnity in her voice was comforting and made me really want to spill my guts to my little sister. Maybe I'd gain some clarity? Maybe it would just feel good to talk with someone about this crazy predicament I'd gotten myself into.

"I'm not brushing you off. Things are just..." Shit, how did I encapsulate the state of my affairs in one or two words? "I don't know. Complicated, I guess?"

"Would talking about it help uncomplicate things?"

"That's just it. I don't think so. I think she and I need to find our way through this mess ourselves. We're the ones who created the problem, you know? We're the ones who have to come up with a solution."

"Oh, no," my sister said warily and then added, "Is she pregnant?"

Fuck it, I decided. I'd just tell her and hope for some useful input. Otherwise she'd keep speculating until she got it right. I didn't want to waste either of our time denying nonsense.

"No, she's not pregnant. Look, I'll tell you, but please don't share this with the folks. I don't want them to get a bad impression of her or get off on the wrong foot. Okay?"

"I'm almost offended you think I would do that. But I'm going to give you a wider margin than normal because clearly you have a lot of balls in the air right now."

"Man, that's putting it mildly," I muttered, but Gray heard me. "Do you remember I went to Las Vegas for a few days? Like a few weeks ago?"

"Yes, of course. Your boss got married, right?" she

clarified.

"That's right. Well, there was a big party afterward—a super loose interpretation of a reception. Everyone got wasted and had an amazing time."

"Fun!" And then she added wistfully, "I love Vegas. I haven't been in so long."

"Well, Agatha and I went to the strip after the reception when everyone else from our group went to their rooms. And, well, we woke up the next morning apparently married. I swear I barely remember any of it, but we have the marriage license complete with the seal from the state of Nevada and both our signatures."

"Ahh, that explains the dayglow-green rings you are both wearing. Okay, so forgive me for oversimplifying here, but can't you just get it annulled? Or revoked or whatever?" my sister asked innocently.

"You're going to think I've gone mad." I took a deep breath and admitted, "But I don't want to."

"Come again?"

"I said I don't want to dissolve the marriage. I want to make it work." I chuckled between sentences. "Hell, if we can make the best out of a really irresponsible decision like this, we can probably take on anything life throws our way."

"Well, that's one way of looking at it. But seems a bit naïve, no? Obviously, I have nothing to draw from here personally, but I'm pretty sure making a marriage succeed takes a lot of hard work."

"So far that seems to be true. And patience. Lots and lots of patience," I told my sister but at the same time couldn't help but notice what was happening to my face. A smile as wide as the 5 freeway in Orange County spread across not just my lips but the entire lower half of my face.

While my wife had the ability to infuriate me, she also brought so much joy and life to my otherwise boring, routine existence. I nodded, basically just agreeing with myself because no one else could see me, but yeah, I wanted to make this work with Agatha. I was determined to make our marriage work.

She just had to get on board with the plan.

CHAPTER SIXTEEN

AGATHA

The day was shot by the time I woke up and felt well enough to get out of bed. I was so thankful Carmen insisted I sleep off whatever hit me at his church. Okay, fine, I knew exactly what happened, but I'd be damned if I'd try to explain it to him and once again be judged for my poor decisions. I could admit to myself, at least, that wasn't one of my finer calls.

It was in the past now, so no use myself up for being so dumb. I certainly learned my lesson and wouldn't be considering cold medicine for a quick edge-smoother anytime soon.

The bedroom was quiet and almost dark. The whole day had slipped away while I'd slept. It felt incredible, though, to have slept that many hours in a row. Why couldn't I do that every night? Knowing at least three others I shared my genetic makeup with also suffered from insomnia led me to believe it was a cell-deep problem. Environment and lifestyle could definitely make it worse, but they rarely made it better. I hadn't found a magical solution yet.

Just then, the door slowly opened, and Carmen poked his head in. Since I was sitting up with all the pillows stacked behind me, he saw me the moment the door opened wide enough.

"Hey, beautiful, how are you feeling?" he asked gently. His cautious smile caused a weird twinge in my stomach, and I stiffened with panic that I'd get sick again.

Okay, not nauseated, I decided after a few moments, but I couldn't quite put my finger on what the feeling was. It could've been guilt. I usually got a hefty dose of that one after pulling a stunt that affected the people around me. I wasn't an ice queen like Shep, after all.

Dropping my gaze to the bedding, I answered, "I'm all right. Much better after so much sleep." I looked up to find his focus squarely on me. "What time is it?"

"Well after five. Closer to six, as a matter of fact. I didn't have the heart to wake you, even though I had at least five personal debates about doing it or not." Again his sheepish smile made my stomach react.

"Truly, I'm glad you didn't. I needed to log some restorative hours. I'm just hoping it doesn't screw with my sleep overnight."

My husband slowly approached the bed and finally sat on the edge by my hip. "You really had me worried, Storm."

"I'm sorry about that. Truly, I am," I replied quietly. When he looked like he was going to start in on a lecture, I put my hand up to stop him. "Please don't lecture me or chastise me right now. I don't think I can deal with it."

He studied me for a long moment. Too long, actually, and I felt uncomfortable under his scrutiny. Finally, he said, "Why would I lecture you for getting sick? That doesn't even make sense."

"Sorry," was all I could come up with and began nervously folding the edge of the sheet back and forth like an accordion.

Silence from both of us for a few more minutes until he asked, "Do you think you can eat something? I can make you some broth or tea or something else that would be easy on your stomach."

"You don't have to do that. I should get up anyway," I replied and pushed the covers down my legs. I don't know why I hadn't noticed before that moment, but when I saw what I was wearing, I asked, "Where are my clothes? My dress..." I trailed off, trying to remember how things unfolded when we arrived home. Really, the last thing I had a clear memory of was barfing on the playground of his church.

"Is it ruined?" I squeaked, afraid to hear the answer.

"No, not at all. A bit wrinkled, but I hung it up in the spare room," he said and thumbed over his shoulder. The way he studied me while he spoke unnerved me. There were definitely things he was holding back from saying, I could tell by his body language. It looked like holding his tongue was causing him physical pain.

"What?" I finally barked, and that one word came out much more aggressively than intended. "Sorry," I muttered and dropped my gaze again. Shit, that was the third time I'd apologized to the man in less than fifteen minutes. Definitely a new personal record, because I rarely used the word in the first place.

Surprise, surprise. Once again, I was so outside of normal with this guy.

Patting his thigh, I explained, "Seriously, that came out way bitchier than I planned." I swung my legs to the side of the bed. I knew better than to just bolt upright after the day I'd had, so I took it step by step.

When I finally stood, I was thankful the world wasn't spinning in a direction that didn't agree with me. My overly attentive mate hovered at my side, though, apparently as concerned as I was.

"All good," I said with a fake, much-too-bright smile. "You really don't have to linger by my side. Seems like all systems are go again."

Carmen gave me a sideways look I couldn't interpret. I couldn't suppress the heavy sigh that escaped and had to consciously instruct myself to hold my head up and shoulders back rather than wither beneath his scrutiny.

By the time we made it to the kitchen, I snapped. The air between us was so burdened with whatever he wasn't saying, I actually felt short of breath.

"All right, Sandoval, out with it," I demanded and leaned against the counter. With my arms folded across my chest, I realized I was sending the wrong body cues, so I dropped them heavily to my sides.

Now it was his turn to deploy an overly bright and phony smile. "Out with what, darling?"

"Don't even try it, man. The energy coming off you is so tense, I think you have something to say and are holding back. For what reason, I can't understand, but I know I'm not picking up on contentment at the moment, like you're trying to sell me with this fake smile."

"Listen, Storm. I just don't want to argue with you. I'm so tired of it, honestly. I know we go from zero to twelve on a scale of ten with our disagreements, and I'm trying to avoid that."

"But you're not denying something's on your mind—"

"I have a shit ton of things on my mind. But given the day you've had—well, that we've had—I don't think this is the time to dig into any of it. Can I get you something? Water? Tea?"

Changing the subject was probably in our best interest. He made good points about our explosive arguing, but problems didn't get solved by ignoring them. I couldn't help that I was a passionate person. I'd always been that way and figured it was part of what a lot of people liked about me. Maybe I was fooling myself?

And that last thought just pissed me off the more I thought about it. Since when did I let a man make me doubt myself? Bullshit.

"Dah?" he said, and I snapped my head in his direction. He totally caught me off guard by using that nickname. Until now, only my family had ever called me that.

"I asked if you want some tea or something."

"Yes, I heard you."

"Then why are you staring off into space and not answering me?"

A stupid grin spread over my whole face, and I knew my yo-yo demeanor was confusing him. So I explained, "You've never called me that before."

"Should I not? I wasn't trying to be disrespectful. I know it's a family nickname, but I like it too. Plus, I'm your damn husband. Isn't that as close as family?"

"I don't mind you saying it. And you know what? A cup of tea sounds lovely. Do you have chamomile?"

"I'll check. I have a whole assortment Gray gave me one year for a gift. I barely ever drink the stuff, so I don't really know what's in here," he explained while taking the lid off one of the canisters that sat on the countertop near the stove. I just assumed they were for decoration, but apparently each one held a little secret.

He busied himself with filling the kettle that I also assumed was part of the kitchen's decor, but apparently people actually used these things. I didn't think my mom ever had a teakettle just sitting on the stove.

While he boiled the water, I riffled through the tea options and found one I liked. "Are you having a cup? Which flavor?"

"Surprise me," he answered with his back toward me.

I grabbed a green tea for him and stood to find two mugs. I still wasn't familiar with where things were kept, so it took opening and closing three cabinets until I found what I was looking for. I grabbed two spoons as well and surveyed the room.

Carmen was a very tidy guy, and this kitchen had his personality all over it when I stopped and looked at it for a moment. The whole process made me grin again, and until he spoke, I didn't realize he had been watching me.

"What are you grinning about?" he asked just as the kettle began to whistle.

"I like it here," I blurted without filtering my thought. Hoping he didn't read too much into my comment, I started to explain more, but he cut me off again.

"I like *you* here," he said earnestly.

His honesty was completely charming. See? Wasn't this better than arguing? Oh, wait, that was his point, not mine. Shit, I guess that meant he was on to something with not wanting to dig into a topic he was convinced would set us off.

We sat in silence while our tea steeped, and some of the edginess dissipated into the atmosphere while the calming chamomile scent wafted up from my cup. I put my face directly over the mug and inhaled deeply. When I looked up from my personal aromatherapy session, Carmen was studying me closely.

Instead of barking the first thing that came to mind, I gave him a soft smile. This one was genuine, and I had a serious hunch he could already spot the difference. Even though I knew the brew would still be too hot, I had to busy myself with something to escape his attention. So I took a sip and immediately regretted it.

"Shit! Hot, so hot!" I patted my bottom lip, hoping to calm the sting.

Carmen was right beside me in a flash. "Let me see," he instructed and pulled my hand away from the burn. He ducked down lower to get a good look and then surprised me by gently kissing me. Instantly I wanted more. There was undeniable physical chemistry between us, and the man's kisses were like an addictive drug. I looped my arms around his neck to hold him close a little longer. He soothed my bottom lip with his tongue before plunging in for a full kiss.

When we parted, we were both grinning.

"Better?" he asked.

"Hmm, I'm not sure. You may have to check again." I smiled bigger and sneaked a quick wink his way. I shouldn't have been surprised when he pulled me to my feet after that bold invitation.

Our height difference was so stark when I was barefoot, so my husband effortlessly lifted me to sit on the island between our cups of tea. He pushed between my legs and bent to kiss me again, and I was happy to oblige.

"You're like a little doll," he said in a low, grumbly voice.

"Is that right?"

"Absolutely."

"Were boys allowed to play with dolls in your house?" I teased and searched his eyes for a clue about what he had planned.

"Hell no!" He laughed and slid my ass to the granite's edge so he could press against me while he plundered my mouth. Jesus, I'd let the man fuck me right here if he wanted. That last kiss was so fucking hot, I whimpered when we parted.

"Your mouth is like a lethal weapon," I told him.

"So many compliments today, Mrs. Sandoval. Careful, or I'll get a big head."

There was some kind of sassy innuendo waiting to be organized in that response, but my head swam with endorphins. I couldn't care to be witty.

"Our tea's getting cold," I finally said for no apparent reason.

I didn't want to stop what we were doing in exchange for sipping tea, but once again, Carmen left me twisted and jumbled and not making much sense. He definitely had some thrall over me I couldn't quite put my finger on. Maybe then I'd be better at warding him off.

Or at least that's what I would do with any other guy. But I was really starting to think he and I had the start of something special here. Maybe if I plugged in and gave our relationship more of an honest effort, we could make this work. I knew I'd been halfheartedly fighting it since we met, even before we were reckless newlyweds.

But what did that look like for a girl like me? I wasn't sure I was cut out for domestication; I certainly wasn't the June Cleaver type of woman.

I wanted a meaningful career and time to myself. Currently I was striking out hard on the first one and had an overabundance of the second while my husband went to work all day. Of course, that's what my own mother did her whole life, but I knew from early on, I'd need more out of each day than changing diapers and wiping up juice spills.

And I got it—for some women, that was a dream come true. Husband who adored them, stay home and raise the children in your own style, not by the head of curriculum at the local day care and on the monthly occasion, lunch with the girls to keep some semblance of social capability.

Yeah . . . not for me at all.

Maybe that was the conversation Carmen and I needed to have before any other. If we had different end goals for this marriage, we were just wasting our time here.

"Hey, where did you go?" My husband was watching me in that scrutinizing way he did.

"Sorry, a million thoughts at all times," I said while tapping my temple. I'd tried explaining this to him before when he busted me faking an orgasm. My brain worked in a way I always thought to be different from most other people.

"You seemed very pensive all of a sudden." He chuckled. "And here I was trying to remember if you had panties on or not."

I shook my head and laughed. Such a guy thing to say.

But now that he'd introduced the topic, why not tease him a little? Pointedly, I looked down at my lap, and he followed my stare. When I started inching the T-shirt I wore up my thighs, he let out an audible groan.

"What?" I tried to appear innocent. That one was a pretty tough sell for me, though.

"You're such a tease," he said with a voice so husky it shot straight to my core. His eyes hadn't moved from where my fingers gripped the material of the shirt.

The feral expression on his gorgeous face gave me the courage to inch it up farther. Then farther still. I leaned forward, looking down at my body, trying to see the view he was getting.

In a flash, he snatched me off the counter and held me in

his strong arms. I wrapped my legs around his torso to ensure I didn't fall. He was easily strong enough to carry me, though. An unexpected giggle bubbled up and out of me, and he met my stare with his matching hungry one.

"Where are you taking me?" I said against his lips before succumbing to his kiss.

Only when we needed more oxygen than we could suck in through our pressed noses, he released me from the kiss and answered, "To our bed. You up for it?"

"Oh, don't go all gentlemanly on me now, mister," I taunted.

"The thought couldn't be further from the ones I'm having," he said as he kicked the door to our room open wider. He stopped by the bedside, still cradling my ass in his hands for support.

"What's wrong?" I asked, alarmed at the way he was looking at me.

"Nothing's wrong. Everything is right," Carmen answered and followed me down onto the bed. I stroked my fingers back through his hair, studying the silky strands as they wove through my hands.

His comment should've set me at ease, but I felt like I had at least three follow-up questions instead. In my mind, I argued with myself about mentioning any of them now or just going with the amazing physical connection we had.

Until a sharp pain caught my attention. "Hey!" I yelped and tried to scramble back from him. The bastard had pinched the inside of my thigh so hard there would undoubtedly be a bruise there by morning.

"Stay with me, Storm," he growled.

My eyes closed as the pain washed through my system.

Whatever inner debate I was having was gone. "Hmmm, okay," I said through a grin.

We spent the rest of the evening in that bed learning a lot about each other's bodies and preferences. If I thought the times we fucked before were amazing, now I had living proof that my sexy husband was just getting warmed up. Finally, I had to beg him to stop, or I wouldn't be able to get out of bed in the morning. The man was a possessed sex god.

And he was all mine.

CHAPTER SEVENTEEN

CARMEN

The temptation to call in sick was the strongest it had ever been. If I could spend another full day with my extraordinary wife, just the two of us, I was convinced we'd both be on the same page where our marital status was concerned, and all her threats the day before about leaving would be long forgotten.

Something changed for the woman yesterday. I wasn't sure if it was the awful events at church, or the time I spent worshiping every inch of her tiny body that did it, but there was a shift in the air between us—and it was definitely for the better.

But I was a responsible man through to the core, and the moment I reminded myself that I was currently the only one bringing in a paycheck, I was trudging to the shower. I still had a few days off but wanted to start socking those away for a legit honeymoon for us. I got the idea the other morning on my run and had been daydreaming about it off and on since then.

It would be the best surprise for her, and from random conversations we'd had, I knew she had never traveled outside the country. She'd explained that her parents had so many children, a trip so extravagant was never in the family's budget. Made sense and gave me a great opportunity to really spoil her.

A soft knock on the bathroom door brought my attention

back to the moment. Agatha poked her head in, and I immediately smelled the coffee in her hand.

"I thought you might like some coffee while you get dressed?" she offered as a timid question.

After I took the steaming mug and set it on the counter, I pulled her into my arms. Her hair was a tangled mess from the sex marathon we'd had, and she'd never looked more beautiful.

I buried my nose in her neck and muttered, "Thank you, baby. So thoughtful."

She wore a tank top and pajama pants, and I swelled with pride when I noticed all the marks on her exposed skin. My grin must've given me away, because she gave me a playful punch to the bicep.

"Pretty proud of yourself, I see."

"I must say, wife, you look pretty well fucked this morning. It looks damn good on you, too."

"My muscles hurt everywhere! You were a maniac. Let's just leave it at that."

Using the coffee mug to try to cover the grin that just kept spreading across my face, I took a big swig. Not sure how she nailed it, but it was exactly the way I would've made a cup for myself.

"How did you know how I like it? This is delicious." I took another sip before rubbing the towel over my head a few times to get my hair moving in the right direction.

"I've seen you make it for yourself a couple of times. Guess I just notice details," she said with a shrug. "Do you have a busy day ahead?"

"I never really know what the day is going to have in store until we're in the middle of it. The joys of being an executive's assistant, I guess. Obviously I see what is already on the calendar for each day, but problems and shit always pop up," I explained between sips.

"Oh, how can you deal with that? Just having to pivot on the fly like that. I'd have an anxiety attack on the hour," she said and forced a laugh. "God"—she shuddered—"that freaks me out just thinking about it. I like a schedule I can count on. I like to know where I will be and when. If something pops up in the middle of my routine, I usually come to a full stop. All productivity stops there because it takes all my focus to redirect my energy."

"I don't think you give yourself enough credit." I was very impressed with how real she was being with me. I powered down the last of the coffee and set the mug on the counter.

But I think my comment unnerved her, because she was very quiet after that. Agatha gave an uneasy smile and snatched the empty cup from where I set it and bustled to the kitchen to put it in the dishwasher.

About ten minutes later, I came through the living room on my way to the front door. "So what do you have planned for today?" I asked my gorgeous girl. I watched as she battled with her first inclination to get defensive but swallowed the reaction down like a bitter pill and refocused.

"Well, I'm finally satisfied with my résumé after working and reworking it a dozen times, so I plan on sending it to every place I can find that's hiring. Maybe some that aren't too." She gave me a sassy little wink after that remark, and I grinned.

I was so proud that she was taking initiative in the job hunting but didn't want to beat it into the ground and ruin the moment. Or hell, maybe even the entire morning with the way one wrong comment could send her straight to irate.

"Awesome. I can't wait to hear about it later. Do you want

me to pick up dinner on my way home for us?" I asked as I slung my bag over my shoulder.

"No, I'm thinking about cooking." She giggled at my skeptical reaction and then added, "Hey! I have some hidden talents you don't even know about yet. My sister isn't the only cook in our house."

"Well, I've tasted her cooking, and if you have a fraction of her talent, sign me up every night!" My excitement probably seemed over the top, but the less we spent on eating out, the better for our budget.

"Okay," my lady said, pushing me with both her small hands on my hip. "Go or you're going to be late. Have a great day." Her normally strong, confident voice turned quiet as my own demeanor suddenly became serious.

I bent down to her height and kissed her chastely. We both lingered there, wanting to deepen the exchange, but we knew I really needed to leave. I groaned low in my throat, and she sighed so hard that her tits heaved up and down in that sexy little top she had on. My groan transformed to a whimper with that delightful view.

We both chuckled, and for me, it was because we were acting like a couple of newlyweds, and I couldn't have asked for a better start to my day. I wanted a life like this more than anything else, but again refrained from beating up a subject we'd discussed before.

Holding out hope she'd come around to wanting the same things I did might have been a foolish thing to do, but at the moment, it was all I had to cling to.

★ ★ ★

"Have you heard a word I've said?" my boss asked impatiently, and I really couldn't blame the guy. By lunch I had recomposed the same fucking email three times. Now, he was standing in front of my desk, snarling at me like an angry guard dog. Not that I blamed him, either. I rarely made mistakes, especially on a task so simple.

"Yes, I heard you. I've apologized and said I would redo it. I'm not sure what more I can say?" I replied, trying my very best to not lose my shit. I was having a terrible time concentrating after attempting to communicate with my wife and being left on read since I'd sent the first message three hours before. The calls I'd tried went straight to voicemail, and the subsequent text messages I'd sent after the first one sat bottlenecked behind the original.

It was taking every shred of willpower I had not to leave and go home and make sure she was okay. After that alien-green emesis episode I'd witnessed the day before, I had myself convinced she was lying facedown, drowning in her own vomit while I dealt with my perfectionist of a boss.

Of course, that thought led to the one that plagued me every time I left her alone.

Was she drinking behind my back? Hell, if she was willing to power down cough medicine to catch a buzz, where would she stop?

And then I'd snap out of it for a few minutes, long enough to convince myself I could trust her. Long enough to fill my own head with bullshit bits of proof we'd turned some imaginary corner and were headed for our happily ever after.

"Dude!" Elijah barked, and judging by the look on his face, it wasn't his first attempt at calling me back to earth.

"Sorry," I muttered. I couldn't even look the man in the

eye at that point. I was fucking up royally, and it was so out of character.

"Maybe you need to call it a day, my friend. I'm not sure what's going on with you today, but clearly your head isn't in the game. You never miss work, man. Take a mental health day and get your head on straight."

"You wouldn't mind? I can finish that email first—" I began to offer, but he held up a hand to stop me.

"Don't worry about it. I'll handle it. But is there anything I can do for you? I may be overstepping here, so just tell me to fuck off, but this has bombshell vibes all over it. Am I in the right neighborhood?"

"Yeah, and again, I'm sorry to let my personal life interfere with my work. I swear this won't become a habit," I insisted while shutting down my computer.

"She okay?"

"I don't know. I can't get a hold of her. For over three hours." I glanced at my phone screen again, like I'd been obsessively doing all morning, then amended my remark. "Well, make that four." I slammed the top drawer of my desk shut so hard that the picture of Gray I kept on top fell over.

"Goddammit," I said and set the frame upright again.

"Okay, calm down a bit, please, or you'll be a danger behind the wheel." He leaned a hip on my desk, blocking me from leaving. He'd get his way if it cost him physical harm, apparently.

"Yesterday she got violently sick at my family's church. She slept most of the day and seemed fine around dinner." I thought briefly about the incredible way we spent the evening and grinned. "Waaay better than fine, actually." I chuckled, trying to give him enough information without saying anything too personal. "This morning she was solid too." I shook my head in confusion. "I can't imagine why she's ghosting me, and every bad scenario I can imagine has been taunting me while I sit here."

Elijah quietly stared at me. When I finally raised my chin toward him, asking him *What?* without speaking, the bastard started laughing.

"You're so fucked it's ridiculous. She's got you chasing your tail, man, and I'm loving it. I remember being in your shoes not that long ago."

"I won't survive too many days like this," I admitted.

"So what made her sick? Anxiety like her sister? Or I guess it could've been a twenty-four-hour bug or something since you said she was fine this morning."

"Anxiety had a lot to do with it, but . . . " I stalled there, and he waited patiently for me to finish the thought. I didn't want to betray her privacy, though. Shit, this was her brother-in-law I was talking to. The very first person he'd go shooting his mouth off to was her sister. I was sure of it.

At the same time, I really needed to talk to someone about what was going on. I was scared I wasn't handling her drinking issues properly, and I didn't want to let her down.

"Spill it, man. You'll feel so much better just getting it off your chest. You know whatever you say to me stays right here, right? I know I'm married to your sister-in-law, but we need to vent from time to time too. You can trust me."

Elijah was the most honest person I'd ever met. There were times the characteristic made him very unpopular because people didn't always want to hear the truth. But I knew if he was vowing something to me, he meant it.

After exhaling a long, slow breath, I admitted my greatest

fear. "I think she has a drinking problem."

His reaction was steady, almost like he might have thought the same thing at some point himself. Okay, that was probably me projecting, but there was no way I was the only one who saw the way my wife could throw drinks down like a frat boy.

"I'm sure you're not saying that without cause. Personally, I've seen the girl shitfaced more times than not, but that's not really a fair observation because we've been celebrating one thing or another every time I've been with the family," he offered with a kind smile. "Also, now that Hannah and I have dried out with the baby coming, it seems like everyone and their mom drinks too much."

I chuckled at that comment. I had experienced the same thing whenever I was the designated driver out with a group of friends. Instantly, I turned into everyone's babysitter.

Maybe I *was* overreacting.

Then I remembered that damn cough medicine bottle I found under the bathroom sink. Yeah, I wasn't overreacting at all. That was not something most people would claim trying in their life, let alone before meeting their new in-laws at Sunday mass!

No matter what, I wasn't comfortable spilling that tea to my boss. He could reassure me twenty more times, but that skeleton needed to stay locked in our marital closet forever.

"Have you talked to her about your feelings?" Elijah asked, and something about the tone of voice or the way he cocked his head to the side while posing it made me bark out a laugh.

"Sorry." I snorted. "You sound so much like a stereotypical shrink it's uncanny. Yes, I've expressed my concern, my displeasure, my alarm on an occasion or two." I shook my head. "She blows me off every time I bring it up."

"Okay, I can picture her doing that. Have you considered getting professional intervention? Are you to that point? I guess what I'm asking is, is the problem that big, or is it something that bothers you and apparently no one else?"

I had to give the man credit. He was very good at getting me to organize my thoughts and feelings on the matter, if nothing else. I thought about the question longer than the others so far and finally answered honestly.

"I don't think it's just me. But these women of ours are very headstrong."

"Preach on, brother. Preach on," Elijah muttered.

I grinned. "She doesn't see anything wrong with her behavior, even though I've seen her turn to alcohol as a coping device on numerous occasions. And seriously, we haven't been together that long. It's not the usual kind of social drinking she cons herself into thinking it is, either."

As I was telling my brother-in-law the situation, I really heard my own words. And I didn't like them. The person I needed to talk with about all these concerns was the woman I'd married.

"I think we can get through it. I'm just worried about her. I've really fallen for the girl. Hard. I want things to work out between us, regardless of how irresponsible our relationship's start was. You know? I'm just worried about her." Repeating that last comment had me questioning who I was really trying to convince.

"Yeah, man, I get it. And I understand the need to care for your woman better than a lot of people do. Trust me." He was quiet for a long pause, and I knew from experience he was really measuring his next remark.

"I'm not sure you want my opinion." He studied me with very attentive ice-green eyes and then added, "But I'm going to give it to you anyway." He laughed. "Go talk to her. Everything you've brought up in this conversation needs to be handled with her."

Leaving out any hint that I'd just concluded the exact same thing, I said, "You know, that's good advice." I smiled and stood, making it clear I was leaving. Now I would push past him if he didn't vacate his perch on the corner of my desk and allow me passage.

Before I was out of earshot, I called back over my shoulder to where Elijah lingered near my desk. "Thanks again, man. You're a pretty good guy, boss."

He spread his arms wide with a mischievous grin to match in size. "I keep trying to tell you." He laughed. The comment was a reflection on a bit he and I exchanged nearly every time he left the office. Though the roles were usually reversed—he was typically the one in a mad dash somewhere, and I was left to hold down the fort.

Thankfully I was well ahead of the heavy stream of commuters that made the daily trek in and out of the city from their suburban homes. I had to remind myself to slow down several times, though. A speeding ticket would be a major hit to our household budget, and I didn't need that extra stress on top of everything else.

Please let her be okay.

Maybe she'd gone back to sleep and was really catching up on rest. Her sleep debt was bigger than the nation's fiscal one, so it was totally plausible.

But what if I found her unconscious? Or not breathing? Could I remember the steps for performing CPR? Would I be emotionally available to do that if necessary?

Christ, I was getting myself more worked up with every mile I traveled. I took a deep breath and blew it out through pressed lips. Yeah ... that didn't help at all. Gave it a few more tries and just felt worse.

My back tires squealed on the blacktop as I circled the apartment complex's parking lot before settling into my designated space. Beside mine sat her little piece of shit car right where it had been parked for days.

So why did my anxiety kick up a notch instead of cool down? I should be thrilled she wasn't out tying one on somewhere. If I ever found out she drove after one of her binges, I'd spank her little ass until it glowed red like Rudolph's schnoz.

Right now, my runaway imagination painted a macabre scene inside the apartment, knowing she was in there but not responding to me.

All fucking day!

Taking the stairs two at a time, I thrust my key into the lock and forced myself to stop. Breathe. Settle down. No matter what I was about to walk in on, coming in that hot wouldn't help either of us.

The apartment was dark and quiet. The blinds were still drawn from overnight, so the only natural light in the entire place came from the slim transom window alongside the door. When I listened, there was no evidence of a show playing on the television or even background music playing while she worked on job hunting.

My pace increased as I checked empty room after empty room and then pulled up short at our closed bedroom door.

I thrust the damn thing open, thinking I'd just rip the

bandage off. The room was dark as well, and the bathroom door was pulled closed. A crack of light could be seen beneath the wafer-thin panel, and I heard water sloshing in the tub. Bile rose in my throat.

Please don't let her be floating in there.

I'd never recover from losing her.

With a stiff arm, I threw the door open and saw her. Okay... first, I heard her. My wife sat up from where she had been soaking up to her chin in bubbles and gave a deafening screech. Immediately I rushed to her and scared her even more.

"Carmen! What is it? What's wrong?" she yelled at what had to be the fullest capacity of her lungs.

"What? I was so worried! Why are you asking me what's wrong? What's wrong with you? Where the hell have you been?" My volume matched hers, and our combined frantic voices bounced around the heavily tiled room like the crashing metal of a ten-car pileup.

Down on my knees at the tub's edge, I gripped her shoulders and shook her. Water sloshed over the lip of the tub and doused my pants and the floor.

She threw my hands off her body with violent force, and I froze. The horrified look on her face would haunt me for years because I was the one who'd caused it.

I dropped back to rest my weight on my heels and cradled my face in my hands.

I was a fucking basket case, and there she was—totally fine. Wet and pissed like a cat caught out in the rain and never sexier—I took a millisecond to notice. But completely fine. My anxious mind had me so spun up, my heart jackhammered in my chest. I couldn't gulp down enough air, and I felt like I was moments from fracturing into a million pieces.

"Carmen?" she asked again, this time much quieter, but I couldn't look at her.

I was angry and embarrassed and at least five other things I couldn't organize to identify. My entire body shook from the adrenaline spike, and I felt her small hands grip my wrists and tug.

"What's going on? Did something happen?" she asked gently while trying to move my hands from hiding my shame. "Please talk to me." That last comment broke me. Well, not the words, but the tone of her voice when she beseeched me.

Tears I didn't want to shed broke free and coursed over my cheekbones and down around my jaw. I couldn't do anything but purge the self-induced madness one tear at a time.

Finally, I lifted my head and met her waiting, imploring blue eyes.

Fuck me, she was beautiful. Her empathy just made me cry harder. What the fuck was going on, though? Maybe this was what people meant when they described a nervous breakdown.

And she was naked and dripping wet, just to add guilt to my heap of misery. I scrambled to my feet and searched frantically in the small room for her towel.

Trying to clear my throat of the raw emotion, I said, "Here, baby. You're cold."

"I don't care." She batted at my towel-clad hands. "Please tell me what's going on. You looked like you saw a ghost when you burst through that door," she said while I ignored her defenses and patted her dry with the towel. If she wouldn't take the bath sheet and dry herself, I'd do it for her. Hell, I'd do it for her every time she bathed if she would let me.

"And why are you home so early?" she added as if it just occurred to her my behavior wasn't the only odd detail here.

"Where's your robe? You're going to get sick. I know how cold you are after the shower."

"Please answer me." She stepped back and out of my reach so I would finally still. I stared at her for long moments, trying to come up with an explanation for my erratic behavior.

I bowed my head until my chin met my chest and wiped my cheeks with the backs of my fists. The embarrassment was so stifling, I couldn't organize my thoughts.

"I was worried," I croaked, knowing damn well that didn't explain much. Her confused expression proved my thought. I filled my lungs with a slow, deep breath and then exhaled. "I was so worried, baby. You can't begin to imagine what I was coming up with in my head while I drove here. I thought for sure you were dead."

And I panicked.

I'd just found this vivacious, intelligent, beautiful human, and the thought of her being taken from me so soon gutted me. A mournful sound came from the center of my chest, and my stunning bride patiently waited for more of an explanation. That sound alarmed her, though, and she stepped in closer to comfort me.

"I tried calling you, and texting you, and you didn't even read them. They just sat there. With every minute that ticked by, my anxiety ratcheted up. Thanks to yesterday's episode, by the time I got here, I had myself convinced you had either drown in your own vomit, or hell, I don't know. I freaked out."

"Oh, baby," she cooed and stroked her hands up and down my arms.

"Where's your phone? Why didn't you answer me?" I

demanded then. Now that I saw she was fine, my embarrassment was morphing back to anger.

Her eyes darted around the room wildly. No way she even saw where she was looking, and no, the device wasn't lying on the floor of the bathroom. "I don't even know, to be honest. Probably still in my handbag from church yesterday. You know that thing is just a nuisance to me." She let out a little chuckle and added, "It's probably dead at this point."

I'd just shaved at least five years off my life from panic, and she thought it was amusing? I sucked in a deep breath to go off on her and put on the brakes before a single stupid word crossed my lips.

Fighting wouldn't solve anything here.

"Carmen, listen," she said while standing. She went out into the bedroom and climbed onto the bed. "Come sit with me, please. Clearly we need to talk about whatever's really going on," she said calmly. "You can't possibly react this way every time I'm not at your immediate beck and call. It's not reasonable."

I joined her on the bed and snuggled up alongside her, laying my head in her lap when she motioned a sort of invitation. I could stay nestled in that paradise for days. She ran her fingers through my hair, attempting to tame the wild mess it had become during my hysteria.

"Talk to me, please," she said quietly and stopped the petting as my cue.

At that point, I had to clear up the things that were eating away at my insides. If I felt more confident that she was taking care of herself when I wasn't around, maybe I'd worry less.

"Can we talk about yesterday?" I asked carefully. I didn't want any of my questions to be the figurative pin from the grenade of her temper.

"Ohhhh kaaaay," Agatha replied with caution. Couldn't blame her, really.

"I know what you did," I admitted and instantly hated how the words sounded on the air. So accusatory . . . and really, they were. I'd leveled the accusation and wanted her to defend her choices.

"Yes, your whole churchy family does. Those poor kids in that classroom are probably traumatized." She chuckled, and again the lighthearted attitude was like nails on a chalkboard.

"I mean, I know why you got sick. And why it was the color it was."

There. That pretty much spelled out what I was doing such a shit job at saying.

"Okay," she plainly offered.

"Just okay? Do you want to say anything else about it?"

"Do you?" Her question ricocheted back so fast, I momentarily wondered if I'd said her part too.

I sat up then, wanting to be looking at her while we had the rest of this conversation. My nerves were settled, and I felt more clearheaded. "I'm not sure where to begin, really. There's a lot I could say—"

She went from red-hot temper to cool, calm, and collected in seconds. It was unnerving the way she could mask her emotions. We'd have to tackle that habit at a later date, though. Rome wasn't built in a day, right?

"I was very nervous yesterday morning, as you know." She looked to me as if she wanted a response, so I nodded. It was the truth. I'd known she didn't want to go in the first place, and I'd insisted she do it anyway. I had to fight the urge to fall on the sword and take all the blame. Even though her resulting behavior was the real problem and only she could account for it.

My wife continued explaining. "While I was getting ready, I found cold medicine beneath the sink. I remembered when we were in high school, we used to shoot that nasty shit." She physically shuddered at the memory. "In a moment of admittedly"—she raised her hand over head as if hushing a crowd—"very poor judgment, I drank some. It didn't end well. The end." She gave a careless shrug like the matter was done and buried.

"Agatha." I sighed.

She took my hands in hers and held them while begging, "I'm going to implore you not to nag me about the decision on top of everything else I suffered for it. Honestly, Carmen, it was stupid. Lesson learned. Can we just leave it there?"

I stared at her for a long time. Longer than she was comfortable with, because she was first to break the gaze and fidget with the bedding.

"Baby, listen. I don't want to be the nag, or the wet blanket, or whatever. I'm worried about you. I don't want to lose you to a decision as stupid as that or worse. Does where I'm coming from make sense at all?"

She had to see that I was doing all this from the right place in my heart. I continued to explain how that bullshit yesterday led to my meltdown today.

"With that so fresh on the brain"—I tapped my temple—"today, when I couldn't get in touch with you, I freaked out. And I can admit fault here too. That was way over the top. I know that. I'm completely embarrassed, honestly."

Her sweet smile was genuine this time. "It was sort of sweet. The way you came busting in here, ready to save the day, all action hero style."

"Yeah, but I left work early, so now I won't get paid for a full day. And I'll have to explain to Elijah why I was acting so crazy—"

"Don't you dare tell him, Carmen. He will turn right around and tell my sister, and my *Gggooooddd...*" She emphasized the word like a teenager mid-rant. "You think *you* overreacted? You haven't seen anything until you see the perfect Hannah lose her shit."

Okay... there was something buried right beneath the surface on that comment too, but we needed to stay on topic or nothing would get solved. I almost wondered if she did that to get the spotlight off herself and distract me with a different topic.

"Calm down," I said and swept her hands in mine again. "I'm always careful not to air our laundry where he can see, you know? Trust me on that."

"Fair enough." She nodded. "But you're going to have to start trusting me too. You can't overreact that way every time you don't get in touch the second you try. I have a life too. It may not meet your approval, the things I've been choosing to do throughout the day, but I'm trying to get my shit together. I really am."

"All right. All right." She made a good point, and it was only fair to give the same trust I was asking for from her. "Can I ask you another question?"

"Umm, I'm not sure I have a choice here. Kinda feels like I'm on the witness stand, you know?"

"Well, I'm sorry about that. It's not my intention." Silence filled the room because I wanted her permission to keep digging in on this drinking issue.

"Go. Shoot. Ask what you want to ask," she finally caved. "Let's get this over with," she muttered.

And I wouldn't let the snarky tone derail me, either. "Have you been drinking behind my back any other times? Besides the cough syrup, I mean."

"No," she snapped instantly. But she also didn't add more.

"I'm really not trying to interrogate you. I just want you to shoot straight with me. You know I've been bothered with this issue since Vegas. I don't want to watch you waste your abundant talent and potential because it's an easy balm to some unaddressed wound."

"Christ, you sound like a shrink," she teased but with enough bite to it to make me pause. I thought she was kidding, anyway...

CHAPTER EIGHTEEN

AGATHA

By now, I was hanging on to my good nature by my fingernails. I'd thought when I moved out of my parents' house, these types of Q&A sessions were done. The last person I would expect to have to answer to like this was my husband.

So why was that bitch Guilt dancing the Watusi all over my heart?

The answer was as plain as the hopeful look on my guy's face. Because I cared about the man. If I shot straight with myself for a change, it was even more than that.

Fucking feelings. Never was good at the things. And this one was growing and gaining momentum like a snowball rolling downhill. These heart-to-hearts he insisted on having were partly to blame. The mind-blowing sex we had the night before and every other time before that added to the big picture too. Then there were the quiet moments we spent together. Not saying anything, just existing in the same space.

Carmen was digging deeper into my heart with every passing day. Now I didn't wonder if we could last a year. I worried it would go too fast and be over before I was ready to cut him loose.

Then what?

"Are you going to expand on that?" he asked with an

expression that made it very clear he wanted me to.

"I don't think it's the issue you keep trying to make it into," I said as calmly as possible. In my head, I started counting backward from ten in Spanish. It was one of the many, many tricks I had to survive conversations I didn't want to be having.

Unexpectedly, he reached out and finger-combed my loose hair across my forehead. It was such a gentle gesture, I let my eyes droop closed and enjoyed the contact.

"Can we make a pact? Regarding the binge drinking?"

Well, that ruined the moment he was building. I'd had all I could take of this topic. "There is no binge drinking. And seriously, Carmen, I've heard all I can handle on this, so maybe lay off or there's going to be a blowout."

That seemed fair. If he thought it was okay to keep needling someone about something, then he'd have to deal with the consequence. At least I was trying to give him a little heads-up on the impending explosion.

"Baby, listen. Ignoring the problem isn't going to make it go away," he said.

Talking to me like a five-year-old was the wrong approach too.

I surged to my feet and shouted, "There is no problem! I said enough!" My voice was loud normally. When I put some gusto behind it, it was like thunder.

However, my ballsy husband was unmoved. He sat quietly in the same spot on the bed and watched me grandstand.

"Are you happy?" I bellowed. "Is this what you wanted? Do you enjoy watching me come unglued? I told you to drop it. I told you there isn't a problem! Therefore, there's nothing to deal with. If you're one of those people who is only content when they're saving someone in crisis, go find someone else.

Don't insist there's one here so you can play the hero!"

When I was finished delivering that mini tirade, my whole rib cage was pumping up and down, trying to allow more air into my lungs. With arms defiantly folded across my chest, I glared down at my man.

Finally, he calmly asked, "Are you finished?"

I shrugged. Then shrugged again. "Yeah, I think so. Are you?"

Carmen rose from the bed and prowled toward me. I wasn't about to step back or cower in any way. But the expression on his face was intense. A little unnerving, definitely commanding, and seriously—hotter than hell.

When we were toe to toe, he bent over my much shorter frame until his lips were right beside my ear. In a dark, sexy timbre, he leveled his promise. "The next time you throw a temper tantrum like a child, you'll be punished like one too. Have I made myself clear?"

He maneuvered so I could meet his serious stare, and I huffed. *Fuck.* His nearness and dark, promising tone scrambled my brain, so I couldn't formulate a response. The only thing I could concentrate on were the goose bumps popping up on my arms and thighs by the thousands. And it wasn't because the air conditioning had kicked on during that little episode.

"Answer me, Storm," he insisted while holding me captive in his gaze.

"*Wha?* What? Answer what?" I sputtered and gave my head a little shake. The bastard knew he had me.

His lips spread into a cocky grin while he repeated the question. "I asked you if I'd made myself clear."

"Yes. Abundantly," I responded. The eye roll wasn't meant to poke the beast looming over me, but apparently it did just that.

Before I could make sense of what he had planned, I was hanging upside down over the bossy man's shoulder. The laugh that poured out of my body seemed to be victim to gravity, because as I hung there, the laughter just drained out.

"Put me down, caveman," I wheezed between snorts. "Seriously, I'm getting dizzy!"

With very little grace, he flopped me onto the bed and followed right down to loom over my whole body with his.

"That's one," he growled just before biting my neck.

I gripped his shoulders while his face was buried in the crook of my neck, originally thinking I'd push him away. But after his wet tongue soothed the first bite, I changed my mind. Now I wanted to hold him there for many more minutes so he could do all the punishing he felt fit.

"One what?" I asked after a long moan sneaked out.

"Keep acting like a brat, and you'll find out," he growled.

"Mmmm, okay." I'd act like the biggest brat he'd ever seen if this was the terrible price I'd pay.

We spent the rest of the afternoon in bed, and by dinner we were both starving.

"Do you want some dinner? I'll go see what I can come up with," I offered while pulling on a pair of yoga pants.

When Carmen didn't answer, I turned to face him. "What's up? Did you hear me?"

"Yeah, I heard you. And yes, I would love something to eat. But if you keep those pants on, I can't really be responsible for my actions," he answered while staring at my ass.

"Do you ever get enough, husband?" I teased and wiggled my bottom for him.

"Woooommaan." He drew out the word while advancing toward me.

But I was quicker for once and took off out the door of our room and into the kitchen, laughing like a lunatic the entire time.

While I was digging around in the freezer, Carmen came up behind me and snaked his arms around my waist. It felt so good to lean back into his body and just be held there. Cold fog lightly billowed out from the open appliance while we stood there entwined.

"This is nice." I sighed and reached back to cradle his face in my palm. He tugged me away from the freezer and shut the door with his foot so he wouldn't have to let go of my body. When he didn't respond to my comment, I turned in his arms and looked up at his very serious expression.

"What's going on? You look very pensive."

In the next moment, I was very grateful for his support because his words might have knocked me off my feet.

"I'm falling in love with you," he confessed. "And it scares the shit out of me."

Dumbstruck. Speechless. Yep, I was both of those. But I also knew this was one of those defining moments people always talk about. It couldn't have been clearer if a clown rode through the kitchen on a miniature bike while holding a sign announcing it.

While that image had me about to laugh, I also knew this wasn't the right time for jokes.

"You're so brave," I told him. And admittedly, it might have been an odd choice in the moment.

"Brave? I just told you I was scared shitless."

I interrupted before he launched into a lecture about paying attention. "You're so brave the way you talk about your feelings. I wish I were like that."

"You can be. Just tell me how you're feeling."

"That puts me in a very vulnerable situation. I don't like that feeling. I think too many times in my life I've been ridiculed for being passionate about things—or people—or maybe taken advantage of because of my feelings?" I shook my head a bit. "I'm not sure if that makes sense."

"It makes perfect sense. I'm sensing a theme here, though." He waved his hand back and forth between our bodies. "Between us."

I cocked my head to one side, basically urging him to explain.

"Trust. We have trust issues. Both of us."

"It kind of makes sense, given the timeline of our relationship, don't you think?"

"Absolutely. But, Storm, listen to me. I'm not going to hurt you. You have to know at this point I'm fully committed here."

I nodded. "I get that. And hopefully I've been doing a better job and reciprocating. I've been trying."

"Does it freak you out? What I just said?"

"No. Not really."

But instead of being content with my response, he let out a sufferable sigh.

"Was that the wrong answer? I'm confused—"

"No. There are no wrong answers when talking about your feelings. How you feel is how you feel."

"Then why the heavy breathing?"

"Every time I pitch one right over the plate for you to take a solid swing at, you bunt."

"Okay, now I'm completely lost. Are you talking about a sport?"

"It's a metaphor, darling." He grinned. "When I start a

conversation that would be the perfect opportunity for you to open up a little, you breadcrumb me with two-word answers."

I saw the point after he explained and truly felt like that was my blond moment allotment for the week. So I tried to explain. "I'm very new to all this open sharing. I haven't been in a long-term relationship."

"Ever?"

"Never. It was never something that appealed to me."

"And now? But see, this is what I'm talking about. I feel like I have to drag every sentence out of you."

"Like I said, this is new to me. Hopefully you won't run out of patience before I'm a sharing shaman like you are." I smiled and poked a finger into his abdomen.

That one made him laugh, at least. And I realized that was a pretty typical way for me to handle serious feelings. I made jokes instead to distract my partner.

But Carmen deserved more from me. I already knew losing him would be a major fuck-up. It would be hard and lonely and filled with regrets.

I couldn't meet his eyes when I said, "I feel the same." If he heard me at all, it would be a shocker. My voice was normally strong and resonant, but that admission sounded like a whisper.

He studied me for a long time until I began to fidget. Finally he said, "And how is that? What is the *same*?"

I met his handsome brown stare and gave him the best pleading look I could. "You know. What you said."

"Say it to me, Agatha. Say it out loud. Baby steps," he encouraged with that boyish smile that melted me every time.

"I—" I studied my sock-covered feet until his entered my line of sight too. He hooked his index finger under my chin and lifted my face to him.

"I'm—" *Fuck! Why is this so hard?*

Because I didn't want to set myself up to be hurt. It was that simple. But it would hurt worse without him, and if I couldn't trust him with my feelings, how did I think I could build a life with the man?

"I'm falling in love with you too." I choked on the emotion balled in my throat.

The moment I saw the joy on his face, I felt better. He beamed like the proud new owner of a fancy car, and my smile unconsciously matched his.

"Thank you," he said after giving me a tender kiss. "I won't betray you. Okay? I promise."

"Okay," I said in a shaky voice and stepped closer to him, hoping he would wrap me in the safety of his arms.

He knew exactly what I needed, and we stood embraced in the middle of the kitchen for many minutes.

"We have something really good here, Storm. If we vow to be honest and open with each other, I know we can make this work."

"And patient. Carmen, you have to be more patient with me."

He gave me that sexy, mischievous smile then and pulled me even closer and kissed the top of my head.

"Yes, wife."

Continue Reading for a preview of the next Brentwood
Bombsells Novel:

Mentoring Maye

EXCERPT FROM
MENTORING MAYE

MAYE

With an outstretched hand on the knob, I was about to tell Joel we could catch up later, but the door was pulled open from the inside, and Professor Chaplin loomed in the doorway with a disapproving scowl.

"If you don't mind, this isn't the social quad. Some of us are trying to work," he hissed bitterly.

"Oh, sorry. You're right. I— I— Uhh..." I stammered like a fool while Joel began backing away. Freaking coward was going to hightail it out of there and not even own up to the fact he was the one making all the noise.

"Ms. Farsey, I believe we have a meeting scheduled?" Dr. Chaplin asked. He gave Joel a once-over and said, "Run along, son. You can talk to your girlfriend when she's done here."

I stepped across the threshold while explaining, "He's not my boyfriend. Honestly, I don't know what he wanted. I was just about—"

He stopped me with a raised hand. "None of that concerns me," he said dryly and took the seat behind his desk in the cramped space. There was a plain folder and two pencils in the center of the desk and nothing else. Not even a laptop. Bookshelves lined the wall behind him, and my eyes darted from title to title on the perfectly aligned spines.

The dude had an eclectic selection for sure, but I was tongue-tied after the whole Joel scene to comment about any of them. Since I was an avid reader, it could've been a way to break the ice with the man, but the opportunity was gone before I could gather my wits.

"Sit down," he instructed, and I dropped gracelessly into the uncomfortable wooden chair. The back was mounted on a semicircle of spindles, which dug into my spine when I leaned back.

"You applied for an internship with the grant-writing program. Is that correct?" he asked while boring a hole in the center of my forehead with his dark, intense stare.

"Yes, that's correct. I'm excited to find—" I began to answer but the man cut me off again.

"You've been chosen to work directly with me for the next ten weeks. I'm applying for three separate grants on behalf of the psychology department and require assistance. Your performance, attendance, and tested knowledge will compose your final grade in my class and can secure a scholarship within our graduate program here at the university. Do you have any questions?"

"Umm, noooo, I don't think so." This was the last thing I expected to hear today and wasn't sure I could handle an entire summer with this jerk. "Not at this time, at least," was my initial response, but I quickly started formulating a host of them, though. "Okay, actually, how many other interns will be working on these grants besides me?"

"It's a one-on-one learning opportunity, Ms. Farsey. You

were selected by the professors of the department for the position, so I suggest you seriously consider the offer as the privilege it is."

Thankfully, my brain came back online, and I asked an important question rather than blurt out any one of the *What the fuck?* type that were clogging up the works in there.

"Thank you." I forced a smile through clenched teeth. "When do you need my decision?"

"Friday, five o'clock. We have a lot of work to accomplish, so if you aren't going to take the spot, I'll still have to interview other candidates."

"Not that this was an interview," I muttered and immediately regretted letting that slip out. When I met his icy glare, I knew he had heard me.

A quick grin sneaked out from his guarded features, but he reined it back in so fast I questioned if it had happened. "No, I suppose it wasn't." He didn't offer anything after that, so silence ballooned between us.

He stood from his much more comfortable chair, and I automatically rose as well. Apparently, our non-interview was over, and I was being dismissed.

"A word of advice, Ms. Farsey," Dr. Chaplin began, and I raised a brow with curiosity about what he had to offer. "If you do accept the position"—he paused until I nodded—"leave the boyfriend at home."

"He's not my boyfriend," I said for the second time, knowing full well the man didn't care what my response was. But my upbringing automatically kicked in, and I offered him my hand to shake. "Thank you for the opportunity. I'll be in touch."

There was no way I would walk out of that office like a

scolded puppy. I felt triumphant to have had the last word. But my bravado crumbled when the door clapped shut right behind me as I left.

My whole body trembled, and I was furious with myself for letting that guy get under my skin. I was even more frustrated with the man himself for acting like such a dick. If he didn't like me, why personally choose me for the spot? Did I really want to spend the next ten weeks in an uncomfortable environment?

ANDREW

I held my breath until the infuriating clacking from her sandals was no longer perceivable from the empty hallway. But her alluring scent was still there when I finally inhaled again. That perfume she wore—day in and day out. It would drive any man insane. It was mystifying how the woman didn't have a trail of desperate suitors following her everywhere she went instead of just one loser who accompanied her to my door.

Similarly mystifying was how I willed my cock to stay flaccid while she sat directly across from me in my cramped office. I had to be the world's biggest glutton for punishment offering her the internship. If there were any sort of divine power in the universe, it would have intervened and swayed her to decline the opportunity. At the same time, we would have both been protected from the raw lust that ignited in my body in her presence.

I'd been teaching for eight years. It was never my intention to land here in my career path, but, well, here I was. Never, and I truly meant ever, had I been attracted to a student. Faculty knew what a tangled web it was to engage with students outside the classroom. In fact, when I was hired at this university years ago, there was an entire day of orientation devoted to not fucking around with your students.

Maybe a refresher course was in order.

★ ★ ★

Two days went by with no word from Ms. Farsey. Twice I had composed email messages reminding her I was awaiting her response, and twice I regained my sanity before sending the messages. But now I was getting pissed because the woman had me tied up in knots and didn't even know it. She would never know it. But if she refused the position, I was in for the longest summer of my life. If she accepted, it may actually be worse.

She'd be a complete fool to turn me down. There was so much I could teach her that would secure her place in the graduate program. I thought surely it would sway her decision when I added the scholarship icing to the cake. Yet here I still sat. Waiting. Waiting to get a message from a woman who was at least fifteen years my junior, likely more.

I'd been fighting the urge to snoop in her personal files in the school's system, but if she made me wait much longer, I could find out where she lived and go pay her a visit.

"Get a fucking grip, man," I mumbled beneath my breath. I was thinking like a horny boy, and enough was enough. If Maye Farsey was too much of a snob to realize the gift I was offering her, I'd move on to the next candidate.

The problem was, she was truly the best qualified of all my class rosters. And she never gave me the impression she was a snob. I'd spent a lot of time—and I do mean a lot—watching her when she was deeply engrossed in whatever she was doing. The woman was immeasurably kind, conscientious, and compassionate. It was also impossible to overlook how often the word *young* seemed to sneak into all my thoughts about her too.

My email pinged that a new message arrived, and my breath caught in my chest. It had been the same routine for the past two days every time that damn chime went off. I had switched the sound off so many times, only to give in and turn it back on to ensure I didn't miss a message while preoccupied.

Not that I had been getting any actual work done. I wanted to beat myself over the head with something big and heavy. I couldn't remember feeling so enthralled by a woman. Ever. When I tried to pinpoint what it was about this female specifically, I spent too long focusing on all her attributes and ended up in the private restroom across the hall with my dick in my fist.

Enough already!

When I opened the email program on the school-issued laptop, my heart rate doubled. The only new message in the incoming queue was finally from her.

Dear Dr. Chaplin,

I wanted to thank you again for taking the time to meet with me regarding the summer internship. After much consideration, I'm happy to accept the offer and look forward to receiving further instruction regarding the hours we will work, location, and so forth. You can respond to this email address, as I check it often. Also, my cell phone number is (925) 555-3038.

Kindly,

Maye L. Farsey

Calmly I closed the lid of the computer and sat back in my seat. With my index fingers steepled beneath my chin, I sat there for long minutes contemplating what I was getting myself into.

Maye L. Farsey. My imagination took off trying to think of perfect middle names that lone letter could represent. Was it an ordinary name like Lynn? Or something more creative like Luna? At this point in my teaching career, I'd seen so many unusual names, I could spend the rest of the day guessing and still not get it right.

Would the temptation of the woman be too great? I could lose my job and therefore, the last ten years of my life. I was being considered for tenure, a goal I had set for myself when first hired. Having a guaranteed contract with the university would take so much worry off my plate. Living in Los Angeles was unreasonably expensive, plus I had been supporting my mother in Nebraska since my father passed away three years ago. Counting on the annual cost of living increases the university offered with tenure would ensure I could stay in the area and continue doing what I loved: teaching and applying for grants on behalf of the school.

When I reminded myself of all the things I busted my ass for over the past decade, and all the responsibilities weighing me down, I felt like an immature boy for devoting so much time to crushing on a student. It wasn't simply amoral. It was career suicide. Ending my career would mean instant financial crisis, and I owed my mother and, frankly, myself, more than that sort of recklessness.

Those thoughts cemented a healthier mindset. Maye Farsey would complete the internship under my direction, and when the summer was over, our relationship would be nothing more than it currently was. I was a forty-year-old man for Christ's sake. My hormones didn't dictate my actions when I was a younger man. They certainly wouldn't now either.

Just to remain on the safe side, I decided to respond to her via email. If I had to listen to that husky, alto voice over the phone, I'd be trapped in my office again until my dick settled down.

Dear Ms. Farsey,

The internship program dictates you work alongside your mentor for at least fifteen hours each week. I've attached a copy of the university's requirements you should have received when applying. Please make yourself familiar with the expectations so we don't have to waste the valuable time we have together.

The first week we will meet in my business office on campus, but the location will potentially change as research becomes necessary. Please secure reliable transportation, as only one absence is acceptable. As you know from my classroom procedures, I do not tolerate tardiness. The same applies for this opportunity.

Our first session will start Wednesday morning at 8:00 a.m. Be prompt. A laptop, notebook, and writing implement will be necessary.

Sincerely,

Dr. Andrew Chaplin

ALSO BY VICTORIA BLUE

Shark's Edge Series:
(with Angel Payne)
Shark's Edge
Shark's Pride
Shark's Rise
Grant's Heat
Grant's Flame
Grant's Blaze

★

Elijah's Whim
Elijah's Want
Elijah's Need
Jacob's Star
Jacob's Eclipse

Bombshells of Brentwood :
Accepting Agatha
Mentoring Maye

Misadventures:
Misadventures with a Book Boyfriend
Misadventures at City Hall

Secrets of Stone Series:
(with Angel Payne)
No Prince Charming
No More Masquerade
No Perfect Princess
No Magic Moment
No Lucky Number
No Simple Sacrifice
No Broken Bond
No White Knight
No Longer Lost

**For a full list of Victoria's other titles,
visit her at VictoriaBlue.com**

ACKNOWLEDGMENTS

Big thanks to the team at Waterhouse Press, who has lent their time and individual talents to make my words shine. I'm also thankful for the Waterhouse proofing, copyediting, and formatting teams. Thank you for your keen eye and attention to detail.

Thank you to the talented ladies on my personal team. Megan Ashley, Amy Bourne, and Faith Moreno, thank you from the bottom of my heart for the daily efforts you put forth to keep me on track. I couldn't do any of this without you.

As always, thank you to the readers. Without you, stories would go untold. I appreciate each and every one of you.

ABOUT VICTORIA BLUE

International bestselling author Victoria Blue lives in her own portion of the galaxy known as Southern California. There, she finds the love and life-sustaining power of one amazing sun, two unique and awe-inspiring planets, and four indifferent yet comforting moons. Life is fantastic and challenging and every day brings new adventures to be discovered. She looks forward to seeing what's next!

Visit her at VictoriaBlue.com